THE ZOMBIE ROOM

THE ZOMBIE ROOM

R. D. Ronald

Book Guild Publishing
Sussex, England

First published in Great Britain in 2012 by
The Book Guild Ltd
Pavilion View
19 New Road
Brighton, BN1 1UF

Typeset in Baskerville by Ellipsis Digital Ltd, Glasgow

Printed in Great Britain by
CPI Group (UK) Ltd, Croydon CR0 4YY

A catalogue record for this book is available from The British Library.

ISBN 978 1 84624 719 4

Acknowledgments

My heartfelt gratitude for their patience, perseverance, advice and guidance (take whichever are relevant from the list) to the following: Amanda Turner, George Elliott, Nickola Gray, Shahid Rasul, Lynne Miller, Sara Jefferson, Rick Nuthman, Debbie Marsh and Carla Wood.

For the people who grouped together to make a trailer for *The Zombie Room*, the like of which has never been done before in the UK. You all gave tirelessly and have my ongoing respect and admiration: Adam Gerber, Amy Swan, Nickola Gray, Maria Ferrie, Luke Garnham, Josh Rafe Coles, Lucy Richards, Lewis Bonner, Nehir Glean, Neville Glean, Kate Jones, Daniel Middlewood, Kieron Hall, Frazan Hussain, Faye Megan Dixon, William Scott Johnson, Simon Flemming, James Watson, Alexandra Ferrie, Sara-Jayne White, Eve Kristina MacDonald, Kevin Longstaff, Kate Smith, Priyha Mohan, Robby Graham, Stuart Ferrol, Laura Jackets, Ellouise Hempstead, Anthony Lawson, Simon Manley, Shaun Robertson, Petr Stach, Jimmy Guy, Mark Leasley, Kim Brown, Danny Kay and Fran Purdy.

1

Tatiana hated her life. She hated working endless hours in the miserably cold factory with the incessant whir and drone of heavy machinery and the never-ending trundle of conveyor belts. She hated fighting off the advances of her lecherous supervisor in a way that did not offend, as she couldn't afford to be out of work. She hated the stack of chores to do every day when she got back home, and she hated never having time for a social life. Time was passing her by, and her vision of the future was anything other than the simple, pitiable lifestyle of her mother. Yet it was her mother's path that Tatiana continued to tread.

She screwed up her face and struggled to hide her revulsion as Murkov's arm slithered around her waist. He was attempting to educate her on how to operate machinery that she was more adept at using than him. It was as pointless as every other time he had tried to engage with her socially. She'd only been making mistakes because the factory was freezing and she kept losing the feeling in her hands. He kept talking, but Tatiana wasn't listening. She mentally willed him to give up and retreat back to his heated office where he could push papers around his desk and let her and the others get on with doing the real work. Murkov reached for her hand to guide it towards one of the levers. Tatiana allowed this but purposely brushed against his sleeve, transferring a grease smear onto the pristine white cotton. He backed away from Tatiana as if she had a contagious disease, muttering about the cost of his imported shirt.

'Get on with your work, Tatiana. Any more mistakes this week and you'll find your pay packet lighter than you would like.'

Tatiana smiled as Murkov hurried back to his office, dabbing at his sleeve with a handkerchief.

Eventually the 7p.m. whistle sounded, announcing the end of the shift, and Tatiana walked briskly through the chattering procession of workers to find her mother. Murkov watched her through his office window but Tatiana deliberately avoided eye contact. She'd seen the naked hunger in his eyes before.

Through a cloud of steam that hissed up from wheezing pistons, Tatiana saw her mother across the crowded factory floor. Unwrapping a headscarf stained with grime and sweat, she laughed with a grey-haired woman from her section.

'Did you manage to stay away from Murkov today?' her mother asked as she linked arms with Tatiana and began their walk home.

'For the most part, yes.'

Her mother's eyes narrowed but she didn't question her. 'Your father is a good man, but you know how protective he is of you and your brother. Do what you can to put Murkov off and mention nothing of it at home. Now come on, if we don't hurry your father will be home before us.'

'Would it be so much to ask for him to start preparing the meal for once? He isn't the only one who works long hours.'

Her mother's traditional values frustrated Tatiana, but if she were to get permission to attend the party on Friday, Tatiana knew it was crucial she have her mother on side.

'Tatty, you know my views on this,' her mother said with a patient sigh. 'Your generation may choose to go a different route, but I was brought up a certain way.'

Tatiana nodded, vowed to try and reel in her sarcasm and let the matter drop. She'd heard it all before and knew her mother's opinion on gender roles would never change.

'I was thinking,' she began after a few moments had passed, allowing the air between them to clear, 'after the National Day celebrations on Friday, that I would go out with Aina? She and some friends are getting together to hang out and play music. I would really like to go along.'

Her mother's dismissive shaking of her head had begun long before Tatiana had finished speaking. 'Your father wants you home. It is a day to spend as a family, not each of us going our own way.'

'But at this rate I'll never leave home. Aina has a boyfriend and already they have talked of marriage. I want my own family one day, a husband, and children, and a nice house, and … and … flowerbeds,' Tatiana said, gesticulating with her hands. 'I never have time for myself, to go out and have any fun. If you keep me locked away like this I'll end up with a man like Murkov and waste my life at some hole-in-the-ground factory.'

Tatiana could see her words had wounded her mother. 'And you think if you had your own family things would be so different?' her mother deflected with a cynical smile.

'I *would* do things differently,' Tatiana said defiantly. 'I will pick a man who will value me as a person, not treat me like a possession.'

'You are only nineteen, Tatty,' her mother said more softly now, sliding her hand into Tatiana's. 'You have so much to learn about the way things are in the world. Your father and I wish only to keep you safe for as long as we can.'

Tatiana could see her mother's mind was made up, and any further talk would do nothing to change it. Sometimes she wished she could run away, break free from the chains she felt her family bound her by, preventing her from becoming the person she wanted to be.

He checked his watch. At 2.34 a.m. Aura nightclub was full to capacity. Nicholas Garrett, or Mangle as he was affectionately known, looked around unsteadily, trying to remember and then locate whoever it was he'd come out with on that particular night.

His nickname came about from the copious amounts of alcohol and narcotics that he consumed during his nights out clubbing, and his insistence that he'd be fine to drive home afterwards. 'Mangle' being the predictable state his car had been left in on no fewer than three separate occasions.

He had so far managed to avoid being arrested, which given his strict middle-class upbringing was a huge relief. He, and whichever friends dared to accompany him on these drink- and drug-fuelled journeys home, had miraculously managed to stumble away from the scenes of vehicular devastation without injury. The only casualties other than the car they'd been in on each occasion were: a set of traffic lights, a garden wall and cherub ordained water feature, and perhaps most bizarrely an empty ice-cream van on an otherwise deserted stretch of country road.

He checked his watch again, having already forgotten the time: 2.35 a.m. No sign of Ross and Danny. Mangle nodded to himself. Yes, that sounded about right, he was fairly sure that was who he was out with. He made his way to the bar for another drink. Most of his night had been spent sweating and gyrating on the dance floor, but now his pill was wearing off, time was wearing on, and the possibility of finding female companionship for after club hours was diminishing.

Mangle knew he was no Adonis, but at 27 and just under 6 feet tall, with short fashionably cut brown hair and a physique kept in decent shape by hours on the dance floor, sweating off any extra pounds gained from midweek lethargy, he knew he wasn't such a bad catch. Besides, his crooked smile and cocky demeanour were most often what endeared him to the opposite sex.

Slowly edging his way through the waiting crowd at the bar, he surveyed the scene. An attractive blonde to his right, but the looming shaven-headed gentleman who scowled when Mangle and the girl made eye contact made him decide to look elsewhere.

A petite oriental girl pushed back out from the bar, carrying pink cocktails. He flashed his best introductory grin, but she looked away, refusing to acknowledge him. Keep looking, he thought. Most other girls appeared to be obviously partnered up, or at least had hangers-on who were attempting to seal the deal.

'Excuse me.' A woman's voice behind him struggled to be heard over the music.

Mangle half turned and felt the intriguing sensation of smooth skin glide over his forearm as she moved past him. A tingling like bubbles in champagne rose up through him and popped on the top of his head.

She was a slim brunette and had now snaked her way almost to the front of the queue. Mangle stepped up his game and followed, easing through as casually as he could so as not to cause confrontation with any Alpha Male-type boyfriends looking to impress. He could only see her from behind but very much liked what he saw. She was around 5 feet 4, in her early twenties, and dressed in figure-hugging black pants and top. The girl caught the attention of the first barman to pass and ordered a bottle of Becks.

'Make that two,' Mangle said squeezing in beside her and ignoring the grumbles from behind. 'I'll get them.'

'Thanks,' she said, turning to look at him, 'but I'm happy to buy my own.'

'Beautiful and independent,' he said, again employing the grin, this time to greater effect.

She laughed warmly. Her eyes were the pale blue of a cloudless desert sky; they watched him curiously for a moment before she spoke again. 'I'm Vicky,' she said, extending her hand.

Mangle wiped his palm on a leg of his pants then took her hand. 'I'm Mangle,' he said without thinking, 'pleased to meet you.'

Her hand felt warm and soft and curiously magnetic. He didn't want to let it go. His own hand, in contrast, was embarrassingly hot and sweaty, but either she hadn't noticed or she didn't care.

The stern-faced barman placed the bottles down in front of them and held out a hand for payment. Mangle released the girl, plucked a twenty from his depleted wallet and handed it over. 'You get the next ones?' he suggested.

She inclined her head in agreement and after he'd collected his change, led them away from the bar.

'Are you here on your own?' Vicky asked, leaning in towards him to be heard over the thunderous roar from the dance floor.

'No, I'm with a couple of friends. Don't know where they are right now though,' he said, and smiled. 'Your eyes are very blue.'

'Um, OK,' she said, laughing again.

'That's because of a low melanin concentration,' he babbled. 'It's a protein. Having pale blue eyes like that with such dark hair is quite rare.'

'Well Doctor Mangle, I'll take that as a compliment – I think.'

'Ha, by all means, but I'm not a doctor, although my parents no doubt wish I was. I had a private school education where you pick up loads of useless stuff like that.'

'So what do you do with this private school education if you aren't saving lives or diagnosing eye colour?'

'I sell bathroom supplies.'

Vicky laughed until she saw he wasn't joking, and then stopped abruptly. 'I'm sorry. I thought you were pulling my leg.'

'Hey, I do quite well: area sales rep, company car, I'm pretty happy with it,' he said defensively.

Vicky placed a hand on his arm. 'I work in a library,' she said by way of conciliation, and added a shrug.

'That's cool. I'm just touchy about the job thing as my parents are a bit stuck up. They expected I'd go the doctor or lawyer route.'

Vicky nodded. 'You have plans after the club finishes?'

'I was going to go back and stay at my friend's place, smoke a few joints and then crash. What about you?'

'Pretty much the same thing, although my friend doesn't smoke. You want me to tag along, or is that really forward of me?'

'It does sound pretty forward,' he said grinning. 'That'd be nice though.'

'It feels kind of weird calling you Mangle. Do you have another name?' she asked, and took a sip from her beer.

'Yeah, Nicholas.'

'Nicholas the bathroom salesman, that's just perfect,' she said and laughed.

'Alright Mangle, who's this then?' a voice from behind him asked, as a pale doughy arm reached around and plucked the beer from his hand. 'Ross, Mangle has been holding out on us again.'

'Alright boys, this is Vicky,' Mangle said as his two friends invaded the conversation. 'This is Danny.' He indicated the short chubby lad with close-cropped black hair in a peak on his brow, who now stood drinking Mangle's beer as he winked at her. 'And this is Ross.' Ross was about the same height as Mangle but slimmer build; he had receding blonde hair that he swept up into tufts, and eyebrows like humps on a camel.

'Nice,' Ross validated with a grin. 'You still coming back to mine after the club, dude?'

'Yeah,' Mangle said. 'Is it OK if Vicky tags along as well?'

'Sure, the more the merrier and all that. We're gonna play Edward Cider-Hands.'

'You have any friends to bring with?' Danny asked, hopefully.

'I did, but I haven't seen them in a while, I don't know if they've already left,' Vicky said. 'Um, you're going to be playing what?'

'Still time before closing,' Danny said, with a glance at his watch. 'Off you go and find them.' He made a shooing gesture.

'OK, come on you,' Vicky said laughing, as she dragged Mangle along with her. 'See you later, guys.'

'A couple of my more delinquent friends from school,' Mangle explained once they'd got out of earshot. 'Have your friends really gone home or did you just not fancy setting them up with those two?'

'They might have gone, but to be honest they're just girls I went to college with. I got dragged out tonight on one of those reunion things, so I'm glad of the excuse to avoid them later on,' she said. 'Now what the hell is Edward Cider-something?'

'Edward Cider-Hands. Those two clowns tape a big bottle of cider to each of their hands. The deal is they aren't allowed to take the bottles off until they're both empty. It's hardly highbrow humour but it can be pretty amusing to watch.'

Vicky laughed warmly. 'Sounds like it could get messy.'

The living-room door clicked shut as Ross staggered towards his bedroom. Vicky pulled her legs up alongside Mangle and slid her toes underneath his calves.

'Will they come back out for anything?' she asked, glancing again towards the closed living-room door.

'No, after all that cider that's the last we'll see of them before noon at the earliest.'

Vicky nuzzled her face against his neck. Mangle could feel her heart beating against his chest, slightly elevated, almost in rhythm with his own. He angled his chin down and she tilted her face up towards him. They kissed for only a few seconds but Mangle felt a rush of adrenalin and found himself short of breath. He wasn't used to this effect from a girl he'd only just met. He ran his fingers through her hair, releasing a smell like springtime. Vicky dropped her hands down and began to unbuckle his belt.

'Are you sure you want to do this?' Mangle asked. 'We did only just meet.'

'I suppose that depends on what your intentions are for after.'

'What do you mean?'

'Well you kinda have to go backwards or forwards after sex.'

'I thought that was during sex,' he said without thinking, and quickly grinned so as not to ruin the moment.

'Ha ha, very funny. I mean a friendship between a man and a woman. After you have sex you either have to move on to a relationship, or you go back to having, well, nothing.'

'Is this a "will you still respect me in the morning" kind of thing?'

'Maybe. I'm just asking if this is only for tonight or something more than that.'

This situation he'd been in more times previously than he could count; but when Mangle told her that he very much wanted it to be more than just tonight, it was perhaps the first time he'd actually meant it.

An alcohol and Ecstasy comedown usually left Mangle with a patchy memory of the previous evening and a feeling like dirt under his skin, but seeing Vicky curled up against him when he awoke filled him with an invigoration akin to the first caffeine hit of the day, and vivid memories of the previous night.

He reached over Vicky and pulled his wallet out of his pants pocket to check how much was left for cab fare home, and winced at what he saw. There was no doubt he wanted to spend time with Vicky, but dates cost, and the last thing he wanted to do at 27 was take her to his place all the time and listen to more of his parents' bullshit. By their reckoning, he should be working for a well-renowned company, with a pension plan, a house and a wife squeezing out grandchild number three by now. He understood that they had sacrificed a lot to pay for his private school tuition, and now expected a return on their investment, but he simply wasn't interested in the idyllic life they had pictured for him, or in being a trophy they could show off among their social circle.

Mangle's usual course of action was to get the latest girl to pay for almost everything, claiming late payment of his wages. After a few weeks the girls would tire of the excuse, but by then Mangle had usually grown tired of them and begun looking around for the next pretty face. But this time he was determined to do it right.

Derek 'Decker' Rankin stood on the corner of Cleethorpe Street, smoking a cigarette and trying his best to look inconspicuous.

He'd earned a modest amount of credibility already through various initiations, but if this went smoothly then he reckoned he'd no longer have to live life as a thug and low-level drug dealer. Brian, John and Tony weren't exactly a gang – that just sounded soft. They were a bunch of entrepreneurs who looked out for each other and got things done.

At 18, Decker was a lot younger than the other three, but even as a scruffy kid running around the streets he'd known their reputation as people you just don't mess with. All three had served stretches inside, but so far the law had never been able to put anything worthwhile together to keep them there.

Decker too had served time, in a young offenders' institute, which he'd tell anyone who asked had been like a holiday. In truth it hadn't been unbearable, and it helped to raise his street profile no end when he got back out. The downside was that it had brought him up onto the police radar and he'd been questioned a few times since for crimes he'd had nothing to do with.

Decker took another drag from the cigarette and flicked the butt against a passing car; it bloomed into a shower of sparks that rained down the side. The brakelights lit up and the car began to slow, but seeing Decker unmoved, the driver had second thoughts and drove on.

Gary Bilaney had wronged the guys in some way. Exactly how, wasn't important. Decker had been told to teach him a lesson. He slid a hand into his coat pocket and ran his fingers over the cold steel of the utility knife, the fresh blade exposed and locked into position to save time. He'd replaced it before he left home, and tested it on a thick sheet of cardboard. Don't kill him, just cause some damage, preferably on the face so people will know. Those were his instructions. He'd been told the spot to wait at and the time to expect Gary to get off the bus, returning from work.

Decker checked his watch. Looking up again he saw the bus making its way slowly around the tight corner at the bottom of the road. A greasy burger wrapper blew against his leg. Decker absently shook it free without taking his eyes off the bus.

The air brakes wheezed as the bus came to a halt, and a few passengers disembarked: an old man in an oversized brown coat mumbled to himself as he walked; a young woman struggled off unassisted with two toddlers and a pushchair. And lastly there was Gary.

He was around 30, reasonably well built, certainly bigger than Decker's more moderate frame. He had on well-worn overalls with work boots and had light brown hair worn in a crew cut. He stopped on the pavement to light a cigarette as the bus juddered uneasily away from the stop, coughing out a cloud of acrid fumes.

Decker strode purposefully across the street towards Gary, forgot to check for traffic and was startled by a car horn that blasted as the driver braked sharply to avoid hitting him. His attention switched back to Gary, who now watched him with a mixture of curiosity and suspicion. Decker's hand went back into his pocket, thumb and fingers rubbing intently on the handle of the knife as if it were a lamp about to release a genie and grant him three wishes.

Gary dropped his cigarette onto the ground and his lips moved silently, as if trying to select the right words to get him out of the unfolding situation.

'N-no,' was all he managed to stammer. 'It was a big mistake, I didn't even mean to do it – you tell them.'

Decker had the knife half out of his pocket now, just a few paces from using it. This was the moment he'd been waiting for. It should be straightforward: just cut him a few times and run. But the rising feeling of nausea inside him was debilitating. His eyes darted left and right, checking no witnesses were close enough to be able to pick him out of a line-up, and then fixed intently on Gary.

Gary had planted his left foot backwards at a 90 degree angle. Was he adopting an aggressive stance to fight back, or was he about to bolt? Decker's nerve ends sang with tension and he swiped his left cuff across his forehead. He stopped in front of the larger man, whose lips were still moving, but Decker couldn't make out what he was saying over the rush of blood pumping in his ears.

Even afterwards Decker couldn't have explained the feeling. It wasn't physical fear: he'd been in enough street fights to know that even without the knife he could probably handle the guy. There might not have been a lot of Decker but he could take care of himself. It wasn't fear of getting caught either. There was no one anywhere near now, and after it was done he'd vanish down the twisting maze of alleyways and back streets, and he knew Gary would never talk.

The thought of dragging the cold steel blade across his face, separating warm flesh as easily as he'd slit the cardboard earlier that day, made his stomach turn over again and he had to swallow the surge of bile that rose up in his throat. Decker had twice in the past used a knife on someone, and never felt like this. Both times he'd been the one who was attacked. Was that the difference this time? Attacking a defenceless man, disfiguring him?

Decker held the knife out in front of him, gripped tightly in his shaking palm. He felt hot and his face tingled; a high-pitched almost electric whine was now all he could hear. He pulled his arm back and swung forward in a low arc.

Gary cried out as blood spilled onto the pavement in coin-sized drops, like a handful of loose change.

'Get out of here,' Decker yelled, or thought he did. He couldn't be sure over the incessant ringing in his head.

Gary turned, cradling his blood-soaked forearm with his left hand, and fled.

Decker staggered a couple of steps, heard a clatter as the knife fell from his hand onto the pavement. He looked down and saw blood on his hand, on his sleeve, on the pavement and across the blade of the knife. Gathering his wits he stooped to pick it up, and ran.

*****

Tazeem stepped spritely up the three red brick steps and into the Mosque to attend Friday prayers. It was considered a compulsory part of a Muslim man's life, but attendance for Tazeem in recent times had become more sporadic than his elders approved of.

The walls inside the Mosque were painted pale yellow and adorned with plaques of verses from the Qur'an, in Arabic calligraphy. A rack of leaflets and newsletters hung on the right-hand wall, and shelving already holding many pairs of shoes was to the left.

Tazeem quickly removed his shoes and made his way to the male ablutions to perform *wuzu*, the ceremonial washing that took place before prayer. He completed the specific routine and walked through to the prayer hall, picking up a spare head covering as he went in.

The prayer hall was a large wide room almost completely devoid of furniture. The floor was covered by a red carpet designed to provide individual prayer mats for the worshippers. Various other prayer mats and Qur'anic texts hung on the walls. The domed niche or *mihrab* in the wall ahead marked the direction of Mecca, showing worshippers where to face whilst praying. Sitting below it, leading prayers, was the Imam. Because the prayer hall had to face towards Mecca, the Mosque had been built at a different angle to the other buildings on the street outside.

Tazeem found a spot towards the far corner of the room next to his friend Latif, and joined in with prayers. Latif was a short man with a rather square shaped head, whose shifty looking eyes were due to an astigmatism he was too proud to wear glasses for, and in sharp contrast to his affable nature.

Once concluded, the Imam Omar stood and faced the room to begin his sermon or *khutbah*. He paused long enough to take in the faces in congregation before him. Tazeem felt the expressionless gaze linger on him for barely a second, but knew his presence had been noted.

*****

'I saw your cousin Ermina with Sadiq again yesterday,' Latif said quietly as they walked towards the hall after prayers. 'They looked pretty friendly.'

'Do you think there is anything in it?' Tazeem asked, trying not to look concerned.

'I don't know, my friend, but she would be wise to steer clear.'

'What are you two whispering about?' Sadiq asked in anything but a whisper as he strode confidently between them.

'Nothing,' Tazeem answered, as he returned his head covering on the way out.

Tazeem had gone through school with Latif and Sadiq, and for years they had been very close. Now at 23 they all had different pursuits, social groups and seemingly work ethics. But Friday prayer at the Mosque would often see them reunited if only for a brief period.

Latif was currently in the process of buying his second business and looked in no mind to slow down his acquisitions. Tazeem worked long hours in family-run shops and oversaw redevelopment of rental properties, but so far had nothing other than a small house in the suburbs he could class as his own. Sadiq, however, never seemed to work any steady hours but was never short of cash, which he'd splash around on his frequent nights out at casinos and nightclubs.

'Were you talking about me? My ears should be burning, yeah?' Sadiq grinned, putting an arm around each of their shoulders.

'So what if we were?' Latif said angrily, and shrugged him off.

'I'm glad to see you made an appearance today, Tazeem. Friday prayer is compulsory for all Muslim men and your absences recently do not meet approval,' the voice of Imam Omar boomed from behind, taking all three by surprise.

Tazeem considered telling Omar he had been attending other mosques while working away, but lying to the wily Imam was pointless; his eyes could pierce and shred the fabric of a lie as easily as a pin passing through a balloon.

Tazeem and Latif retrieved their shoes and left the Mosque,

while Sadiq lingered in the doorway, talking jovially with some of the others.

'I don't know how Sadiq manages to convince old grey-hair of his righteousness without any feeling of compunction,' Tazeem said, as they walked back to the car park.

'I know what you mean,' Latif nodded. 'Even though I've done nothing wrong, standing near Omar brings on a feeling of much guilt. Sadiq is without doubt lacking a social conscience.'

Tazeem let the matter drop. He could identify with Latif's misplaced guilt around the Imam, but a social conscience was not something that he paid particular attention to. He said goodbye to his friend and climbed into his eight-year-old silver Mercedes, then drove off to one of his family's stores to put in an afternoon shift.

Tazeem relieved Mavis, a local alcoholic who took shifts at short notice, happy to receive payment in alcohol. He took his place behind the cash register. There were a couple of customers browsing towards the back of the store but no one required immediate service. He took out his wallet and withdrew a number of credit cards bearing different names. Picking two at random, Tazeem reeled off around 30 Lotto scratch cards from their display cases on the counter and rang them up at the till, using the credit cards.

This was a low-risk scam he'd run successfully for a while. He'd fraudulently apply for the credit cards at addresses of properties where he was overseeing repair work, then use the cards a few times to buy large numbers of scratch cards while working at various shops. He was under no illusion that this would bring about great riches or early retirement, but the extra cash made his life a little easier.

Tazeem pulled out the silver *taweez* locket that he wore on a chain around his neck, left to him when his father died. He didn't believe in superstition, but using the partly serrated edge to scratch away the foil coating revealing the numbers and symbols beneath had become a part of the ritual for him. Mavis waved at Tazeem to attract his attention. She'd retrieved her coat from the stock-room and now stood beside the door holding up two 1 litre bottles of Smirnoff for his approval. He nodded and she left, cradling the payment for her shift.

Before long a scattering of silver shavings had gathered beneath his chair. The winning cards he filled in with false names and addresses, and mixed them in with other cards awaiting collection by the lottery company. He took the amount he'd won from the till; money for old rope.

2

National Day celebrations were in full swing by the time they arrived at the stadium. Usually they queued for hours to get decent seats, but Tatiana's father managed to call in a favour and had got them reserved seating right next to the presidential podium. He was a hard-working and very principled man, although not particularly smart, and certainly would never provide his family with any great wealth. She knew he would always do right by them, put food on the table, clothes on their backs and provide well intentioned morals to live by, but Tatiana found his frustratingly narrow-minded views clashed with her own opinions so much that she often felt oppressed and claustrophobic. His point-blank refusal to allow her to go out with her friends after the celebrations was no exception.

Her father's pride grew along with the excited roar of the crowd as they entered the main arena. He stopped momentarily to breathe in the atmosphere, as the warm proximity of so many people mixed with the inviting smell of cooked food from vendors, and patriotic music played over the public address system.

He affectionately patted her younger brother Eski's shoulder, and walked on. Tatiana's mother linked arms with her and they followed a few steps behind. Her mother didn't have the same interest in politics as her husband, and tolerated rather than supported his passion. The most important issues for her happened within the home, while political promises rarely seemed to deliver anything tangible, as far as she could see, that directly influenced their lives for the better. Her father began to sing along with many other men in the stadium. He looked expectantly at Eski, but the boy was too young to recite the words from memory.

The presidential grandstand, to the left of the entrance, was slightly elevated. Virtually all of the seats were taken, but her father calmly proceeded through the crowd, confident that his friend would not have let him down. Sure enough, four adjoining seats close enough to the grandstand to reach out and touch, remained unoccupied by anything other than reservation place-markers. Her father beamed as he ushered his son along the aisle, her mother next, then Tatiana, and finally he took his seat.

A speaker bolted to a wooden post on the walkway a few rows in front buzzed and crackled. Tatiana winced and covered her ears. Grumbled complaints from nearby spectators indicated it was likely an on-going occurrence. Nothing would spoil the day for her father, though, who had got to his feet and was clapping and singing to the next song.

A large workman in dusty blue overalls jostled his way through the spectators gathered on a dividing walkway between blocks of seats. The exuberance of the crowd did little to lift his visibly sullen mood; Tatiana found his indifference rather curious and continued to watch his approach. He had a burly physique, with a thick muscular neck, and the scowl he wore made his features scrunch up like a fist. He carried a heavy-looking grey toolkit that was scuffed and dented along one side, and wore big black boots.

He stopped at an electrical circuit box at the foot of the post, put down his toolkit and opened up the box. He fiddled around inside with various tools, during which time the speaker continued to pop and fizz, eliciting louder protestations from the crowd. Tatiana felt almost an affinity with the man. No wonder he looked miserable, having to work on a holiday and receiving nothing but complaints for his efforts. After another moment the sound cleared and static-free music once more poured from the loudspeaker. An ironic cheer and a smattering of applause failed to lift the man's spirits as he began to pack away his tools.

Tatiana continued to watch as he took a cylindrical metal device from the bottom of his toolkit and placed it within the circuit box. He closed the outer door, but not far enough to lock it, stood, picked up his tools and hurried back the way he had come.

Tatiana thought this peculiar. She looked around her, but nobody seemed in the least concerned. She assumed it must be a gadget to prevent further interference. Reasonably placated by this, she glanced around and smiled at the happy faces. The workman had stopped at the far end of the walkway and was looking back in the direction he had come from. Perhaps he'd forgotten one of his tools, she thought, and was considering whether to go back now or just to get it later. Whatever his dilemma, he'd started back towards them. Again he put down his tools, but this time stepped tentatively toward the circuit box, in the manner of one approaching a vicious dog. He knelt, teased open the door and reached inside.

After further adjustments within the circuit box, the workman was on his feet and hurrying away, his toolkit discarded behind him. He'd travelled no more than half a dozen steps when he ventured a look over his shoulder. At that exact moment there was a bright white flash, and Tatiana's whole world changed.

'Danny, yeah, did you arrange for him to be there tonight?' Mangle asked into the hands-free headset of his cell phone.

'I did, yeah. You're still sure about this?'

'I am,' Mangle said, sounding more convincing than he felt. 'So what's the plan?'

'He'll meet you at the club and you can sort out collection. Are you on your way up there already?'

'I managed to line up a job nearby, so I can get the office to pay for the fuel.'

'Nicely done. A bit out of your area though, isn't it?'

'Yeah, but I convinced the boss that if they sign up with us then I may be able to get their other stores as well. Besides, I'm better off out of the way. Arthur, one of the other reps left his car running outside the office this morning and someone stole it. The boss is fuming. I'm happy to let the dust settle before I come back tomorrow.'

'OK man, let me know how you get on,' Danny said, laughing. 'Speak soon.'

Mangle terminated the call. He thought about calling Vicky just to say hi, but he'd only left her an hour ago, and less than a month into their relationship he didn't want to seem too clingy.

It may have only been a few weeks but they were the best he could ever remember. Vicky had been fantastic. They were planning a future together, and against her parents' wishes she'd used her savings to put down a deposit on a house for them both. Mangle had promised to match the amount to buy furniture and fix the place up and they'd use their combined wages for mortgage repayments.

His parents appeared to approve of Vicky at first, after all she was very presentable, well-spoken and charming, and she seemed to give Mangle a previously bereft sense of direction. However, after she mentioned working in a library, and offered little inclination of career ambition, he noted more than a slight chill had crept into the atmosphere. Frankly, he didn't care what they thought, but until he and Vicky were able to move in together, keeping the parents placated was essential.

Mangle pulled up outside the showroom after spending four hours on the road. It was a decent-sized shop in what looked to be a popular industrial estate with good highway links to two nearby cities. A large order and continued custom might actually prove as lucrative over time as the deal Danny had arranged at the club later that night.Taking his suit jacket off the hanger behind his seat, Mangle put it on, straightened his tie and smoothed the creases from his pants. It was time to impress.

A nearby steeple bell tolled four o'clock as Mangle arrived at the hotel. He didn't realise churches still announced the hour; perhaps just in more rural locations. The company had booked him into an out of the way hotel to save on city centre prices. It would mean an expensive cab ride to and from the club, but given the order he'd logged that afternoon, nothing was going to spoil his mood and the smile that had taken root after his meeting seemed quite content to remain.

The hotel, Antonine's Lodge, looked to have been formed from a cluster of old farm outbuildings. The sign outside boasted 16 bedrooms in the main building, a spacious bar and well stocked wine cellar in another, and an excellent restaurant that served *the best beef dishes for miles around* in a third.

'A room for Garrett,' he told the woman behind the large oak desk as he walked into reception.

She returned his smile emphatically, probably believing it was for her benefit, fetched his room key and again grinned. Mangle plucked it from her hand and whistled as he walked across the blue-carpeted lobby and up the stairs toward the rooms.

His room, No.11, was reasonably sized but painted a garish red, matching the red and green tartan drapes secured by red tasselled cord that hung either side of the bow window. Two club chairs sat inside the bow, and a small table which was crowned with hotel-themed stationery, two bottles of spring water and three complimentary miniatures of spirits. The room was quite homely in daylight despite the overbearing colour scheme, but once night fell he guessed it would quickly become oppressive.

Mangle sat in one of the chairs and took in the panoramic

view of the landscape for a few moments, before taking out his phone to call Vicky.

'Hi,' she said, picking up on the second ring. 'Did you get booked into your hotel OK?'

'Yep, I'm looking out on lots of fields and big brown fluffy things eating grass, from my incredibly red room.'

'That sounds like fun. I wish I was with you.'

'Well I'm sure it would be fun if you were here, but as you aren't, I'll have to make do with my complimentary notepaper and some tiny bottles of Macallan whisky,' he said, picking up one of the miniatures and squinting at the label.

'Aren't you going out tonight to see what the locality has to offer?'

Mangle felt his conscience fleetingly brushed by guilt. Vicky had no idea what he had planned for later that night. If she did, she'd never have let him do it. But this was a necessary step to lay down a building block to begin their life together.

'I might do a little later if the room continues to shrink at the rate it's currently doing.'

Vicky's musical laughter spilled out of the earpiece, and before he realised what he was doing, Mangle said, 'I love you.'

He'd hung up in a panic and turned his phone off right away. Now, getting out of the taxi outside Sabotage nightclub, Mangle debated turning it back on. If Danny needed to speak to him he wouldn't be able to get through. But if he turned the phone on, Vicky was bound to call and he wasn't ready to have that conversation just yet. What had he been thinking? He'd never before told a girl he loved her and meant it, and he'd certainly never said it first. His stomach turned over again like a washing machine on a slow spin cycle. Mangle reckoned he just needed to get this deal over with, hopefully have a good night's sleep and talk to Vicky in the morning, maybe during his trip back home if he felt up to it.

He took his place in line outside the club. The cash for the deal was tucked down his boxer shorts in case a pat-down from the door staff revealed the suspicious bulge. He wrinkled his nose as a waft of cheap perfume crawled over him from the group of giggling women queuing in front. The woman closest to him was wearing fake tan and there were streaks down the back of one leg. He felt like he knew a secret. This deal was the only thing he'd ever kept from Vicky, and he felt burdened by it. The queue shuffled forward a few steps and a motorcycle went past, sounding like a fly buzzing against a window pane. The entrance to the club was a nondescript brown double door that opened up between two high-street stores. Above was another brown rectangle the same shade as the doors that the club name was now illuminated through it in brilliant white. During the day you'd probably walk right by and not even notice the place, but at night it was a central hub of social interaction.

The queue moved again. This time the group of women and Mangle passed through the doors, paid at the kiosk and were admitted inside.

Danny had told Mangle to wear his blue sweater, brown pants and black shoes, so his contact would be able to identify him. Perhaps not a great fashion selection, but he was fairly sure there wouldn't be anyone else in the same attire.

Inside, rough stone walls were covered by wood panelling from waist height down to the grey slate floor. Large mirrors were hung throughout the club, reflecting the same faces from many angles at once which gave Mangle a slightly unsettled feeling. Sparse patches of illumination were created by the seemingly random placement of downlighters in the ceiling. Mangle ordered a bottle of Becks at the bar and went to stand in one of the lit spots to wait until he was approached.

Three beers and twice as many checks of his watch later, Mangle was finally tapped on the shoulder. He turned around to see a wiry-framed youth wearing a blue V-necked sweater and light brown pants, with black trainers.

'Danny said I was the one supposed to dress like this and you'd approach me,' he said to Mangle.

'Yeah, well, he told me the same thing. Fuck it, we're here now so let's get it done.'

'You not wanna chill out in here for a while first? It generally picks up late on but it's worth hanging round for. My girl is bringing a friend out with her, I could hook you up.'

'No thanks, man, I'd rather get this done and head off.'

'Sure, whatever. Follow me out in five minutes. Walk outside, go left, then down the street there's a car park just round the corner. I'll see you and wave over.'

'Right, yeah, OK,' Mangle said uncertainly.

'You didn't think I'd bring it in here, did you?' the man asked Mangle with a smirk.

'No, I guess not,' Mangle lied.

The man nodded, and left the club. Mangle checked his watch once more; he'd finish his beer and then leave. He'd already been anxious enough, but now he had to walk to a secluded spot with all the cash and trust this stranger would be honourable enough to not club him over the head and take it. He took another drink from the bottle with an unsteady hand.

Walking out of the club, Mangle paused. His gut feeling was to turn right and flag down a cab. He told himself it was just nerves and that he'd be fine. He turned left and kept a lookout for the car park.

After a few minutes he caught sight of the meeting place down a narrow side street, and again ignoring his instincts walked towards it. A single mercury vapour lamp cast a cold blue glare onto the tarmac, revealing most of the parking bays to be empty. Six cars were dotted around but not enough light penetrated within for him to see if any were occupied. Mangle kept walking, but slower now. His breathing had quickened and the night air felt colder as he sucked it in.

He heard a soft hum as the driver's window on a nearby Saab went down, enough that he could identify the occupant as the man from the club. Mangle opened the door and got into the back seat behind the driver.

'I stink or something so you have to sit in the back?'

'You have the stuff?' Mangle said, ignoring the question.

The driver slid back the cover on the centre console and withdrew a package wrapped in brown paper before saying, 'Cash first.'

Mangle pulled out the uncomfortable bulge of money from his shorts and held it out to the driver.

'Fantastic,' the man said sarcastically. Gripping it between finger and thumb he dropped it into the console he'd taken the package from. 'You couldn't have put it anywhere else?'

Mangle opened up the crinkled brown paper. A resealable plastic bag full of white powder was inside. He opened it, licked a finger and dabbed it into the powder before tasting it.

'We good?' the man asked from the front.

'We are,' Mangle confirmed. He resealed the package and got out of the car.

'OK, see you next time.'

'Not me. Strictly a one-off,' Mangle told him.

'Yeah, you'll be back,' the man laughed as Mangle closed the door.

Mangle jammed the parcel down into his pants pocket and hailed a cab from the main street. He flirted with the idea of calling Vicky on his way back to the hotel, but decided to wait until morning.

Surprisingly, sleep came easily and he rose the next day at 8 a.m. feeling refreshed and looking forward to getting back home. He paid the bill to a cheerful receptionist, and on the way out to the car turned on his phone. He half expected it to burst into life and begin ringing as soon as his finger left the power button, and felt somewhat disappointed when it remained silent. Throwing his bag containing the package onto the back seat, Mangle started the engine and began the drive home.

After an hour the phone rang, but checking the caller ID Mangle was disappointed to see it was Danny, and not Vicky.

'Well?'

'All OK, no problems,' Mangle said.

'You were supposed to ring last night and let me know.'

'Right, sorry. It was late and I had the phone turned off.'

'Well played, man, don't worry about me fretting here all night.'

'OK, you're right, I should have called, but it's done now. I'll be back in a few hours. I'll swing by your place first to get rid of this.'

'Alright, see you soon.'

The morning sun was bright and Mangle reached for his Aviator sunglasses. He cracked the window a little to feel the breeze and turned up the stereo. By the time the phone rang again he had forgotten all about expecting her call.

'Nicholas. I tried calling back yesterday but your phone was switched off.'

'I know. I'm sorry. What I said kind of slipped out, and I didn't know what to say.'

'Did you mean it?'

'Yeah, I guess I did.'

There was a moment of silence over the line, and at first the blue lights and siren behind didn't register.

'I guess I love you too,' she said, and he could hear the smile in her voice.

The police car kept pace a car's length behind and began flashing its headlights.

'Vicky, I'm gonna have to call you back. I must have been speeding or something, I'm getting pulled over.'

His whole focus had been on the conversation, and now pulling the car onto the hard shoulder, Mangle experienced a sensation like waking from a dream. He waited for the police officer to approach the car, and wound down the window.

'Is this your car, sir?'

'It's a company car, but mine, yeah.'

'Can you explain how the registration plate for this vehicle is in the stolen car database?'

'Stolen?' Mangle said, incredulous. 'No, wait. I know what

must have happened. There was another company car stolen from outside the office yesterday; whoever reported it must have given these details by mistake.'

'I'm going to need to take you into custody until I can have this verified. Please get out of the car.'

Mangle cursed his luck. Just when everything had started going his way. The new account for work, Vicky telling him she loved him, and everything last night had gone great too.

That was when it hit him like a bucket of ice-water. The bag.

'My bag … on the back seat.'

'Leave everything where it is,' the policeman instructed. His partner led Mangle to the patrol car behind and opened a rear door to put him inside.

'It'll just take a second, my … my stuff for work,' he stammered. A guilty sweat beaded his forehead and his hands felt heavy and numb.

'Are you OK?' The second cop asked.

'Yes, I'm fine,' he said forcing a smile. 'I had a late night, that's all.'

The cop pushed Mangle into the back seat and closed the door after him. Mangle watched as he walked up to his partner who was talking into a radio. A few seconds passed, and he could see the second officer's mouth gold-fishing as he spoke to his partner. They both turned and looked at him through the windshield. Instinctively, Mangle looked away. He tried to focus on anything outside of the car, to appear natural, but there was nothing to see: a featureless grass verge on one side of the car, passing vehicles on the other.

He risked a look back at the officers again. They both still watched him, but now neither was speaking. Whatever had been written on Mangle's face must have been clear for them to see. The first cop began talking into the radio again and his partner reached into the car and withdrew the bag from the back seat.

Mangle's heart slammed against his ribcage. Suddenly the impact of what had seemed like a simple task, something to alleviate short-term financial problems, weighed down heavily with its long-term consequences.

The cop emptied the bag onto the grass verge. A crumpled shirt fluttered as it was caught by the breeze. His toiletry bag dropped on top of it. The cop unzipped it, emptied it out. His folders containing all the new customer sheets and order invoices that he'd completed the day before were dropped beside everything else; the pages flapped anxiously. It was like watching his life become a train wreck.

The cop opened the bag again and peered inside. His smile spread like warm butter. Looking back he winked at Mangle, before reaching in one last time and taking out the brown paper package.

Decker wasn't a big fan of cannabis, but when Brian passed around another joint he thought he'd look stupid if he refused. Taking a small inhale he quickly blew the smoke out and nodded approval, before handing it to the blonde who was draped across his lap. He took a swig from his can of beer to get rid of the taste while the blonde – Pamela had he been told she was called? – took two greedy hits from the joint and passed it to her friend.

'You want one of the girls to fetch anything for you, Decker?' Brian asked.

'Yeah, man, good stuff,' Decker said, his head swimming from the cannabis. 'I mean, no, I'm good.' The others laughed at his inexperience.

Decker ran a hand over the still healing tattoo John had done on the back of his neck with a sewing needle and a bottle of Indian ink. Reward for the way he'd handled things. 'Carpe Diem', in a murky black italic script: 'Seize the day', John had told him it meant. They all had the same tattoo. John had rolled up a shirt sleeve to show off his own, Bri had tapped his breastbone, and Tony pointed to his shoulder blade.

Decker smiled and shrugged off their laughter. Their humour was only barbed if you sat on the outside, and now he was one of them. During the three weeks since the stabbing, Decker's standing with the others had risen exponentially. He didn't just see them during the day now, doing jobs and running errands, but hung out with them in the evenings as well. There had been better parties, better drugs and better girls. People's attitude towards him had changed as well and he now knew what it felt like to be on the receiving end of the fearful, respectful and envious looks he'd been giving to men like Brian since childhood.

'You ever hear anything from Bilaney or the police then, Deck?' John asked, lying prostrate on the sofa opposite.

'Nothing. There was no one around and it was done professional. Besides, he wouldn't dare say anything anyway.'

'He might not, but his brother is well pissed,' Tony said. 'He's been making all kinds of promises to get back at you.'

'Yeah?' Decker asked sitting up straighter in the chair. The blonde kissed the inflamed skin around his healing tattoo and giggled. He pushed her away.

'You not heard?' Tony asked. 'His brother Alex runs heroin over a few estates with some of his friends. Last I'd heard he was just a snot-nosed kid. Guess he came up. Bit like you, Deck.'

'You're not worried are you?' John asked goadingly in Decker's direction.

'Course not. Maybe he just needs some of what his brother got to put him in his place.'

The blonde giggled again and put her arm back around his neck. The boys thought it was pretty funny too and laughed along. Decker reckoned he'd saved face. It wouldn't do to show any weakness. Now he had his spot at their table there was no way he was going to give it up.

An electronic chirping from his pocket alerted Decker that someone was calling him. The ring tone on his cell phone was a classical number, to show he was cultured. He didn't know what it was but recognised the tune from a bread commercial that had been on the TV when he was a kid.

'Speak,' he said after flipping the phone open.

'Decker, you have to come now.'

'What? Who's this?'

'It's me, Becky. There's a bunch of guys outside say if you don't come out they're gonna burn the house down. They have cans of petrol here, Decker. I'm really scared. Should I phone the police?'

His head was spinning from the cannabis, alcohol and sudden alarming news. Becky was his older sister. It must be Alex Bilaney and his crew. He had to confront them. If Becky phoned the police they'd only come back again later, but next time she might not get a warning. Had someone told them he would be there, or was this a ruse to scare him, or lure him out?

'Don't phone the cops, Becky. I'm on my way.'

'Hurry then, please, Decker. The twins are upstairs.'

'Decker, what's going on?' John asked as he hung up the call. All three had perked up at the prospect of trouble.

He was out of the door and halfway down the stairs before he realised the others were following. He shouted an explanation over his shoulder. Tony's old blue and white Dodge Charger sat by the kerb outside. A bleep as the door locks released, and they all jumped inside. Tony turned the key and the engine immediately roared into life. The tyres squealed in protest as he wheelspun out into a line of oncoming traffic.

Becky lived about a mile away, and Tony rocketed along the narrow suburban streets at breakneck speed. Decker was panicking at the prospect of someone hurting his sister, and worse still his niece and nephew, but looking around the car the other three seemed thrilled at the potential onset of violence.

Tony spun into Becky's street, and what Decker saw made his heart feel like it was being wrenched from his chest. Her garden was within sight at the bottom of the small cul-de-sac. A small grey saloon was parked at an angle across the path and three figures were standing on her lawn, one of them holding a burning lump of wood.

This was far from being a nice middle-class suburb – public

drunkenness, domestic and casual violence never registered as something the locals needed to call the police about – but even here someone would surely have reported this by now. Whatever he was going to do it would have to be quick.

Tony's Charger bucked and lurched as it mounted the kerb then slid to a halt on the grass. Before the car stopped Decker was already out and running up the path. Shouts of encouragement rang out from behind him as a barrage of taunts and threats were fired from in front. His head was foggy. He had to shut them all out, try to focus.

A piece of wood lay in the overgrown front garden, part of an old window frame, a straight cut line with a ridge and patches of white paint clinging stubbornly to the edge. Decker bent and snatched up the makeshift weapon. Flailing blindly he screamed threats of his own, although what he shouted he couldn't exactly be sure. Looks of uncertainty now shrouded two of his adversaries. They stepped back, no longer vociferous with their taunts. The third man, the one holding the burning stick, stepped forwards.

Whoops and cheers came from his friends behind, drunk on their revelry of narcotics and battle lust. Decker swung and Alex held up his makeshift torch to deflect the blow. A shower of sparks and burning flakes of wood rained over them. More cheers came from behind, shouts of 'Do it, Decker! Do it!'

Alex swung the burning club at him. Decker stepped back as the flames combed his face with a sound like the billowing sail on a ship, the smell of burnt hair. He swung out in retaliation, catching Alex off balance. The piece of wood struck Alex across the side of his head. If there was a sound on impact then Decker couldn't remember it afterwards, but he did remember the judder of vibrations up his arms as the heavy wood thudded against Alex's skull.

Alex spun sideways and crashed down into the long grass. Three flecks of white paint lay on his scalp, and for a second looked like flower petals, as if he'd fallen asleep in a meadow.

Decker looked blearily around the garden, still clutching the window frame. The grey car carrying Alex's friends pulled away and began accelerating up the street. John, Brian and Tony were frantically climbing into the Charger. They were shouting something at him. Decker just blinked, then a moment later they drove away. Decker wasn't sure at first why they had left him.

He turned and saw Becky, crying in the doorway of her house. What was he doing here? Turning back he saw flashing blue lights at the end of the road, and realised the ringing in his ears was the sound of approaching sirens.

Central café, although not particularly central to anything, was a place where Tazeem occasionally liked to go and relax. Tazeem greeted the owner, an Algerian man he knew called Bassam, and took a seat at a table near the rear of the shop. The interior was painted in pale yellows and browns with domed arches along the walls and arched doorframes. Large ceramic tiles covered the floor and the furniture was wicker, the tables topped with thick, round glass.

Tazeem ordered mint tea. He knew Ermina never arrived on time, so had delayed his own arrival to avoid, or at least minimize, his inevitable wait. He was on his second glass when she made her entrance.

'Hey, cousin,' Ermina said as she dropped into the chair opposite.

'Would you like to order something?'

'No, I have other plans for lunch. So what do you want to see me about?'

She looked calm but her demeanour was prone to rapid change if things didn't go her way. Tazeem knew this. He had to be cautious, or risk her walking out.

'I just thought it would be nice for us to catch up. We rarely spend time, just the two of us these days.'

'Hmm, I guess so,' Ermina said, reached across the table and took a sip of his mint tea. She wrinkled her nose, put the glass back down and fished in her bag for cigarettes.

'So what are your plans for lunch?'

'I'm meeting Sadiq. I don't know where we're going, though.' A smile hinted at the corners of her mouth as she lit up, the tip of her Marlboro Light glowing orange. She had obviously guessed this might be the reason for their meeting.

'You seem to be spending a lot of time with Sadiq these days.'

'Is that just an observation or should I expect it to be followed up with questions?'

'Look, Ermina ...' he began, carefully.

'No, you look, Tazeem. Sadiq knows how to treat a lady, and he isn't shy of putting his hand into his pocket.'

'It's not his pocket I'm worried about,' Tazeem said, and immediately knew he'd made a mistake.

Ermina tutted, rolled her eyes and folded her cigarette-holding arm across her chest.

'You know the kind of lifestyle he leads. I'm worried about the image you may get from hanging around with him.'

'Sadiq looks after me. That was what you said you would do, ever since we were kids. You don't run your own business or have any investments. A few hours here and there working in shops and you expect to look after your mother and me as well? Tazeem, you're a joke,' she said bitterly. 'Even your dopey friend Latif is doing OK for himself.'

'Sadiq doesn't run any businesses either,' he protested weakly.

'No, but when a chance comes along he isn't afraid to take it. He steps up,' Ermina said, gesturing flamboyantly with her cigarette as she stood up.

She turned on her heel and stalked out of the cafe, almost knocking a plate from a timid waiter's hand. He nodded and smiled as he put down the plate and quickly retreated to the kitchen.

Tazeem slid a hand into his pocket and withdrew the lottery card. The Lucky Leprechaun: three matching Leprechaun symbols guarantees a cash payout of 250k, promised the shiny yellow lettering that danced along the top of the card. The idiot faces of three cartoon leprechauns grinned mockingly back at him.

Tazeem's mother and Ermina's father were brother and sister. Ermina's mother died in childbirth and Tazeem's father had also died when he was very young. As a result, Tazeem was encouraged to look out for Ermina as if she was his sister. Their remaining parents were old now, and Tazeem felt the pressure of being head of a household despite never having agreed to it. He knew he had been shy of providing from time to time, but he had never anticipated that might cause Ermina to look to a man like Sadiq for comfort or financial security. His hand lingered a moment longer on the card before he slipped it back into his pocket.

The doorbell rang and Tazeem – or 'Paavan Patel', his newly created identity – walked along the narrow hallway to open it. He had managed to forge or otherwise obtain a fake lease for the vacant flat he was in, a driver's licence and a birth certificate, which he used to open a bank account. Even with all the documents he still felt uneasy claiming the prize from the winning ticket.

'Mr Patel?' a bronzed, smiling face asked as he opened the front door to a succession of blinding flashes from a camera.

'Yes,' Tazeem confirmed, 'are the pictures necessary?'

'Just a few shots,' the grinning man continued. Tazeem turned and walked back into the house, signalling for the bronzed man and the photographer to follow. The less people witnessing this the better, and next door's curtain had already begun to twitch.

The syrupy man settled onto an armchair, and began to talk as he flicked through papers that needed signing.

'Tazeem Hamid,' a voice bellowed along the hallway.

Shit, they must have left the front door open, Tazeem thought.

'This is the police.'

Three officers burst into the room. The lottery employees looked at each other as if they'd slipped through a crack into another dimension.

'This is Mr Patel,' the now nervously smiling face grinned uncertainly at the policemen.

Tazeem took out his freshly acquired identification and presented it to one of the officers.

The officer squinted at the driving licence then laughed as he tossed it onto the floor. 'You're having a laugh. If this was any fresher the ink would still be wet,' he said, and twisted Tazeem's arm behind him, encircling his left wrist with handcuffs.

'A witness at the shop saw you in possession of a load of scratch cards, Tazeem.'

'I work there, they must have seen me sorting out cards at the shop. I never gamble. I just found this one.'

'Exhibit A,' the officer almost sang as he pulled out the Taweez locket that hung on the silver chain around Tazeem's neck.

He yanked on it and the chain snapped. Being careful not to touch the locket itself, he closely inspected the edges. Sure enough, tiny foil shavings remained in the groove from the last time Tazeem had used it to scratch the cards.

3

The lingering civil unrest following the explosion, the finger-pointing and political backlash, possibly contributed to Tatiana falling through the cracks of an already flimsy social care system. The newspaper headlines were dominated by what had been labelled 'The Daisy-Cutter Assassination Attempt' because of the type of device used in the blast.

After three months, when her visible wounds had healed, Tatiana grew tired of her solitary existence in the hospital. One afternoon she slipped out and didn't return. Back at the rented accommodation she had previously called home, she found the family's belongings rotting in boxes by the side of the road. Anything valuable had been taken, and the house was being prepared for another family to move in. No one had told her so, but Tatiana knew in her heart that her parents and brother were dead. She'd looked in every ward during her recovery, but held out no hope of finding them recovering under the white linen sheets of a hospital bed.

Tatiana felt a sudden tug at her sleeve. She spun around, startled, and recognised the face of the grey-haired woman who had worked at the factory with her mother. The woman's eyes swam with sympathy and confusion. Tatiana watched as her mouth soundlessly formed words, but she could hear nothing. The woman's lips fell still and she stared blankly at Tatiana, her forehead creased with concern as she waited for a response. Tatiana shook free of the woman's grip and ran.

This was the same treatment she had received in hospital. As she'd carried no identification and appeared unable, or perhaps unwilling, to answer questions, priority had eventually switched to the other victims of the blast. Tatiana felt she had been forgotten.

With only a handful of coins in her pocket, Tatiana took a bus into the city. The future hadn't crossed her mind while in the hospital. She'd been numbed from pain, grief and confusion, but the growling in her stomach proved a nagging reminder that she had to adapt to a new way of life, and adapt fast.

The city was dark and wet when Tatiana stepped down out off the bus. It was surreal to see cars passing by over the wet tarmac without hearing the familiar swish of tyres. Tatiana turned away from the kerb and was enveloped by the aroma of fried chicken from a nearby takeaway

She walked up to the serving hatch and looked over the menu. Without taking the remaining coins from her pocket, Tatiana knew she didn't have enough for even the cheapest item listed.

The man in the serving hatch had waxy skin and black hair, a thick tuft of which also sprouted from each of his nostrils. He began waving his arms to attract her attention. Tatiana guessed he must have been talking to her as she looked forlornly at the prices. The man gestured at the menu behind him, pointed at her and gave an exaggerated shrug. Tatiana withdrew her coins and held them out to show him. He stole a quick glance up the street and then beckoned for her to come around behind the counter. Tatiana ducked into the alleyway and saw a door open up a little way ahead.

Maybe he's looking for staff, she tried to reassure herself as she walked toward the door; a chance to earn some money and pay for somewhere to stay. Tatiana stepped inside a cluttered storeroom. Large brown sacks of potatoes were lined up along one wall next to a battered looking refrigerator and chest freezer. The floor was dirty and the air smelled sour.

She felt large calloused hands on her arm and neck, and spun around to face the man. Unperturbed by her incredulous expression, he fumbled with the buttons on her shirt as he tried roughly to undress her. Tatiana beat at his hands, and seeing his belt and pants already unfastened she staggered backwards and fell heavily against the wall. He shouted at her, the tendons in his neck as taut as tow-rope, and spittle flew from his lips. He pulled a crumpled wad of notes from his pocket and brandished them at her. His fury raged. Tatiana staggered to her feet and bolted out into the alley.

Her breath felt hot and acrid in her throat as Tatiana fled toward the main street. She stole a look backwards to make certain she wasn't being pursued, ran headfirst into a passer-by and they both tumbled to the ground. Panic gripped Tatiana and she felt danger all around her. She looked up at this new potential threat, but saw no malice in the young girl's quizzical gaze back at her.

Tatiana checked for her pursuer. The man stood uncertainly by the doorway; his pants had slid down a few inches, revealing a band of pale, hairy flesh. Seeing the anxiety on Tatiana's face, the other girl got to her feet and shouted at him. He dragged up his pants and disappeared back into his store.

The prospect of spending the rest of his life in jail wasn't something Decker was able to process. Six months, or a year, or even ten years, he thought he could begin to wrap his head around. At least then there was an after. But life … to remain within the same four walls until he drew his last breath just didn't make sense. There was no after, there was only a before; and 24 hours in every day to relive the before, over and over again.

His first week in Portmarsh was the longest and most unbearable of his life. He was locked in a one-man cell for 23 out of every 24 hours. For the hour a day when the door was left unlocked for him to socialise with other prisoners, Decker still remained alone in the cell. It was almost as if by attempting to make something of the situation he was in, and get to know fellow inmates, he would be accepting his fate. A fate he still found too unbearable to comprehend.

He didn't wash, just splashed cold water onto his face as a distraction from the oppressive brick walls and banging cell doors that echoed continually throughout the wing during daylight hours. He didn't talk to the guards when they checked on him by opening the metal panel in the door. He ignored the inmates who spoke to him when they brought his meals three times a day, and did little more than pick at the food which was tasteless at best.

After a week he was moved to a different wing and into a shared six-by-eight with a grizzled old con called Alf. He had faded tattoos that stained most of the visible skin on his hands, arms and neck a dull blue, sharp eyes and a thick beard that made his mouth look like an axe wound on a bear.

The first two weeks few words were exchanged, which suited Decker fine. Letters arrived and lay unopened in a pile beside his clothes and toiletries. The fragments of conversation that passed between him and Alf were like pieces of a jigsaw puzzle that didn't fit together. Too much in-between was missing.

Alf had his routine of reading, exercise and crossword puzzles that he slotted in around naps and social. As soon as the cell door opened at 6 p.m. he was out, and he never returned before exactly 7 p.m. Decker continued to keep away from the rest of the jail population.

'You scared of them?' Alf asked him one night when he returned to the cell.

'I'm not scared of anyone, you or any of the fuckers out there.'

Alf let the words drift around the cell for a while without reply.

'How long you been in?' Decker asked eventually.

'Thirty-three years.'

'How long have you got to go?'

'I doubt I'll ever get out now. I made a lot of mistakes on the outside, then a whole lot more in here.'

'Don't think I'll ever get out either,' Decker stated.

'Maybe not. Some don't. I've had my share of parole hearings and I'm still here.'

'Why didn't they let you out?'

''Cause it took me a long time to realise that in here you need to learn through wisdom, not experience.'

'What the fuck does that mean?'

'It means you're in here 'cause you fucked up, and if you keep fucking up till something in your head finally works out you need to change your ways, then a whole lot of time is likely to have passed you by. On the other hand, there's no shortage of people in here who are gonna fuck up for you, so if you keep quiet and watch them make the mistakes, you can learn. Wisdom rather than experience.'

'What's that make you, a fuckin' prison philosopher?'

'No, just an old man who would do a lot of things different if I had my time over. You got family on the outside?'

'Yeah.'

'Forget about them. Make the most of where you are.'

'What's the point in forgetting the only things that matter? What will that solve?'

'If your world is out there and you are in here then the only things that will gather within these walls are time and bitterness. Eventually, that bitterness will eat away at you and leave nothing behind but resentment and hate.'

'That's pretty much how I feel now, so what's the difference?'

'You might think that's how you feel now, but hold onto it for a month, a year, see how time magnifies those feelings. You'll end up fighting; no doubt you'll start using drugs, which of course you'll eventually be caught with, then there's the abuse towards the guards. Right now you're probably thinking none of that matters 'cause your life is over anyway, but it isn't. One day your parole hearing will come around, and everything you've done in here will all be listed on pieces of paper in front of them to make a judgement on whether you deserve another chance. It's up to you to always have that thought in the back of your head. Otherwise you'll end up another wasted life, left in here to rot.'

'You mean like you?' Decker asked with a sneer.

'Yeah,' Alf said looking down from the top bunk. 'That's exactly what I mean. You have to make up for what you've done, and not just to get out of this place, or once you do get out you'll end up coming right back. I can still remember what the judge said to me in court all those years ago: "If you can learn, change and atone, then maybe you still have a chance at life."' Alf had turned back around and stared at the ceiling of their cell. He let out a long slow sigh, before adding, 'It just took me too long to realise that he was right.'

Over the first few years Decker adapted better than he'd expected to life in prison. He began replying to his letters, although there had been none from Brian, John or Tony. His sister Becky still blamed herself for what happened that night, regardless of the number of times he tried to reassure her that there was nothing she could have done. The words in his mother's letters seemed to carry some of the burden of his guilt as well.

Decker struck up friendships with a number of people inside, but heeded Alf's caution to choose his words wisely and his friends even more so. A lot of talk between the inmates was showmanship, exaggeration or just downright lies, but Decker felt he was learning to recognise which was which.

So far he'd managed to avoid being put on report for anything; something of an achievement considering the drug use and violence that was endemic among the prison population. Inevitably there had been confrontations. But so far Decker had always turned away from conflict in open areas where the prison guards would see. When anyone wronged him, or challenged the respect he'd begun to accumulate, he would wait and visit one-on-one in their cell with no witnesses. Sometimes this was enough to force his would-be opponent to back down, but regardless, the situation was always dealt with.

As time went on, he began to take his personal fitness a lot more seriously and also gave up smoking. There was little he could do about the prison diet, but always took his share of fruit and vegetables and opted for the healthier options.

He began a work programme training as an electrician, and was allowed the privilege of regular access to the gym. His previously lean frame and stringy muscles gained shape and began to bulk out. He also signed up to the library programme and under Alf's guidance began to broaden his knowledge through books.

Decker was halfway through the seventh year of his sentence when Alf was diagnosed with cancer. They hadn't been cell mates for almost a year, following Alf's transfer to a minimum security facility, but still kept in contact by letter. Despite giving up smoking at the same time as Decker, Alf had contracted lung cancer. He'd suffered from deep hacking coughs which had worsened in the last few months they had shared a cell. In one of his last letters, Alf said that the prognosis wasn't good and he had perhaps six months to live. The letter was impersonal, and had more lines devoted to criticising the food and complaining of an inmate who had cheated him at a hand of cards.

Decker swept a hand over his eyes and brushed away the tears, but despite the pain he felt at the news, he couldn't help but smile at Alf's carefree way of dealing with it. Alf had no family, certainly none that kept in touch, and despite Decker having his mother and sister on the outside, Alf had become the most important person in his world – the father figure and role model he had never known as a child.

Just an hour out of his cell each day for 'social' was fine by Mangle. The other inmates, for the most part, looked like the kind of men he'd cross the road to avoid having to walk past, let alone sit down and chat with. One problem with this was that the hour they had for recreation was also the only time they had access to the phone, and by the time his cell had been unlocked, a substantial queue had always already formed.

For the third day of his incarceration Mangle stoically took up his place at the end of the line. No guards patrolled near the payphones. All calls were no doubt recorded so there was no need to listen to outgoing conversations from the wing. This may have created the illusion of privacy for some of the prisoners who seemed a little carefree during their calls, but it also meant that twice before, larger inmates had decided Mangle had been saving their place in line and stepped in front of him, and the hour of recreation had ended as he stood waiting for their calls to finish.

Mangle checked the clock that hung on the whitewashed stone wall at the end of the wing. He was the last in line, with eight minutes before the bell sounded, announcing their return to cells. An irate man yelled threats into the receiver in front of him in a Jamaican accent. Mangle glanced around but nobody was paying him any attention. The man's volume level increased along with his displeasure at whatever it was that he'd heard, and then the Jamaican began hammering the handset against the steel outer housing of the phone. Mangle rushed forward and tried to calm him while anything remained of his first chance at outside communication.

'Fuck you,' the man spat, and pushed past Mangle, leaving the receiver dangling at the end of its armoured cable.

Tentatively, he held the handset to his ear, pressed to terminate the connection, then listened. The sweet sound of a live line was music to his ears. Mangle fumbled some coins into the slot and again glanced at the clock. He began punching buttons.

'Hello?' He was relieved to hear Vicky's voice answer the call.

'It's me, this is the first chance I've had to phone and explain.'

'You don't need to explain, Nick, I heard what happened.'

Her tone was matter-of-fact and Mangle thought perhaps she didn't understand the situation he was in.

'I just want you to know I did it for us ... '

'How the hell could this be for us? I phoned your parents and your mother blames me. She says I must have got you mixed up in this. I work in a fucking library, for Christ's sake. That's hardly a den of iniquity.'

'I'll call her and explain it was nothing to do with you.'

'You'll be lucky. She told me to pass on the message that she and your father have had enough. She's supported your lack of character and loose morals and tried to encourage your non-existent ambition long enough, blah-blah-blah. Now you have to stand on your own.'

'OK, well at least we still have each other. And I'm finished with drugs, I won't have anything to do with anything like that ever again,' Mangle stammered into the handset, and he meant it.

The wiry Jamaican bellowing at the top of his lungs and attempting to demolish the phone had elicited no interest from other inmates, but the fretful tone creeping into Mangle's voice had begun to turn heads.

'We don't have each other, Nick. I could never trust you again after what's happened. I can't pay the mortgage on my own and I have no way to get back the deposit I put down on our house. Dad says the only thing I can do is cut my losses and go for a quick sale at a much lower price. I've applied to be transferred to a library down south. I'd appreciate it if you didn't call back. I don't want to speak to you again. It's over.'

Tazeem waited patiently during the rigorous pat-down preceding his prison visit. He moved along to the collection desk, where he handed over his watch and signed next to his prisoner ID for collection on the way back out. A buzzer sounded and Tazeem's section was led forward into a long, brightly coloured, thinly carpeted room. Feeling anything other than concrete and steel under his feet was like walking barefoot across a dewy lawn.

Rows of orange and green plastic chairs were bolted to the floor down the length of the room, with small Formica tables squatting in-between them. Tazeem sat where he was instructed to, and waited for his visitor to be shown through. Soon, conversational voices battled to be heard over the noise of shrieking children in the soft play area at the end of the room.

Ermina headed the next clutch of visitors. Her sullen gaze swept the room before she spotted him and stalked over.

'Nice to see you too,' Tazeem said as she perched stiffly on the edge of her chair.

Ermina placed a single cup of coffee down in front of her. Tazeem looked down the line at drinks and confectionary that had been purchased internally by family and friends for other inmates to consume during the visit.

'You've made a real mess of things, Tazeem,' Ermina said.

Tazeem thought about protesting but her susceptibility to turbulent moods silenced him. 'Didn't you think about how me and my father, and your mother, would cope if you were locked up?'

'You were the one talking about taking risks, about stepping up when a chance was presented. The reason I took the chance was to provide for the family.'

Ermina displayed the knowing smile of someone conversing with the village idiot, and shook her head as she picked up her cup. She blew onto the hot coffee but put it back on the table without taking a drink. 'Luckily for you, Sadiq is taking care of me.'

Tazeem took a breath and swallowed down his bitterness before it could be verbalised.

'Look, Tazeem, we can all see how you've failed up to this point, but that's not to say it's all over for you.'

'What do you mean, "failed", and who exactly is the *all* you're talking of?'

'Me, Sadiq, my father, your mother. I've spoken to Sadiq and he'll take over your responsibilities while you're in here. He's working on some pretty exciting things, actually, so when you're released you'll come to work for him. With a more capable and dominant man leading the way we will all benefit, Tazeem.'

He sat back in the chair, dumbfounded.

Ermina checked her watch. 'I have to go. I just wanted to come in and tell you not to worry, and that I'll move into your house to look after it for you. I won't be visiting again, though, I can't bear this place,' she said distastefully, and wiped her palms on the front of her skirt. She reached across to take Tazeem's hand.

'No contact, table four,' a leather-faced guard bellowed down the row.

Ermina abruptly withdrew her hand. 'Goodbye Tazeem,' she said as she stood up. 'Try to stay out of trouble.'

4

For two months Tatiana lived with Sasha, the girl she'd run into after her encounter with the man at the fried chicken booth, her little sister Polina, and Natalia, whose small rented apartment they all stayed in. Sasha and Polina had been made homeless after their mother was killed during a brutal robbery. No one was caught for the crime, so their father sought his own vengeance. He beat the name of a man from a drunk in a bar, hunted him down and murdered him. Whether his act of retaliation was in fact directed at the perpetrator of the atrocity, Sasha and her sister didn't know. After their father was arrested, they took what money they could find and what belongings they could carry, and fled, fearing if they were put into social care they may be separated forever.

Polina had been friends with a deaf girl at school and understood sign language. Tatiana picked it up quickly and eventually, through Polina's patience and dedication, was able to read the girl's lips as she spoke the words she was signing.

Tatiana felt a sudden vibration through the arm of the couch, and Polina sprang up from the seat beside her and rushed from the room. Tatiana followed her. In the tiny bathroom, they saw

Natalia crouched in the shower cubicle with her face in her hands. Polina swept aside the ragged shower curtain, sat in front of her and tried to ease Natalia's hands away to see what was wrong. Finally she relented. The left side of her face was swollen and scraped. Her make-up was smeared and streaked from the tears that ran down her cheeks, and her chest rose and fell rapidly as she tried to catch her breath.

Tatiana knelt down and took her hand as Polina ran to fetch Natalia's asthma inhaler. They knew what had happened. Natalia had suffered in this way before. Tatiana led her through to the sitting-room and they sat down on the couch. Polina came in and handed her the inhaler. Natalia shook it and took two blasts. Her breathing levelled out and she eased back against a cushion. She would talk about it when she felt ready.

'At first he was nice man,' Natalia said eventually, after wiping her face with a cloth Polina brought her from the bathroom. 'He even took me for meal first, they never do that, then to hotel room where we start to do it. He was struggling to … perform.'

'He was a limp dick,' Polina said and giggled.

'Don't talk like that. If Sasha was here she would make you eat soap,' Tatiana scolded. She took a breath and then more softly she said, 'Polina, why don't you go to your room and try to get some sleep. Your sister will be back soon, she will come sit with you.'

Obediently she left the room so that the older girls could talk.

'She's too young to understand how dangerous it is,' Tatiana said. Natalia nodded. 'You can't go on like this, Talia. Who knows what might happen next time.'

'I know. Have you thought about coming away with me?'

'To buy visa is so expensive. You've been so kind to me already, I would never be able to repay you.'

'We won't have enough for full visas, but we can get working deal. In this country men only pay women for sex, but overseas women get paid good money just for dancing. I have enough for down payment, and we can go to a place I hear of, Garden

Heights. We can work in club as dancers to pay what we owe, then afterwards we are free to do what we want.'

Tatiana nodded her agreement to Natalia. The prospect of leaving both scared and excited her, but she knew there was now nothing left for her in her homeland but grief, and memories of what she had lost.

The inmates were led out to wait in reception for the transport to arrive. Mangle was the only one from his unit and the last to congregate with the other prisoners. He was uncuffed from the accompanying guard, who was around 30, with a round face and plump wrists like those of a baby or an old woman. The handcuffs left indents where they had nestled between the folds of flesh. The other prisoners were already shackled together in pairs, except for one, and Mangle was attached to him.

'Evening,' the inmate said, as they were handcuffed together.

It was morning, but Mangle still nodded, acknowledging the ice-breaker. His travelling companion was burly but not brutish, and had no visible tattoos on his hands and arms which seemed at odds with his powerful prison physique, although there were two words on the back of his neck: 'Carpe Diem'.

Their belongings were sealed and tagged in clear plastic bags and taken down onto the bus. A register was called, which seemed a little pointless at this stage, but they answered to their names anyway and then filed down one pair at a time. His companion was called Derek Rankin.

The day was cold and a tablecloth of cloud permitted only a smudgy grey light to permeate. Climbing on board a vehicle for the first time in over two years filled Mangle with a warmth of memory, and he tried to savour every detail. The world seemed a much larger place than the one he'd left the last time he passed through the prison gates.

The bus seats were divided by a central aisle. Each seat was taken up by a pair of cuffed inmates. A guard occupied the third seat in every other row. Mangle and his companion took their seats on the second to last row. The pudgy-wristed guard took the inside seat on their row. Once the last two guards had climbed aboard, the door was locked and the engine started up.

All of the prisoners were silent and looked out of the windows almost in enchantment as the bus began to move. Mangle guessed most of them had probably not seen anything outside the prison walls for a lot longer than himself.

The bus was designed for anything but comfort, and Mangle could soon feel the heat from the engine below his seat. Diesel fumes reached up through tiny gaps between the metal plates on the floor, making him nauseous.

The guards chatted quietly amongst themselves while the prisoners mostly maintained silence. The guard on Mangle's row flirted with a female guard who sat diagonally across the aisle, in front of them. A shaven-headed man with a pock-marked face and a spider-web tattoo on his neck was cuffed to an Asian in the seat beside her. The flirting was awkward and Mangle cringed at the guard's heavy-handed approach toward the woman, who in Mangle's estimation was way out of his league. She smiled politely at his attempts at humour, but he recognised the want-away look in her eyes from similar situations he'd been in at night-clubs.

There was a break in the conversation as pudgy-wrists perhaps reassessed his battle plan, and the female guard turned back around and faced forward. Undeterred, or maybe just desperate enough to have one last try, pudgy wrists poked her on the shoulder. When she turned he pointed sneakily towards the Asian sitting to her left, screwed up his face and wafted a hand under his nose. Bizarrely, this seemed to work and she let out a light-hearted laugh that turned a few heads further down the bus. The Asian man turned his head momentarily, but unaware that he was the reason for her laughter, looked back out of the window.

Mangle had never seen the man in Portmarsh, as they'd been housed in different wings, but he felt more of an affinity to him than to the racist guard he sat alongside.

'Hey man, what's your name?' Mangle asked across the aisle, but the Asian didn't turn around.

'Tazeem!' Mangle's companion said.

The Asian turned around, startled at the unexpected contact. He nodded over at them.

'And I'm Decker,' the man said, extending his uncuffed hand.

Reedland Grange was a minimum security prison for offenders considered to be of low risk to the public, coming towards the end of their sentence and preparing for reintegration to the community. Rather than a 23-hour lock-up, they were made to work at a variety of jobs around the prison and get accustomed to a six-day working week, to make the transition back into society less turbulent.

'Tazeem, hey.'

He was on his way back to work for the afternoon kitchen shift and turned at the sound of his name.

'Mohammed, how you doing?'

'I'm good, man. How come you never hang out with the brothers after work?'

'I do sometimes, just depends on how I feel.'

'Nah, you're always with that white boy. What's up with that?'

'Nothing up with it, man, he's my friend. His cell is on my landing and we both work in the kitchens. So what?'

'Spending so much time with a Kafir, it's not right. You should stick to your own.'

'Whatever, man.You don't even know him. You just bag him out 'cause he's white and has different beliefs.'

'You're a Muslim. It's white people who locked you up in here and now you look to make friends with them?'

'It's the law that locked us up in here, the same as it did Mangle. I'm gonna be late for work, man, I'll see you at Friday prayer.'

'Yeah, make sure you don't miss it this week. Remember where you belong, Tazeem.'

Tazeem hurried on to the huge brick building that housed the kitchen and vast dining hall. Some of the other workers were smoking hand-rolled cigarettes by the door before the start of their shift, and greeted him as he walked by.

'What was up with Mohammed?' Mangle asked as Tazeem came in and put on his apron and hat. 'I saw you just before I came in to work.'

'He's just being a prick, nothing new there.'

'I don't think he likes me,' Mangle said, grinning.

'Yeah, probably not. He doesn't seem to like anyone with your milky complexion,' Tazeem said, and laughed.

They both took up their station in veg prep. Tazeem sliced a turnip in half and began expertly to manoeuvre the sharp blade of his knife around the purple skin, revealing the firm yellow flesh underneath. He glanced at the three huge sacks on the floor. It would be a long afternoon.

Part of the rehabilitation programme at Reedland Grange involved improving the level of literacy and numeracy of the inmates, to enable them to function in an average workplace. Tazeem took his usual seat at the far corner table, took out his notebook and waited as the other inmates came in and sat down. The tables were arranged around the walls in a U formation, the teacher's desk at the front and the whiteboard directly behind her. Mohammed was one of the last to enter, and sauntered over to sit beside Tazeem.

The teacher was in her fifties, short in stature, and had an easy-going manner that could change gear to that of a drill sergeant in a split second when required.

'For the new faces in this class I'll remind you that these classes are compulsory, you must attend, but that doesn't mean you can't enjoy it. I am here as your teacher, not as your enemy. Isn't that right, Les?' she said, aiming a theatrical glare at one of the larger inmates.

Tazeem knew Les from working in the kitchen. He had shoulders as wide as a doorframe and a neck as thick as a bull's, a sloping forehead, overhanging brow and a blunt nose, and carried a perpetual scowl wherever he went.

'Yes, Miss,' he grunted in reply, failing to acknowledge her attempt at humour.

'You'll all be working at different levels, so if someone asks a question that you yourself find easy, you will not mock them. The goal here is the same for you all, to improve your own skills and increase your chances of getting and keeping a good job on the outside.'

An ironic ripple of laughter went around the room that the teacher ignored.

'Anyway, for those of you that don't know, my name is Annabelle McCulloch. You can call me Miss or Annabelle. Not Anna, not Belle, and definitely not Tinkerbelle, so please don't think you're the first one to come up with that.'

A more enthusiastic laugh warmed the room. Tazeem was impressed at how the teacher managed to forge a link with her students, despite the visible hostility most had entered with. With the introduction over, the lesson started.

Tazeem looked over the worksheet he'd been given and began writing. Mohammed started talking to him in Urdu, so Tazeem ignored him. He knew it would incite ill feeling from inmates able to hear but not understand what was being said, even though Mohammed wasn't talking about anything in particular. He knew the result would be the same; it was clearly a calculated move, epitomized by the half-smile Mohammed wore as he spoke.

'In English please, you two,' Annabelle said looking over towards them.

'Yeah, it's fucking English class, not Bunkoo-Bunkoo,' a voice from the far side of the room snapped.

Tazeem looked across and saw Les leering back at them. Mohammed stood up and began to hurl insults at Les in Arabic until Tazeem put a hand on his arm. 'Leave it, Mohammed. You knew this would happen.'

Mohammed sat back in his chair with a faint look of pride at how easily he had managed to elicit some petty racism from the room.

'Alright everybody, pipe down.' Annabelle said, authoritatively. 'OK now, Les, I want you to tell me which words are the adjectives in this sentence.' She turned and began to write on the whiteboard: 'The quick brown fox jumped over the lazy dogs'.

The distraction appeared to work and the room quietened again as Les switched his attention to the whiteboard. His brow at first crinkled and then furrowed deeply in concentration, or perhaps frustration. A few mutters went around the room, which further deepened the ridges in his forehead.

'It's quick and brown, Miss,' Tazeem said, in an effort to relieve the mounting tension.

'Fuck off you Paki cunt, I was just about to say that,' Les roared, and flipped the table over as he sprang to his feet.

Mohammed seized the opportunity and did the same, hurling a torrent of racial slurs that only he and Tazeem could understand. Annabelle pressed the panic button on her desk and a siren began to wail in the corridor. There was an immediate jingling of keys like incoming sleigh-bells as guards sprinted towards the classroom.

Les was standing in the middle of the room, gripped with fury. Veins pulsed in his temples and spittle had gathered at either side of his mouth, lips pulled back tight over snarling teeth. So far he had managed to resist the urge to pummel Mohammed, who continued to taunt and abuse him.

Tazeem backed away, keeping out of the altercation. They all knew that any violence would result in them immediately being shipped back to a high-security facility, possibly with time added onto their sentences.

The first guard burst into the room, quickly assessed the situation and walked purposefully toward Les, who seemed unaware of his presence. Two more guards followed a few seconds later. Mohammed had fallen silent and adopted his 'butter wouldn't melt' look, playing the victim to avoid punishment.

The first guard put his hand on Les's shoulder and quietly but forcefully urged him to follow them. For a moment his fixed stare flickered between Mohammed and Tazeem before something appeared to click back into place inside him, and he allowed himself to be led from the room.

'You reckon he'll get shipped out then, Decker?' Mangle asked at the lunch table after Tazeem had finished telling the story.

'Hard to say. He's got a screw loose, no doubt, but he's kept out of trouble since he's been here so they might give him another chance.'

'I guess that answers the question,' Tazeem said pointing towards the door.

Les walked in with the guard who'd arrived first in the classroom earlier. The guard exchanged a few words with Les and then left the dining hall. Les picked up a blue plastic tray and took his place in line without looking around the room.

'He'll have been in front of the Governor. Looks like Les is here to stay.'

Tazeem looked down and pushed the remaining food around the plate with his fork. He hadn't really wanted Les to get shipped out, but after staring into those coal-black eyes, seething with rage, Tazeem didn't relish the prospect of working alongside him in the kitchen.

5

'How do you know where to go?' Tatiana asked as they walked briskly through the city streets on a cold, wet Sunday morning. Broken bottles, discarded items of clothing, and used condoms were a visible record of the previous night's enjoyment for some, and misery for others.

'The girls on the street talk about it a lot,' Natalia said, turning to face her. 'It is what most work for these days. Drugs and alcohol are not the only way to cope with their lives; there is hope for the future.'

Natalia led the way towards an old stone church, although any evidence of stained glass windows was covered over by thick wooden boards. A grim-faced man in a black leather trench coat stood smoking a cigarette by the door. He stopped them from entering as they tried to walk past.

'What do you want?' he asked, and flicked his cigarette butt over Natalia's shoulder.

'I have money, and we want deals for working visas,' she told him, and produced two envelopes. The man opened them, flipped through the bills and slid both envelopes into an inside pocket. 'We want to go to Garden Heights,' Natalia said.

The man's laughter sounded like a landslide. 'You don't get to choose. Your contracts will be auctioned to the buyers; you will go where they have work.'

'We're dancers,' Natalia protested. 'That is the work we have come here to do.'

'Yes, dancers,' the man nodded as he ushered them past.

Inside, the pews had been dumped haphazardly in a pile in one corner. Six folding tables were surrounded by moulded plastic chairs, occupied by expensively dressed, expressionless men. A dark-haired girl wearing just her underwear stood shivering in the centre of the floor.

'Seven hundred,' said a man with a pencil-thin moustache from one of the tables.

'Eight hundred,' was the response from two tables over.

Pencil moustache glared at the man who'd outbid him, before saying, 'A thousand', through clenched teeth.

'Fifteen hundred,' came the immediate reply. Pencil moustache folded his arms and shook his head.

'Sold,' said a skinny man with a cigar as thick as his wrist from the front of the room, as he tapped his ash onto the floor.

The girl tentatively picked up her clothes and followed the buyer through a door at the back of the hall.

'You,' the skinny man said, pointing at Natalia. 'Lose the clothes, you're up next.'

'We're a package deal,' she said defiantly, and grabbed Tatiana's hand. The skinny man's gaze swept the room for any objections but no one spoke up.

'Alright then, both of you strip.'

Tatiana looked to Natalia as she hesitantly reached for her top button. 'I'll take them,' a white-haired man wearing a purple cravat said in clear, unaccented English. 'Five thousand for the pair.'

'This is your lucky day,' the skinny man said with a squinting leer and a wave of his arm. 'Follow him. You're leaving for Garden Heights.'

*****

Decker set off early the next day to collect a half jar of coffee, owed from the previous night's card game on A wing. He decided to knock for Tazeem and Mangle to walk into work together on the way back. The corridor was narrow and dimly lit and smelled faintly of bleach as the cleaning crew had recently mopped the floors. As he approached Tazeem's room, he saw some white lettering on the dark blue paint of the door. He gave three slow knocks and waited for Tazeem to open up.

'Decker, what brings you up this way?' Tazeem asked when he saw who it was.

Decker didn't answer but pointed to the door.

'"Paki go home." Not exactly original and I'd be more than happy to go home if it wasn't for all the guards and fences.'

'It looks like toothpaste so it'll come off, no problem. Suppose you should go fetch one of the guards, they're meant to log any racial stuff.'

'Nah, I'll just wash it off. Don't wanna make the situation any worse than it is. Besides, if Mohammed or any of his lot see it, things will kick right off.'

Tazeem came into the kitchens about ten minutes after the start of shift looking jaded and squirrely. Decker had knocked at Mangle's door and explained what had happened as they walked to the kitchens, and told him not to mention anything for now. Mangle's immediate response was outrage, as he and Tazeem had become pretty close. Being imprisoned day after day, month after month, with the same people, tended to amplify the impact and importance of situations that surrounded them. Friendships bonded quicker than they would on the outside. Decker still received letters from guys he'd served time with early on in his sentence, proving that the prison cliché, 'out of sight, out of mind', wasn't necessarily true.

Rivalries and disputes were also magnified, though, and could quickly turn into blood feuds. Having spent most of his adult life looking for warning signs to avoid trouble before it began, Decker's gut feeling told him to distance himself, but something he'd learned from Alf returned to him now: 'Family are one thing, but blood will still let you down. But true friendship, that's real family, and if you find someone who will stick by you no matter what, then you do whatever's necessary to hold onto them.'

He had a good feeling about Mangle and Tazeem, and he admired the way Mangle was determined to stand shoulder to shoulder with his friend, but having seen just what could happen when things went off, he knew neither Tazeem nor Mangle were prepared.

Decker watched them from his spot by the ovens, going through their usual veg-prep duties. Les was working alongside Jim, chopping portions of meat from a huge side of beef. Jim was a lifer, the same as Decker, and had perfected a knife juggling routine over the many years he'd spent working prison kitchens. He watched as Jim effortlessly tossed and caught three bloodstained cleavers. Les ignored him, having seen the routine any number of times before. He raised his own cleaver up high before slamming it down into the chilled cow carcass. If the writing on Tazeem's door was anything to do with Les, then he was giving nothing away.

Decker checked the timers on the ovens and went outside for some fresh air, as the atmosphere in the kitchen was thick from heat and humidity.

Under other circumstances the countryside view from the doors to the kitchens could have been described as tranquil, with clumps of hazel and beech trees and fields of barley under a panoramic blue sky. Most shrubs had been removed from within the grounds as prisoners used them to hide contraband that was thrown over the 30 foot fence from outside. Decker watched two squirrels scamper around the trunk of a solitary elm; another ran expertly along the chain link fence.

The serrated howl of a siren behind him snapped Decker out of his moment of relaxation. He turned and ran back into the building, hearing shouts from inside even over the deafening alarm. His first thought was that someone must have been stabbed.

The kitchen staff, contracted from outside the prison system, weren't trained to deal with physical altercations. All three huddled within the main office. Lawrence, the head cook, was stammering into a radio held between shaking hands. Decker rounded the bank of ovens to see most of the inmates gathered along the far wall beside the industrial-sized dishwashers.

Jim stood in the doorway to the raw meat section with a gleeful look on his face, two cleavers gripped loosely in his left hand. Les stalked in the veg room, brandishing another cleaver so tightly that his knuckles showed up as white as ivory. Mangle was trying to talk him into dropping it and Tazeem, with a long red slit down his right forearm that splashed blood like rose petals onto the cream-tiled floor, orbited the large aluminium shredder in clockwise revolutions.

No prison guards were on the scene yet, and judging from the intent on Les's face they would arrive too late. Decker backed against the ovens and began to edge nearer, attempting to stay out of Les's line of sight. If he could make it unseen to the raw meat room, he'd be within half a dozen steps of Les.

'Leave it, Decker, this is none of your business,' Jim said in a voice loud enough to carry as Decker moved past him.

He glared at Jim, who now adopted a smug grin, and then looked back at Les who had turned 45 degrees to keep both Tazeem and Decker within his field of vision.

'Fuck off, Decker, don't make this Paki one of your pet projects.'

Decker kept edging closer and said nothing. He knew he would either have to watch Tazeem get cut open, or he'd need to rush Les, who was now very aware of his presence.

Something scuffed against one of the benches behind him and Decker spun halfway around as Jim made to grab him by the neck. Decker gripped Jim at the wrist and elbow joint, dropped to one knee and threw his assailant over his shoulder. A satisfying snap from the forearm and resulting scream of pain told him Jim would be no more trouble, but Les had made the most of the distraction and was almost on top of Tazeem. Decker got to his feet and rushed towards them just as Mangle seized a tray of chopped lettuce and threw it in Les's face. Les momentarily lost composure and flailed wildly with the large steel blade.

Decker jumped him from behind. Wrapping his right forearm around Les's throat he flexed his bicep tight against the carotid artery and gripped Les's wrist in his left hand. Tazeem swung forward with a chopping board, knocking the cleaver out of Les's hand, and then backed into the corner beside Mangle. Spittle frothed at Les's mouth as he swore vengeance on Decker through clenched teeth.

'Easy, big fella, you're almost out,' Decker said, clinging tightly to him.

Les sank to his knees. Then his hands, which had been clawing at Decker's forearm, fell limp by his sides.

'Decker, get the fuck off him and back up against the wall,' a guard yelled, arriving just as he was no longer required.

Decker relaxed his grip and Les slumped forward face first onto the blood-splashed floor. Decker held up both palms and slowly backed away as two more guards arrived and ran to the fallen men. Another moved cautiously behind to cuff Decker.

'Well, look who it is,' Mangle said, glancing up from his chicken biryani.

'Alright boys, you miss me?' Decker said, putting his tray down at his usual seat at the table with Mangle and Tazeem.

'Always, man. So what happened?' Tazeem asked, looking concerned. His hand instinctively moved to touch the bandage covering his lacerated forearm.

'I went before the Governor yesterday and gave my statement. He'd already had all the reports in from the kitchen staff and you lot, and Les and Jim's twisted version of events. I'd been in solitary for two days so I had no way of corroborating with anyone, and what I said must have tied in or I'd be on a bus out by now. I take it there's been no sign of those dickheads?'

'Nah. You think they're already gone, then?' Tazeem asked.

'Definitely. How's your arm anyway?' Decker asked, gesturing with his fork after spearing a piece of chicken.

'Eighteen stitches, but I'll live. It would have been a whole lot worse if you hadn't stepped in,' Tazeem said, briefly making eye contact with Decker before looking back down at his plate.

'Don't worry about it, all in the past now,' Decker said dismissively, and scooped up a forkful of rice and curry.

Tazeem saw Mohammed watching from a few rows over, then shaking his head and returning to a conversation at his table.

When there was a knock at Tazeem's door later that night he thought it would be Mangle returning the shower gel he'd borrowed earlier, but was surprised to see Mohammed waiting in the corridor.

'Salaam alaikum Tazeem, kya haal hai?' Mohammed said in Urdu with mock formality and a wide grin: 'Good evening Tazeem, how are you?'

'Mohammed, what's up?'

'Just come by to say hello, man. Why does something have to be up?' Mohammed said, switching to English.

'You're right, it doesn't. OK, come in,' he said, and held the door while Mohammed entered.

Tazeem sat on the bed and muted the volume on the small TV set. Mohammed settled onto the solitary plastic chair. Tazeem knew there would be a reason for the visit, and waited for Mohammed to get to the point.

'So how are you, Tazeem? You're out pretty soon now, aren't you?'

'I'm doing OK, man, only a few weeks to go now.'

'How is your arm healing?' Mohammed asked. 'It looked a pretty bad wound.'

'It's getting better,' Tazeem said and ran his left palm along the length of his bandaged right forearm. 'There'll be a scar there once it's healed but that's not so bad.'

'I saw you at lunch today, with the two white boys. You didn't look so happy. Has what happened made you realise your mistake in hanging out with their kind?'

'No, Mohammed,' Tazeem said, making sure to keep his voice level.

He knew if he brought up Mohammed's part in stirring up the trouble in the literacy class then he'd have him here arguing his point for half of the night. 'That was just the action of one man. Decker and Mangle are still my friends.'

'I had a visit today,' Mohammed said, waving away Tazeem's words, 'from my cousins who live up in Garden Heights.' Tazeem waited through Mohammed's pregnant pause.

'They asked me to tell you that Sadiq says, hi, and of course your cousin Ermina.'

'Right. I haven't heard from him since I've been in jail. Is he doing OK?' Tazeem asked, doing his best to ignore the smirk Mohammed wore at the mention of Ermina's name.

'He's doing very well for himself, very well. My cousins have been working with him a lot over the last year. Once I am released I expect to be spending more of my time up there, so no doubt we'll run into each other.'

'What's he got going on?'

'The usual sort of things, but he's working with some diligent people and they're expanding all the time. You could do a lot worse than to hook up with him once you get out.'

'So I've been told. I guess I'll wait and see what my options are.'

The following day they had a break between two and three in the afternoon while there was a staff meeting about kitchen security. It was a warm June day, so Tazeem, Mangle and Decker sat on the grass outside of the dining hall, waiting for the kitchens to reopen.

'How long have you been inside for, Decker. About ten years?' Tazeem asked, and took the last bite of his apple.

'More than, yeah,' Decker nodded solemnly.

'What you gonna do when you get out?' Tazeem asked, and tossed his apple core towards the trees for the squirrels.

'I have no idea. If the parole board were asking I could trot out a host of stuff based around the qualifications I've got while I've been inside. But the truth is I just don't know.'

'What about you, Mangle? Three years behind bars and now only a month till freedom again. You gonna go back into the bathroom supplies trade?' Tazeem asked, turning to him.

'Yeah, I enjoyed it, got to travel about a bit and the pay was OK,' he said, leaning back against the wall, which was warmed by the afternoon sun. 'You ever hear from the guys you were involved with before you got locked up, Deck?'

'I did eventually, after I'd been in for a few years. Maybe guilty conscience or something once they realised I wasn't gonna roll over on them. I'm gonna keep well clear if they let me back out, though. Getting involved with them will only ever land me back in here again. I've seen enough of the type come and go over the years, but they're always back inside again before long.'

'Do you think your chances are good at the next parole hearing?'

'I hope so. Done everything I was supposed to do, kept out of trouble – well, apart from that the other day, but the Governor said he'll vouch for my innocence after reading all the reports. I don't think there's anything else gonna be achieved by keeping me in.'

'A reformed character,' Tazeem laughed.

Decker grinned and chewed on a long stalk of grass. 'They all say that when it's parole time, obviously, and I know a lot of them never will be, no matter what you do to them or however long you keep them locked up, but I really think I am. Remorse comes from inside you, but you have to go looking for it. It can't be programmed or beaten or forced into you,' he said wistfully, and then laughed.

'That sounds like another line you picked up from old Alf,' Tazeem said.

'My first ever cell mate, yeah. He'd leave these nuggets of wisdom lying around like breadcrumbs for the birds. He'd say something really off the cuff, just throw it out there like it was nothing. But then at night when I was trying to sleep the same line would go round and round in my head. At first I thought I was going nuts being locked up all the time, but then I'd catch him every once in a while just give me this knowing look, and I'd realise he knew exactly what he was doing.'

'Maybe you reminded him of himself when he was younger.'

'Yeah, that's probably what it was. Learn by other people's mistakes, he'd always say. Wisdom over experience.'

'You gonna see him when you get back out?' Mangle asked.

'Wish I could, man. He died a few years ago – cancer.'

'Sorry to hear that, Decker,' Mangle said, and meant it.

'I never really knew what grief was until he passed. I lost my grandparents when I was younger and I kind of went through the motions, I suppose, like I'd seen other people do when confronted with death. But I never really felt it in here,' he said, tapping a fist against his chest. 'Anyway, what about you then, Taz? Must be just over two years you've been off the streets for now, so what you gonna do when you get out?'

'Mohammed has been trying to get me involved with a guy I've known since I was a kid. But I reckon it would only end in tears. I've got an idea I've been thinking on, though.'

'Not exactly a reformed character yourself then, Taz?' Mangle laughed.

'You do what you gotta do to survive,' Tazeem said with a wink.

6

Tatiana and Natalia were bundled into the back of a grey van alongside four other girls. Although the prospect of going to Garden Heights had provided a moment's respite in her anxiety, Tatiana was no longer so sure it was a good thing after looking into the faces of the other girls. Trepidation hung on them like wet cloth. Natalia saw it as well, but did her best to force a reassuring smile. Two benches had been fastened to the floor on either side of the van, which looked more accustomed to transporting goods than people. Natalia sat facing Tatiana to make it easier for them to communicate. She reached over and took Tatiana's hand as the engine coughed into life and the van began to judder as it idled.

'We will be travelling for some time,' said the well-spoken man who had purchased their contracts, closing the passenger door after climbing in up front. A layer of wire mesh separated him and the unhealthily pale driver from the girls in the back. 'There will be two rest stops on the way for you to use the toilet facilities. There will be no interruptions to our journey other than that. Do not address myself or the driver unless we speak to you first. Is that understood?'

A mumbled affirmation seemed to be enough for the man and he turned to face forward. The van pulled out of a rear parking lot to the church and set off down a deserted street.

After a while, Tatiana gave up trying to watch the other girls for any sign of conversation. An earlier scattering of platitudes had abated and her fellow passengers turned their focus inward, their eyes dropped to the floor. Even Natalia, who had been so upbeat about the voyage, had sunk within herself and made little attempt to talk.

Tatiana watched their progress along the featureless highway, and tried to guess where they were. She had never travelled so far from what she had known as home, but felt no excitement at the expanse of an unfamiliar horizon. A few times she saw the man who'd bought them talking into a cell phone, but had no way of knowing what was said. He occasionally turned back to look at them, but his expression betrayed no indication of his intent.

Long hours and drab scenery passed by, and light drained from the day like water from a bath. The temperature dropped and the girls instinctively huddled closer together to conserve body heat. At some point Tatiana fell asleep, and the next thing she realised was lurching awake as the girl she had leant against gave a startled jump. The back doors to the van stood open, and warm morning sunlight crept inside. The girls got to their feet and climbed out at the behest of the driver. His skin looked almost translucent in the bright daylight, with a roadmap of thin blue veins visible at his temples.

The air, fresh and thick with salt, revealed their close proximity to the ocean even before Tatiana saw the boats. The white-haired man and a much larger man stood with their backs to them a little way off, talking to whom she guessed, from his posture and get-up, was captain of one of the boats. He wore dark grey waterproofs with zigzag orange fluorescent stripes. The other man, from his build and the quality of his suit, Tatiana supposed might be the white-haired man's bodyguard.

The driver of the van pushed her forwards and Tatiana stepped into line with the others. Another man in grey waterproofs appeared at the top of a gangway and beckoned them onto a boat, down a set of stairs, and instructed them to sit and wait. Six other girls already sat in what appeared to be the living quarters. There were four beds, a table and four chairs, and a small TV fixed onto a wood-panelled wall. The panelling wrapped around on three sides, with inbuilt shelving that housed books and knick-knacks, and there was a galley area to the rear of the room. Tatiana and Natalia exchanged relieved looks. If this was to be their accommodation while they travelled to their new home, then it would be a little cramped, but certainly liveable.

Around ten minutes later the captain, who introduced himself as Jacob, and two other men came down the stairs. One of the girls, perhaps emboldened by the absence of the white-haired man, asked how they should decide who got to sleep in the beds. The two shipmates stepped forwards as if to demonstrate. One walked past the girls into the galley and the other followed, stopping only to deal a swift punch to the side of the girl's head.

Tatiana felt but did not hear the collective cry emitted around the room as their companion fell to the floor. She spun to face the captain to plead for his help, but he now stood holding a silver pistol in his left hand.

Tatiana looked back to the crew who were busy with something at the back of the galley. Part of the rear wall swung inwards, revealing a large fibreglass container behind. Even the girl who had been assaulted had her full attention on what the men were doing, and some of the girls moved closer for a better look. A sealed trapdoor above indicated they must be on a trawler, and this is where the haul of fish would be dropped for storage whilst at sea.

But the thick chain fixed around the wall, and the many sets of manacles attached to it, revealed that it was no longer fish that would be kept in the ship's hold.

*****

Despite not having received any reply to the messages he'd left at the office, Mangle remained hopeful that he could still get back his old job. He'd served there for almost six years, and aside from a number of damaged company cars, and of course his eventual arrest, he'd had an unblemished record.

Tracey looked up and flashed a brief but cryptic smile before quickly looking over at the boss's closed office door.

'Is Alan expecting you?'

'No, he hasn't replied to my messages so I thought I'd show him that I'm just the same old Nick by coming down in person.'

'Good luck, then. You'll probably need it. What you did was stupid, and as far as the rest of us are concerned you've paid for it now, but the way Alan has been talking you'd think you'd been selling drugs to schoolchildren.'

Mangle flinched at the comment, then brushed a hand down the front of his suit and adjusted his tie.

'You want me to buzz him for you?'

'Please, Tracey,' Mangle said, taking a deep breath.

She pressed a button on the console at her desk and then crossed her fingers in a display of solidarity before speaking. 'Mr Worther. I have Mr Garrett here in reception for you,' she said briskly into the phone, her voice taking on the slightly pinched quality of a railway platform announcement.

'Nick, yes. OK, I will.' She carefully placed the phone back into the cradle as if it were something very delicate. 'He'll see you now, go right up.' Tracey forced another smile, although her eyes betrayed an indication of what he had to expect.

Alan Worther had been in charge at Pristine Bathroom Supplies for as long as Mangle had worked there. He was a small man, in both stature and personality, and made no pretence of being a friend to his colleagues. In his own words, he was there to lead, and as long as their wages were paid they should expect nothing more from him.

His office was an efficiently sized cube up a flight of steps from reception, with one small window obscured by permanently closed blinds. Mangle climbed the last two thinly carpeted stairs and knocked on the maple veneered door.

After the customary three-second pause he was instructed to enter. Alan sat with both elbows resting on his matching maple veneered desk, his fingers steepled against his lips.

'Nicholas Garret,' Alan said, before Mangle had a chance to compose himself and speak first. 'So you're out then.'

'Yes sir, I've paid my debt to society and I'm back.'

'Well, that's a matter of opinion,' he muttered, briefly looking away before turning back to focus directly on Mangle. 'So what can I do for you?'

'Well, considering the length of my employment here and previous good record, I had hoped to have my old job back.'

'I'm afraid that won't be possible. We're a traditional company here and once news of your arrest and the specifics regarding it got around we had a real battle not to lose a great deal of custom.' Alan was being reserved, possibly even diplomatic, in what he said but the delight that danced in his eyes revealed his true feelings.

'I can only apologise for that, sir, but given an opportunity I'd like to put everything I have back into my job and make up for any problems my indiscretion has caused.'

'The position has been filled anyway,' Alan said, shaking his head. His eyes slid over a framed wedding photo on his desk. 'Arthur, my son-in-law has stepped up to your old position, and has proved to be a valuable asset to the company. He's respectful, punctual and he's learning fast. We have nothing for you today I'm afraid, Nick. And to be honest I'd rather you didn't come back again. Do we understand each other?'

'Perfectly,' Mangle nodded, and closed the door on his way out.

Although he'd made it quite clear that immediate family were all he wanted to see, for just a few drinks at his mother's house, and that they definitely weren't to make a fuss, Decker's mother and sister hired the community hall and invited pretty much the entire neighbourhood.

Driving up in the taxi and seeing all the streamers and 'Welcome Home' banners fluttering outside was almost enough to make Decker instruct the driver to keep going. He hadn't anticipated anything like this. All the handshaking and backslapping that he'd had in the two days following his release had proved more unnerving than the barrage of animosity he had envisioned.

Decker's Uncle Sam waved his arms when he recognised his nephew in the cab.

'Just here will be fine,' Decker said, reaching for his wallet.

'You sure?' the driver asked comically, seeing the look of distress on Decker's face.

The door was pulled open by his enthusiastic uncle, who leant in and thrust some money at the driver.

'Take it easy, Uncle Sam.'

'No need for all that uncle stuff, you're a grown man now. Call me Sam. Now come on, everyone is waiting.'

Sam ushered him up the three concrete steps and through the graffiti-covered front doors.

Decker squinted and raised a hand against the bright lights that temporarily blinded him as they entered. A crackle from around the hall as the PA system came to life, and the gathered masses began a tuneless chorus of 'For he's a jolly good fellow'.

'What the fuck is going on?' Decker asked, but his uncle detached himself, singing along, and slipped into the crowd.

Decker was edgy. He nervously waited for the song to end. As the final line was bellowed out his mother stepped forward and clutched the hand that he was using to shield his eyes. The spotlights were lowered and he was dragged off and introduced to everyone, a continuous stream of names and faces he barely remembered from childhood. Declarations of how brave he'd been protecting his sister, and how glad everyone was that he was home, rang in his ears. For his mother's sake, Decker put up with the fawning adulation of her friends, but as soon as a lull presented itself he stole away to get a drink and retreat to a quiet spot.

'What's wrong with your face? After all that time in prison I'd have thought you'd appreciate all the trouble people went to here for you to welcome you back home,' Sam said, spotting Decker hunkered down in a chair behind the buffet tables.

'It's not that I don't appreciate what everyone has done. I just wanted to get out and settle into a quiet life. All the fuss, people telling me I did the right thing, all of this,' he said, gesturing around the room, 'it just isn't right.'

'It'll all calm down soon enough. This is more for your mother's benefit, she just wants you to see she's proud of you, despite everything.'

'Yeah, I know. I just wish she'd have told me instead of putting on an exhibition.'

'Here's another blast from the past decided to make an appearance,' Sam said sternly, looking towards the door. He stood up straight and pushed his shoulders back.

Brian led the way, squinting around the now gloomy hall. John and Tony followed, looking unsure of themselves. Decker stood up and waved, catching Tony's eye. The three made their way over.

'I'll catch up with you later, Decker,' Sam said and walked towards his mother, who looked on anxiously.

'Decker, you're looking well,' Brian said.

Tony and John nodded and murmured agreement.

'Thanks, guys. I've had plenty time to spend in the gym over the years – tried to keep myself in shape.'

'Glad you didn't suffer too much.'

'There was plenty of time for that as well,' Decker said, his mouth stretching into a straight line.

'Anyway,' John said, 'just wanted to say we're glad you're out, and as soon as you're ready to get back to work we'll make sure you're sorted. You've been away a long time but we intend to make things right.'

'Yeah,' Tony agreed. 'Don't want you to think we don't appreciate the way you kept our names out of everything. You took the heat and did your time like a man.'

'Thanks for thinking of me, boys, but from here on I'll be staying out of trouble.'

'It's early days,' Brian said dismissively. 'Get settled and then we'll talk again.'

Decker nodded and watched as the three made their way back around the crowd. Tony stopped to heap some food from the buffet table onto a paper plate, then caught up with the other two by the door.

'You mean that about going straight?' Sam asked, returning to Decker's side.

'Yeah. I've done more than enough jail for this lifetime. I just want to get a regular job and forget about that chapter of my life.'

'Good for you, Derek. I don't think your mother would be able to handle you going away again.'

'I don't think I could either.'

Tazeem entered Central Café, sat at a table, and after a quick glance at the menu gave the waiter his order of a cassantina salad and green mint tea with roasted nuts. The clock on the wall opposite showed that Latif was a few minutes late, but as Tazeem looked back towards the door he saw his friend coming in.

'Tazeem, my friend, good to see you looking well after your ordeal,' Latif said as he sat down on the chair opposite.

'Thanks. How have things been out here while I was away?'

'There have been changes which I'm sure you've heard of. Sadiq has become integral in a lot of businesses and he's less than forthcoming about his activities.'

'What do you mean?'

'The initial impressions after he took over so many of the housing projects were good. Rental income was up and problems with tenants vanished almost completely. He would always deliver his positive reports right after Friday prayer, so many of the elders would overhear. He would make a point of letting it be known that he was interested in expanding and taking on other ventures. Offers quickly came in, which he snapped up.'

'It sounds like he's doing very well.'

'Yes. He's working with a lot of the younger members of the community as well as bringing help in from abroad – seems like more every day. One of the workers from my shop has begun to get involved with his dealings. Also, there have been things I've heard …'

'Things like what?'

'Some of the company he has been keeping, affiliations with suspicious men at some new strip club he's tied up with.'

'And Ermina?'

Latif nodded. 'He spends more and more time with your cousin, throwing money around wherever they go. They seem inseparable these days. And with her looking after your house while you were away ...' he said, and gave a what-did-you-expect shrug.

Tazeem drank the last of his tea and replaced the glass with a clink. 'Do you have plans of your own for returning to work, Tazeem?' Latif asked gently, to get their conversation back on track.

'I have something I've been working on,' he nodded. 'I need a couple of people to help get it off the ground, but I think I may have the right ones in mind.'

Mangle drove past the whitewashed exterior of the Bear and Crown pub, turned onto the gravel drive and pulled up in the car park behind. He walked in through the rear doors and was embraced by the smell of traditional home-cooked roast that conjured up welcome memories of Sundays at his grandmother's house as a child.

He ordered a pint of Satan's Sister, which the chalkboard behind the bar recommended as: 'One of the Most Sinister Real

Ales of the Week We've Ever Served', and took a seat at a corner table near a small arched window overlooking fields.

'You find it alright?' Decker asked, walking toward the table carrying a half-finished pint.

'Eventually, although I'm a bit surprised you knew about the place.'

'My uncle brought me here a few times as a kid. Good food and good beer, he always told me, plus I wanted to avoid anything local,' he said, sitting down opposite Mangle.

'Is there a reason for you wanting to keep a low profile?'

'No, nothing like that, just that life since I moved back into my mother's has been a bit of a goldfish bowl. I thought it was bad in jail, with everyone knowing everyone's business. Guess I was expecting things to be different on the outside.'

'Are you finding it hard to adjust?'

'Maybe. It's just not like I thought it would be. I was prepared for all this bitterness and resentment, but it's like they regard me as some kind of hero for killing a heroin dealer, and that's harder to deal with.'

'Have you had any luck job hunting?'

'Nothing, man.Even with my qualifications from inside, without references no one will give me a chance. Did you get your old job back?'

'No. The boss decided I was a lost cause and told me pretty much that, when I went and asked. That wouldn't have been too bad but he's pissed in the water for all the other companies I might have approached as well. Guess we're pretty much in the same boat,' Mangle said morosely, and gulped a mouthful from his pint.

Decker exhaled heavily through his nose and gazed out of the window.

'Have you thought about getting into anything less than legal?' Mangle asked cautiously after a few moments of silence.

Decker's eyes sharpened as he turned to look at Mangle. 'I'm having to fight off the advances,' he said, looking away again at the foam sliding slowly down the inside of his now-empty glass. 'The three I was mixed up with before prison, I thought after an initial appearance at my welcome home party they'd leave me be, but it's like they want to cash in on my local celebrity status and have me dealing drugs. "Don't mess with Decker, look what happened to the last person that did," some shit like that. I want no part of it, but they won't leave me be.'

'Have they threatened you or something?'

'Not threats or anything, just phone calls, appearances at the door. If I keep getting this much open attention from known criminals then the police will get interested and it won't take them long to pin something on me, not with a previous murder conviction hanging over my head. The guys know that, the same as I do. No doubt they figure that before long I'll realise I'm better off with them and come trotting back into the fold.'

Mangle didn't say anything but went and brought them two fresh pints from the bar.

'Can you see any way out, then?' he asked, putting the glasses down onto the table top.

'I've been thinking about it a lot. What else is there to think about?'

'And?'

'And I thought about Tazeem. He'll no doubt have stuff going by now. An afternoon shift in the kitchens and he'd have hatched enough plans to fill a notebook,' Decker said with a half-smile.

7

Tatiana no longer noticed the acrid stench of the pooled vomit and urine on the floor of their watertight prison. The dipping and lurching as the small boat negotiated its way across the choppy sea had made several of the girls seasick, and the duration of the voyage with no access to a bathroom had seen some of them release their bladders.

Conversation between Tatiana and Natalia was stolen in urgent moments when enough sunlight penetrated through gaps in the trapdoor above to allow Tatiana to lip-read. Natalia had communicated details of a phone conversation the white-haired man had while they were in the van. He'd argued with Jacob, the man they now knew was the captain, about treatment of girls on previous voyages. Some had died in transport, and others he'd described as being 'spoiled'. Whether this was true, or a ploy to make the girls behave, it had proved effective, as none of them had put up any resistance. They were filed into the room, their possessions taken away, even Natalia's inhaler, and chained by their hands and feet.

Natalia's breathing was shallow and uneven on the side of Tatiana's neck as her friend nestled against her. Tatiana nudged her until Natalia opened her eyes.

'Your breathing is getting worse. I will shout for one of the men to come.'

'No,' Natalia said. 'You can't make any trouble. The man said in the van that if we do, one of us could get really hurt.'

She insisted she would be fine, and would try to stay calm and sleep through it. Reluctantly Tatiana agreed, but did her best to stay awake while Natalia slept.

The vomit and urine pool in the concave bottom of the hold had deepened when Tatiana next awoke. It sloshed around, soaking into their clothes as the boat bobbed over the rolling waves. A sudden shaft of sunlight penetrated the gloom from above just as the girl chained directly in front of her threw up, the dry heaves lasting long after her stomach had purged itself.

Tatiana turned to Natalia as they were again thrown into darkness. She nudged her friend and waited for her to respond. After a moment, Tatiana pushed against her more insistently, but Natalia still wasn't roused. Barbs of anxiety tore at Tatiana's insides as she shouted at Natalia to wake up. The ship lurched again and the pool beneath them soaked Tatiana's thigh. A shard of light cut through for only a moment, but long enough for Tatiana to see Natalia's vacant staring eyes, and lips that had turned a matching shade of blue.

Decker pulled the white Volkswagen up to the kerb outside Kang's convenience store at 10.24 on Tuesday morning, and he and Mangle climbed out. Mangle wore a freshly dry-cleaned business suit. He checked through a list of points on his clipboard and casually glanced up and down the street. Decker, in black gloves and plain blue overalls, did likewise as he retrieved a toolkit from the boot of the car. An electronic beep sounded to announce their arrival as Mangle led the way through the door into the brightly lit store. Briefly checking his clipboard again, he approached the counter.

'Mr Kang?' Mangle asked the concerned-looking oriental man who was serving, as he flipped open a wallet displaying his photo ID.

'I am Kang. What is this?' he asked, jabbing a finger towards Decker with his toolbox. Decker also flashed an ID card, and looked around the store.

'No need to be alarmed, Mr Kang, we are from G&E Utilities. This is simply a courtesy call to ensure your power supply is running optimally.'

'All is fine, no need. Good day,' Kang said, making shooing gestures with his hands as if trying to scare away a flock of pigeons.

'This won't take more than a few moments and we will be on our way,' Mangle said, and smiled reassuringly. He turned toward Decker who was walking through a doorway at the rear of the store overhung with opaque hanging plastic flaps.

Mr Kang uttered something in Korean to a small child who scuttled off through a door behind the counter, and judging from the hollow thumping sound that followed, the child quickly ascended a flight of wooden stairs.

Decker located the electricity meter and examined it before opening his toolbox. Mangle stood beside him, again scanning over the printed sheets on his clipboard.

'There are some broken seals,' Decker said with a disdainful shake of his head.

'OK, we'll have to remove it then,' Mangle confirmed.

Decker fished a large torch and cable cutters out of the toolkit, as muffled voices speaking quickly in Korean came from the floor above. Mr Kang stood behind Decker, stammering something about waiting for his brother, as Decker clicked on the torch, handed it to Mangle, and then flipped the breaker on the power supply, throwing the whole store into darkness.

The soft hum from the rows of freezers subsided and was replaced by nervous silence downstairs and echoing footsteps from above. Ignoring the panicked Mr Kang behind him, who had reverted to speaking in Korean, Decker clipped all of the cables going into the meter, detached it from the wall and put away his cable cutters.

The footsteps above reached the stairway and began their hurried descent, before darkness and gravity conspired to cause their owner to tumble down the remaining steps. Mr Kang fell silent behind Decker and Mangle, and then quickly took off through the store in the direction of the noise.

'You got everything?' Mangle asked.

Yep,' Decker confirmed, and picked up the toolkit and the disconnected electric meter.

They walked through the now pitch black store, illuminated only by the circular beam of light from the torch that Mangle held, and the rectangular glass panel on the shop door. Decker walked back out to the car to start the engine as Mangle sorted through pages on the clipboard before picking the correct one to detach.

A creak sounded behind the counter and a different Korean man limped through the doorway, aided by the first man they had spoken to, and headed towards Mangle.

'I am Mr Kang. This my store,' he said to Mangle by way of explanation. 'That my brother,' he added, throwing a disparaging glare at his nervous-looking companion.

'Hello, Mr Kang,' Mangle said in an efficiently polite tone. 'I'm afraid we discovered evidence of tampering on your electric supply and have therefore been forced to disconnect you.'

'All my food go bad. I must have power on.'

Mangle slid the sheet across the counter and spun it around to face the owner.

'Here is the contact number of my associate, Mr Lawrence, if you wish to speak with him. I will make sure a correct bill is sent out to you in the next day or two after the meter has been examined.'

'Day or two – no. No good. Must have power back today.'

Mangle paused as if in thought before speaking again. 'I'll tell you what, Mr Kang. If I move some appointments around I can have the meter inspected and a correct bill delivered by courier just after lunch. As long as you clear the balance before the close of business today, we can have your supply reinstated before this evening.'

'Yes, yes. Thank you. Today, yes,' Kang said to Mangle, before looking nervously towards the freezers.

Mangle calmly walked out of the gloomy interior and climbed into the car.

Twenty minutes later they pulled into the maze of small industrial units they'd collected the Volkswagen from earlier that morning, where Tazeem was waiting for their return.

'Everything go OK?' Tazeem asked pulling down the metal shutter on his unit, after they'd parked the car up inside.

'He panicked a bit, but other than that it went fine. Barely even looked at the IDs,' Decker said, dropping the car keys onto a scuffed, paint-spattered wooden desk, and putting the toolbox and meter onto wall-mounted shelves behind it.

'You gave him the sheet explaining disconnection, with the phone number?' Tazeem asked, sitting down in a black swivel chair behind the desk.

'I did,' Mangle said. 'I still don't see exactly how this is going to work though.'

'Well, my contact, Mr Lawrence, who actually works at G&E Utilities, will be on the other end of the phone should Mr Kang decide to call. He removed the customer record for Kang's address from their system this morning and added his supply code to that of an existing supply to the factory over the road, so the power is still connected – or it was till you two turned up – but they won't receive any more bills from G&E.'

'OK, I've got it so far,' Mangle said, sitting in one of two plastic chairs opposite.

'Right. Well now his supply is off and he has a shit-load of frozen food that is gonna go really smelly really quickly, unless he gets the juice switched back on.'

'Which explains all the flapping about when I flipped the switch,' Decker said, sitting in the chair beside Mangle.

'So now I have him sweat for an hour or two, then courier out what looks like an authentic G &E Utilities bill, except it won't be their bank details on it but an account I've set up.'

'So he pays that bill this afternoon … and then what?' Decker asked.

'You two go back to the shop today. You know how to reinstall the meter, right?'

'Yeah, fully qualified for all kinds of electric stuff courtesy of a course I took in prison.'

'Well, once you've reconnected him, Mr Kang is a happy camper 'cause his food isn't spoiled. He continues paying the bills that I'll send out to him each month. Meanwhile, the shop's electric supply is being paid for by the factory over the road, who have such a high consumption they won't notice the increase.'

'So everyone's happy and it doesn't even look like a crime has been committed?' Mangle asked.

'Exactly,' Tazeem said, gleefully rubbing his hands together. 'My friend at G&E gets a healthy slice of the pie and we take the rest.'

'Wow,' Decker said, shaking his head. 'And what do we do after that?'

'After that, my friends, we move on to the next one.'

'But neither myself nor Decker have jobs yet. If we start earning money with nothing to show where it came from, then Probation will be on to us right away,' Mangle said.

'Just leave it with me,' Tazeem reassured them.

Over the next few months Mangle and Decker worked to Tazeem's plan and together they established a network of businesses that supplied them with a substantial regular income. Convenience stores, back-street garages and even modest high street shops were targeted, relieved of their supply on the pretence of tampering or a faulty meter. Amended bills were immediately dispatched, followed by quick payment and reconnection within the hour. They also attended their day jobs at e-Bit, Latif's computer store.

A probation officer visited twice to check up on them and was impressed with the positive reports he received from Latif.

'What's the name of the place, again?' Decker asked, as he drove along the congested street looking for the shop Tazeem had assigned them that morning.

'Eazywash Laundrette,' Mangle said, reading from the paper in his hand. 'There, park behind that van.' He pointed to a vacant parking space just before the shop.

The sign above the door looked hand-painted and quite old. Inside was similarly unkempt, with unpolished floors and machines that appeared to be as old as the building itself and perhaps as old as the attendant. She wore a blue gingham uniform and had her grey hair pulled back in a net so tightly that her forehead appeared botoxed. She peered suspiciously at them through a cloud of cigarette smoke as they walked into the deserted store.

'What do you want?' she snapped at Mangle, whose suit apparently identified him as trouble.

'Nothing to worry about Mrs …' he said, but she didn't fill in the blank. 'It's simply a courtesy call from G&E Utilities to make sure your power supply is working within regulated guidelines.'

This was the standard line he used in these situations, which partnered with a flash of his credentials and a flash of his smile would allow them access to the meter. She shook her head and stubbed out the cigarette into an overflowing ashtray perched on top of one of the machines. Mangle again reached for his ID and presented it to her for further examination. She gave it barely a glance before again saying no.

'You don't seem to understand, Mrs …'

'Ethel.'

'Ethel, you have to let us inspect the power supply or your electricity may be cut off.'

'I don't trust those photo things,' she said, and Mangle obligingly put it away.

She picked up a dog-eared copy of the Yellow Pages, licked a nicotine-stained index finger and began leafing through.

'That's perfectly understandable,' Mangle said and removed a sheet from his clipboard. 'Here is a letter explaining our visit and a phone number of my boss who will answer any questions you may have.'

He hoped Lawrence was alone and able to take the call. Usually they didn't take this much persuasion.

'I don't want that either. Those high-up idiots never know what's going on. It's the people on the floor that really run things,' she said, jabbing her bony finger on top of the machine she leant against and issuing a rattling cough. 'You think my boss has a clue what to do if a machine breaks down in the middle of a shift? No chance. I'll talk to the girl who answers the phone. She'll be able to tell me what's going on.'

Decker swapped his toolbox from one hand to the other, and looked anxiously at Mangle.

'There's no need for that Ethel …' Mangle said, but she had found the number for G&E and begun to dial. 'Look, this is obviously a bad time so we'll call back when it's more convenient.'

'Hello?' Ethel said into the receiver, and then to Mangle, 'Don't you go anywhere till I know what this is about.'

Decker had already opened the door and he and Mangle were through it before the overhead door closer snapped it shut.

'We must have done twenty places already and we almost get sprung off a little old woman?' Decker said, hurriedly starting the car.

'She had nothing to lose by double-checking, I suppose. We just didn't expect it as no one else had done that.'

'So that's the end of our run, then?' Decker asked, after Mangle had explained to Tazeem what had happened.

'No, we just need to go further afield and be more selective with the businesses we choose,' Tazeem answered, unperturbed.

'More selective in what way?' Mangle asked.

'It's something I had planned on doing anyway. We'll just step up the time frame,' Tazeem said, leaning back on his chair and crossing his right ankle over his left knee. 'We only go for businesses that have something to hide. Places that don't want anyone poking around.'

'What do you mean by that?' Mangle asked.

'Yeah, let's have some examples,' Decker said, shaking his head.

'Alright: clothing stores importing counterfeit goods, shops selling cigarettes smuggled into the country to avoid paying tax, frozen food outlets buying up cheap out-of-date stuff and changing the dates to resell. There's any number of back-street businesses that don't want anyone official looking too closely at what goes on. Removing their power will make them pay whatever bill we hold under their noses, to restore the status quo quickly.'

Mangle frowned and scratched his chin. 'It sounds a lot more workable, but how are we gonna find out where these businesses are? I doubt they simply advertise the fact.'

'Just leave that to me.'

Friday morning, and Decker and Mangle met Tazeem back at the lock-up at 07.30 a.m. as instructed. He'd arranged another job, but had remained tight-lipped about the details.

'Good morning. Right on time – well done.'

'Where we off to then, Taz?' Decker asked, striding into the garage.

'Here's the paperwork,' Tazeem said, handing the clipboard to Mangle. 'It's a wholesale food distributer.'

'A cash and carry,' Decker said.

'Exactly.'

'So what's the situation with them? You said only businesses that have something to hide,' Mangle asked.

'This particular place is taking a shipment of wine courtesy of a stolen eighteen-wheeler that's been getting a makeover for the last few days.'

'Really?'

'Yeah, the truck has been rebranded to look the same as one that delivers from one of their regular suppliers, same plates and everything. The wine will be stashed in the warehouse out back and collected by some of the manager's more trusted customers, who will sell it on, and everyone makes a quick profit.'

'So what's our role, then?'

'Same as usual: turn up and go through the whole electric company thing. The timing is crucial. If you arrive there and create a scene just before the delivery is about to land then the manager will pay anything to make the problem vanish.'

The large car park in front of ValueNet was mostly empty, but Decker drove around and pulled up near the delivery entrance at the back. The building was vast and constructed of orange brickwork with corrugated sheet cladding. The majority of orders were received online and shipped out in a procession of ValueNet vans, half a dozen of which were parked in front of the warehouse entrance, being loaded up by staff. Decker and Mangle walked briskly past them, looking for either the electric supply or someone in authority.

'Can I help you?' a burly man with stooped shoulders and a patchy beard said as he hurried across to them. He introduced himself as the manager.

'Yes, we're from G&E Utilities,' Mangle said, and went through their regular routine.

'This really isn't a good time.' The manager shook his head and smiled through his distress.

'We'll be as quick as possible and then be right out of your hair,' Mangle beamed at him.

A quick glance at his watch, and the manager ushered them across the delivery dock to a corner of the warehouse.

'We'll be very busy here soon, could you hurry this along?' the manager asked, switching his ample weight from one foot to the other in the manner of a child who needs to urinate.

Mangle patted the nervous manager on the shoulder and regaled a reassuring platitude as Decker went about his business. A murmur of concern from Decker a moment later was all it took to accelerate the manager's heart rate further, then Decker threw the switch that plunged the entire place into darkness.

'I'm sorry, but I've had to remove your supply,' Decker said, stepping back into the warehouse carrying the disconnected meter under his arm. 'It looks like there's been tampering.'

'That's ridiculous,' the manager said, with a look of surprise.

'We'll have to call out a team right away to check on this. They'll need to determine exactly how underpaid G&E has been and have the account reimbursed before power can be restored.'

'No, we can't shut down business. The place will lose a fortune,' the manager stammered, realising the other ramifications. 'You have a team coming here?'

'Yes, some engineers will come and diagnose what has happened. They may be here for several days,' Mangle confirmed, as he scribbled notes onto his clipboard.

The manager took a step back and struggled to come to terms with what had been said. His brain was freewheeling as he searched for any way out of the mess, like a mouse in the grasp of a cat.

'There must be some other solution we can come to here,' he said with a pleading smile.

'Well, we could have the meter analysed back at the department, but the data may not be as accurate as an investigation conducted on site.'

'That's OK, do that,' the manager stammered as he grasped the lifeline.

'You do realise that this will lead to an updated bill that could be in excess of the actual power consumption?'

'That's fine, I'm sure you'll do the best you can,' the manager said, a vague hope beginning to take root within him. 'So there will be no team called out now? And how long until power is restored?'

'It shouldn't take long at all, provided the account is cleared right away. I'll courier the bill to you as soon as possible.'

*****

'And that was it?' Tazeem asked when they arrived at the lock-up. 'No phone calls to check on you or anything?'

'Nope, the guy was so horrified that he would probably have stripped naked and run around the car park singing Abba songs if we'd told him it would get the supply reconnected.'

Tazeem laughed and sat back in his chair. He pushed a piece of paper and a pen across the desk towards Mangle. 'How much do you think we should charge him?'

Mangle looked at Tazeem and then at Decker.

'It's a big place,' Decker said with a shrug.

'It is,' Mangle nodded, and wrote down a figure on the sheet and pushed it back over to Tazeem.

'I like the way you think,' Tazeem nodded at the number Mangle had written. 'But let's think a little bigger,' he said, and added a zero.

8

Tatiana could no longer feel the pain in her bruised face as the boat chugged calmly into the docks. She had seen the other women yelling at her to be quiet as she wailed for help at the sight of her dead friend. Finally the men came and beat her unconscious, but no one was released from the hold. When she awoke, she was still chained and pressed up against Natalia's cold, vacant-eyed corpse.

Once the boat had been moored, the shipmates opened up the hold, unlocked their chains and filed them out. Natalia's body was left soaking in the pool of filth as the other girls were led up the stairs, across the gangway and onto the dock. It was dark outside but the moon provided enough light that Tatiana could see the white-haired man, now wearing a bright blue cravat and a Panama hat, standing watching from a short distance away. Beside him were two Asian men with their hands in their pockets, and another who looked oriental. The captain had already gone ashore and stood nearby, but looked uneasy.

The oriental man came across to the girls and gave them a quick once-over, pausing for a second at the sight of bruising on Tatiana's face, then signalled for them to be loaded into a waiting van. After a headcount the white-haired man grabbed the captain's arm. Tatiana was the last to take her seat and looked back at the scene outside. The captain looked concerned, yet defiant, as the white-haired man talked sternly to him. She caught only snatches of what they said as the exchange was animated, and both men were moving as they spoke. 'This is the last time,' said the white-haired man. The captain was protesting his innocence, but it appeared to fall on deaf ears.

One of the Asians seemed amused by the exchange. He walked up to the captain and gave him a friendly slap on the shoulder, his fingers glittering from a flamboyant adornment of diamonds. The white-haired man looked anything but amused, and asked the oriental man something about a clinic. He shook his head, and all three men walked out of her line of sight.

Tatiana faced forward. None of the other girls were talking. They seemed acceptant of whatever fate awaited them. Whatever it was to be, Tatiana thought, surely the worst must now be behind them.

Mangle walked into the Bear and Crown and ordered a beer. As the barmaid proudly began to recite the available list, Mangle waved a hand indicating that any would do. She returned somewhat sullenly a moment later with his glass, and he gave her a handful of coins. After a brief glance around the bar he saw Decker occupying the same spot they'd sat in previously, and he carried his dripping glass over.

'We'll have to stop meeting like this, people will talk,' Decker said, as Mangle put down his glass.

'Very funny. Even if I was that way inclined I'd be way out of your league.'

Decker laughed and took a drink from his own glass.

'Did you manage to arrange a new flat to move into yet?' Mangle asked.

'I found one that's suitable, but when I move in I want to do it with a clean slate, you know?'

Mangle nodded as if this was something that had been bothering him as well. 'It was a good job this morning and we've had a good run,' he confirmed, 'but maybe it's best not to test our luck.'

'The knocks are still coming on my mother's door from Brian and that lot. My reason for not getting mixed up with them was to avoid the inevitable prison sentence that would come from the association. Now we've got some money behind us it would be stupid to risk everything for the sake of greed,' Decker said, looking thoughtfully into his glass.

'Are you going to pack it all in and just keep working at the shop for Latif?'

'That's what I've been thinking. You reckon Tazeem will be pissed?'

Mangle shrugged solemnly. 'We should probably talk to him and find out.'

Tazeem arrived early for Friday prayers and met Latif just inside as he was removing his shoes.

'Latif, how are Derek and Nick working out at the shop?' he asked, crouching to unloosen his laces.

'Hello, Tazeem. Very well, actually. Nick is working on the desk with customers and Derek is helping out in the stockroom. They are both very diligent, thanks for recommending them.'

'Well hello there, cuz.' Tazeem looked over his shoulder to see Ermina walking towards them.

'What are you doing here?' he asked her.

'I got a lift down with Sadiq and some of his friends; he's parking the car outside. Don't worry, I'm not staying, just thought I'd pop in and see if you were here so I could say hello.'

'What friends?' Tazeem asked, but before she could answer Sadiq entered with a group of men.

'I'll see you later, Tazeem,' Ermina said, and turned to leave.

As she sauntered by Sadiq he reached down and gave her a slap on the ass which roused a chorus of laughter from his friends. Ermina tossed a playfully disapproving look over her shoulder.

Catching Tazeem's glare from across the room Sadiq began to walk over, but Tazeem and Latif quickly moved on to the ablutions and from there straight into the hall.

They found two free prayer mat spots and took their places. Sadiq and the others were last into the hall and first out again following the prayers. Tazeem and Latif intentionally dallied in the hall, hoping to give them enough time to leave so they wouldn't be subjected to another instalment of how successful Sadiq had recently become. His boastings had been tolerable when the claims were fairly baseless, but now that he had actual achievements behind him he had become even more insufferable.

Thinking they had waited long enough, Tazeem and Latif finally made their way back through to the entrance hall and collected their shoes. It was a sunny day and some clusters of men remained talking outside as they left.

'Hello boys.' Tazeem and Latif turned and saw Sadiq beaming at them from just to the right of the main doorway. 'And how is business going for you two?'

'I can't complain,' Latif said, flatly.

'And you, Tazeem?' he said, turning a shark-like grin in his direction.

'I'm doing alright.'

'That's interesting, your cousin said you may have been struggling a little lately since you got out of prison. No need to be proud, my friend, I'm always willing to extend a hand of support to a less fortunate brother.'

'Very noble of you, Sadiq, but you can save your help for someone who needs it,' Tazeem said, taking all of his effort not to spit the words back at him.

'Very well,' Sadiq said with a mirthless smile. 'My organisation is expanding very quickly, I'm sure there will be further opportunities for you to come on board.'

Tazeem was understanding when Mangle and Decker sat down with him the following week.

'To be honest I didn't expect you both to hang around this long,' he said, to ease any guilt they may have felt about leaving him in the lurch. 'I have got one last job lined up, though. How about that, then we divide up the proceeds?'

Mangle looked over at Decker and shrugged his shoulders.

'It's OK with me,' Decker said.

'Alright, I'm in,' Mangle confirmed.

It was arranged for Thursday morning. They arrived early, were briefed by Tazeem and drove to the location he'd given them, a warehouse in Bluebell Industrial Estate that he'd heard was receiving shipments of stolen goods from offshore. Same type of set-up they'd been to numerous times before: go in, kill the power, threaten an immediate investigation, then they bend over backwards to pay the bill.

Decker drove the car through a maze of mostly unused units as Mangle read out directions from a sheet on his clipboard. He turned right and pulled up outside number 18 near a white Mercedes van with the logo of a frozen food supplier on the side. It was the only vehicle on the site.

The concrete approach around the building was cracked and patches of grass and other weeds clumped where grateful seeds had been given the opportunity to grow. Mangle walked ahead while Decker fetched his toolkit. Nearing the building he became aware of raised voices inside and stopped, waiting for Decker to catch up.

'What's going on?' Decker asked as he stopped beside Mangle.

'I don't know. It sounds like someone's pretty pissed off though.'

'You heard anything they said?'

'No they aren't speaking English.'

The sound of a large metal bolt being thrown was followed by the steel door from the warehouse being flung open. An enraged Asian man strode out, then became aware of Decker and Mangle standing in front of him. For a moment they all stood unmoving and silent before the man regained some of his wits.

'Spahee! Spahee!' he cried, wild-eyed, and took off running across the deserted site and through the treeline beyond.

Decker and Mangle looked from the disappearing figure back at each other, unsure whether or not they also should beat a hasty retreat. A large white man with a shaven head was joined at the door by two more Asians. He had ragged scar tissue on the left side of his face and neck that was shiny like plastic. The man quickly glanced around outside, noted the presence of only one other vehicle, and demanded to know what they wanted.

'Ahh … hello. We're from G&E Utilities,' Mangle said, gathering himself and slipping into their rehearsed routine.

'Whatever you are selling we don't want,' the man growled at him in heavily accented English.

'We are from the electric company,' Mangle explained again, speaking slower and more deliberately. 'We must come and inspect your supply. For safety, it is required by law.'

'No,' the man said, screwing up the left-hand side of his face in a grimace that made his scars crinkle like cellophane. He began to close the door; the two other Asians had already vanished inside.

'If you do not allow me to inspect the meter I will have to return with the police.'

This had the desired effect and the heavily set man paused while pulling closed the steel door. Again his eyes drifted around the car park, before coming to rest on Mangle.

'You are electric company man,' he said, as if what he'd first been told had only just begun to resonate.

Mangle remained silent but flipped open his ID. Decker, standing behind him, did likewise and rattled his toolbox.

'You come in and look at supply, then you go.' It wasn't phrased as a question, but Mangle confirmed this was their intention.

'Alright,' the man said and took a step backwards, allowing barely enough room to pass.

Voices were raised behind him, again not in English; Mangle thought he heard two different languages, but couldn't be sure what. Barely taking his eyes from them, the scarred man barked a few words over his shoulder and the voices fell silent.

Taking this as their cue, Decker began to walk inside.

'I'll be right there,' Mangle said and took out his phone. Decker looked at him quizzically, but continued walking. 'Hello Clive,' Mangle said into the silent handset after first going through the pretence of dialling a number. 'Yes, we're at the job now. Yes ... yeah ... just a few minutes and we'll be on our way back. OK, see you soon.'

Mangle put the phone away. The scarred man was standing just inside the warehouse, watching him intently. Breathing in, he squeezed past and walked along a narrow corridor. The warehouse had been segmented into rooms of various sizes. Each room had a door, and what looked like a small window obscured by a curtain. The light in the corridor was minimal and came from three bulbs suspended on chains from the ceiling high above. A large stack of wooden crates was piled near the rear wall.

Mangle saw Decker just ahead, crouching to take his torch and other tools from the box. He knew what was coming next, so again quickly scanned the interior to orient himself before the impending darkness fell. There was no sign of the two Asian men. Mangle kept his eyes on the scarred man, who appeared to be in charge, as Decker began his lines about the meter having been tampered with.

Mangle instinctively knew this was a bad idea, but like a runaway truck, it was too late to stop the inevitable. He backed up against a wall as the realisation came over the scarred man of what was about to happen. Decker had already turned on his torch and now he stood with the cable cutters in hand and flipped the switch. Immediately, complete blackness engulfed them.

The scarred man ran forward and grabbed Mangle by a fistful of his shirt. Decker's torch beam swung wildly backwards and forwards as he spun around, illuminating glimpses of the warehouse. Frightened screams sounded from numerous women somewhere within the building. Mangle tried to calm the man who had grabbed him, explaining that the matter could be sorted out in no time.

The two Asian men and another white male came out from separate rooms, shouting things Mangle couldn't understand. Decker's beam of torchlight bounced from one to the other. The doorway behind one of the Asian men stood open, briefly revealing the frightened faces of a number of women sitting huddled together on the floor inside. One looked to have sustained a heavy beating, her face swollen and bruised. Mangle looked away. If they were to get out of this, he knew he had to think fast.

He spoke to the scarred man, who still held him almost off the ground. 'Let's go outside and I'll explain how we can solve this for you right away,' he said, patting the man gingerly on the shoulder, hoping what little light flitted around the room would show his face to be calm, although he doubted he was that good an actor.

The scarred man again shouted orders and the other three held their ground. Decker had dropped the disconnected meter and looked ready for a fight, but it was one Mangle was certain they couldn't win. Still holding a handful of Mangle's shirt, the scarred man pulled him towards the warehouse door. 'You stay,' he turned and shouted at Decker.

'You try to trick me. You say just look,' he said to Mangle after opening the door a few inches to let in some light. His breath was thick and smelled like rotting meat.

'No, I didn't trick you. Your supply had been tampered with, but I can still fix this for you. I need to return to the office and have the meter inspected. This will tell them the actual consumption, and I'll have a new bill brought out by courier right away.'

'You go nowhere,' the man laughed, 'you will fix now.'

'I'm sorry, we can't do that,' Mangle said, hoping the man wouldn't call his bluff. 'Taking the meter away and giving you a new bill to pay is all I can do to prevent the police being involved.'

The man stared at him a moment longer, his focus switching from eye to eye.

'Manipulation of a meter is a criminal offence,' Mangle said, almost apologetically. 'Sometimes they can become damaged accidentally and can look like intentional tampering. I'm sure that's all this is. Once the bill is paid your power will be switched back on and there's no involvement from the police.'

The man maintained his grip on Mangle and bellowed over his shoulder, 'Can you move them yet?'

'No, it's too early,' another voice answered back. 'The clinic isn't ready.'

The man relaxed his grip and his appearance softened like tide-eroded stone. 'I apologise for any mistreatment. I am a little stressed right now. You say you can have this taken care of and this will all be forgotten about. So how much?'

Mangle explained again about needing to first return to the office, but the man looked less than convinced. 'Bring money,' he shouted to the others. Moments later another white man, almost ghostly pale in complexion, approached carrying a fat brown envelope. The scarred man opened it, took out a thick sheaf of notes and flicked through them. 'This will pay for our electricity to be mended. You will take it, go away and make it right. No more intrusion.'

Mangle nodded dumbly as the stack of money was replaced into the envelope and handed to him.

'What's going on?' Decker called out to him.

'Fix it back up,' Mangle replied. 'We're done here.'

9

Even though they waited until dark, the men still seemed agitated as the girls were hurriedly shoved back into the van outside. Whatever had happened back at the warehouse when the lights went out, Tatiana was pretty sure it had been beyond their control. Thoughts of freedom flirted momentarily, before Tatiana shook them away. She was no longer even sure what freedom was, but immediately mistrusted her surfacing feelings of hope.

Some of the girls seemed scared, one or two slept, and the others looked as if they shared Tatiana's own numbed acceptance of their fate. The van was again driven by the pale man, and two of the Asians rode up front alongside him.

It took just over an hour to arrive at their destination. They travelled through a bewildering cityscape, with buildings bigger than any Tatiana had previously seen; but other than the lights shining brighter and the buildings rising taller, the looks on the faces of the night people they passed were the same as those from the city streets she knew back home.

The oriental man stood beside the van as the girls disembarked. From his thin, steel-rimmed spectacles, white lab coat and authoritative stance, Tatiana guessed he must be a doctor, and the place they'd arrived at, the clinic. It was a large stone building at the end of a winding gravel drive, shrouded to the front by a thick belt of pine trees. A few cars were parked in an otherwise vacant lot, but there was no sign of any other people. The man introduced himself as Dr Chu, and then led the girls into the building, along a disinfectant-scented corridor and onto Accommodation Wing A. In there, they were instructed to remove their clothes and put on the regulation blue cotton jumpsuits.

During the next week, the women were subjected to various medical examinations and blood tests. Twice a day they were given injections, thankfully Tatiana thought, no more from the bizarre looking contraption that was used upon their arrival. Once each day they underwent a treatment session in one of the outbuildings known as the Audiology Suite. The women were filed out and led into the darkened room. Inside there was a huge screen and a number of plush chairs, like a small yet expensive-looking movie-theatre. Each chair had an unobstructed view of the screen and its own set of headphones. The girls were seated, straps were fastened around their wrists and foreheads, preventing them getting up or looking away from the screen, and the headphones were placed over their ears.

Afterwards, Tatiana always remembered this part, but only snatches from the succession of images that began flashing onto the screen, and, no matter how hard she tried, she could not recall anything else of the sessions. Although twice since, she had woken in a panicked state during the night, feeling as if she was again back in the chair.

An older woman called Laura was assigned to stay with them much of the time. She slept in the same wing as the girls, wore the same uniform, albeit in a different colour, hung out with them socially, and exercised with them outside, although she wasn't made to wear one of the outdoor collars. Laura intrigued Tatiana as she detected none of the underlying menace that appeared to lurk within the other staff, yet she also didn't appear to be imprisoned there. She referred to Tatiana as Tatty; her mother had called her that, and Tatiana liked it. It felt like a connection to her past. Laura underwent the same Audiology sessions, and was given the same injections twice a day as the other girls.

For the first two days, they had been rounded up and injected, told that their immune systems would be unable to cope with the influx of foreign bacteria, and that further injections were optional but should be immediately sought if any of the girls felt unwell. Tremors had been the first indication that there may be something in what had been said, followed shortly after by knotting stomach cramps. Tatiana was determined to resist the clinic's influence. She watched Laura and her fellow captives as they lined up one by one, and were injected by a satisfied-looking nurse. On the fourth day Tatiana vowed that no matter how hard it got, she would not seek out the medication, but found that the attention she then garnered from the gathering cluster of perplexed medical officials might ultimately prove more hazardous to her health than allowing the continued subjugation of her blood stream.

The next day, Dr Chu gathered the women together and told them that their progress had been good, that some of them were ready to begin the next phase of their re-education.

It had been just over a week since their final job. Tazeem had tied up any loose ends, so no threads of evidence could be traced back to them. In his opinion, they'd got in, made a tidy sum, and then got out before anyone was caught, so he considered the project a big success.

Tazeem got to the restaurant half an hour before Mangle and Decker were due to arrive, allowing him time to talk with Latif alone. He'd told Latif a few days ago that his two friends would be working exclusively for Latif now, and although no specifics were mentioned, Tazeem was pretty sure Latif had got the message: whatever arrangements or illegal dealings they'd been involved with were coming to an end. Latif saw this as a reason to celebrate and had invited them all to attend the reopening of his restaurant, Mailsi.

Tazeem was impressed with the contemporary remodelling. The tables, chairs and bar were dark rosewood, with pristine white tablecloths. The walls were smooth and painted pale green, with columns and curved support beams finished in burnt orange. Soft light was supplied by wall lamps throughout the restaurant, providing an endearing and intimate atmosphere.

'Very nice,' Tazeem said approaching Latif at the bar. 'But there's no way you designed all of this. I've seen what trouble you get into even selecting your own clothes.'

Latif laughed and ordered a bottle of Becks for Tazeem and another Pepsi for himself from the barman. 'Very funny, my friend, but nevertheless perceptive,' Latif said, and signalled a waiter to prepare the corner table for them.

'It is surprising that Sadiq hasn't tried to get a slice of this place to add to his growing empire,' Tazeem said, sipping his beer.

'Oh, he has tried. He wanted to fund the whole refit but I said no. It has stretched me to breaking point but I'd rather that than trust that man. And his erratic behaviour convinces me even more that I did the right thing.'

'What has he done now?'

Latif took a moment as he searched for the right words before leaning forward and speaking softly. 'It has been said for a while now that he has become a little too accustomed to the cocaine he has some of his henchmen selling.'

Tazeem nodded; he had heard similar whispers as well.

'His habit appears to have got the better of him now; he often mutters to himself and his twitches have got a lot worse. The men who follow him are fickle. They were attracted by his money and power, but this sign of weakness could be enough for an ambitious member of his entourage to try and step up into Sadiq's place. They are like jackals, after all.'

Tazeem sat back and smiled, took another drink from his beer and waited for Latif to admit to some exaggeration, but his friend remained stony-faced and serious.

'He said he would call in tonight for the reopening. If you're still here you may see for yourself,' Latif added, with a dismissive wave of his hand, evidently happy for Tazeem to witness the level of Sadiq's decline on his own.

Mangle and Decker arrived shortly afterwards and they all ordered their meals. The restaurant filled steadily as they ate and Latif quipped that he was pleased with the turn-out, although not nearly as pleased as his bank manager would be. The friends dutifully laughed, then ordered dessert and a further round of drinks.

Sadiq made his grandiose appearance before the end of the night. He arrived with a clutch of henchmen and walked from table to table, engaging guests in small talk, slapping backs and asking if everyone was enjoying their meals. Latif excused himself, somewhat irritably, and went to the bar to see that they were served on the house. Tazeem tried to pay little heed, but the way Sadiq entered a room attracted the focus of everyone's attention. His expensively tailored suit, designer haircut and, of course, the customary array of diamonds that decorated his fingers and wrists, drew the eye; and the effortless way he worked the room, held it. Had Latif's earlier words not prompted closer scrutiny, Tazeem might have missed the tremor in Sadiq's hands and the frequency with which he touched and rubbed at his nose.

The parade of faces Sadiq interchangeably associated with were generally of less interest to Tazeem, until he spotted Mohammed, who, immediately once they'd made eye contact, came across to the table.

'Isn't this just like old times,' he said, his comment weighing heavily with irony and light on nostalgia.

Mangle and Decker looked up from their conversation and gave their obligatory greetings.

'Still like to keep mixed company, then, Tazeem,' Mohammed said, and snorted a contemptuous laugh.

Tazeem let the remark pass without comment, which he'd

learned in Reedland Grange was the best way to deal with Mohammed.

'How is business for you these days, Tazeem? Did you give any thought to the conversation we had that day?'

'Business is OK. I get by.'

'Sadiq is doing very well, and those working with him likewise. You'd be a fool not to acknowledge that and take a seat at his table.'

'I'll bear it in mind,' Tazeem said coolly. 'It's nice to see you again, Mohammed, but let's not spoil tonight for Latif with any bickering.'

'I agree. I didn't come across to pick an argument,' Mohammed lied, 'just to say hello to some old jailbird friends.' With that he turned and walked back to the bar.

'He hasn't simmered down any since his release, then,' Mangle commented.

'There's that guy from the shop as well,' Decker said, 'the little guy from the stockroom who never says much.'

'Latif says many of the younger members of our community are falling in with Sadiq. He's establishing quite a workforce,' Tazeem said. 'Come on, let's finish up and go.'

'Hello Tazeem,' Sadiq said as he breezed up to their table. 'Mohammed says you might be interested in working for me.'

'I'm afraid he must have misunderstood,' Tazeem said, dabbing at his mouth with a napkin.

'That is a shame. You were always very creative, I'm sure we could do very well together.'

'I don't think so,' Tazeem said with a smile and a note of finality.

Sadiq reached inside his jacket pocket, withdrew three flyers advertising a strip club and dropped them onto Tazeem's plate. 'A new venture. You and your friends drink all night for free. Go and enjoy yourselves. Have a look at what else is out there for those prepared to take the chance,' he said, before returning to the bar.

'You want to check it out?' Decker asked when they were back outside.'

'I wasn't intending to. What about you?' Tazeem asked Mangle.

'Free drinks and naked dancing girls, how bad can it be?'

It was just past eleven when their cab drew up at the club, South of Seven. It was easy to miss, the entrance being recessed back from the main street with doormen who stood just inside the club. The sign above the door looked like a large block of black marble with the name of the club cut deeply into it. Fiery red letters slowly lit up and flickered as if being written by an invisible hand, before extinguishing for a moment until the cycle began again.

Tazeem held the flyers they had been given by Sadiq, and presented them to the doormen. One of them nodded, and said to keep them for use at the bar.

A thick red carpet like an infected tongue ran the length of the large stairway up to the club. At the top a heavy glass door opened into a large oval room. Inside, everything was chrome and red. Scarlet spotlights hazed down from the ceiling onto the cushioned chairs arranged around the stage. Men sat alone or in groups of two or three, eyes fixed on the women spiralling around polished chrome poles in the centre of the room.

The dancers used their hands and tightly toned thighs suggestively as they spun around, carefully surveying their audience. Sultry music came from hidden speakers, adding to the intoxication of their movements. Around the outside of the room other beautiful women wearing little or nothing at all flitted between the infatuated, intoxicated men, sometimes luring them away for a private dance. The men would follow obediently, weighed down by lust and credit cards.

Tazeem led the way to a small table against the far wall. Within moments a waitress wearing only white lace panties and a clip-on white collar and black bowtie sauntered over to take their order. Tazeem placed their VIP flyers on the table and Mangle asked for three vodka and cokes. After a lingering look she turned and sashayed off to fetch the drinks.

'Is this your friend's place?' Decker asked Tazeem.

'I don't know if he owns it or runs it, or exactly what it is he does.'

An electro-pop track overlaid with sensual female vocals began to play as the next dancer strutted out onto the stage.

Decker looked as mesmerised as the other men in the room, unsurprising after the number of years he'd spent in all-male company. Mangle watched the other women as they circled, like birds of prey deciding on their next kill. He noticed a raised, darkened area to the back of the room, just beyond the incandescent red glow, which he presumed was for actual VIPs, not just guys lucky enough to have been given flyers for free drinks. A group of men sat there talking, seemingly oblivious to the floor-show.

The perky waitress returned with their drinks on a polished silver tray perched on perfectly manicured fingernails. She plucked the glasses one by one and placed them onto the table, waited for a few seconds before realising she wasn't about to get a tip, and walked away again, this time with a less graceful gait.

Seductive groaning now accompanied the track as the woman gyrated on the stage, grinding her crotch against the pole. The back-stage door opened and a man led out two girls wearing string bikinis, one pink and the other turquoise. They were attractive, but Mangle's attention lingered on them for another reason: they carried themselves very differently to the other girls they had seen. Their movements were disjointed, uncertain. They seemed acutely aware of their semi-nakedness. One lagged behind a little and was grabbed firmly around her wrist by the man leading the way. He escorted them around the outside of the room, stopping for a few words with the other girls and to point out things to the two in tow.

One song blended into the next and another dancer came out onto the floor and began her routine. She wore silver sequined heels that matched her bra top and panties. Mangle watched absently for a moment or two before glancing around the room. The girls the man brought out had been left in the shaded section of the club and were being turned and examined by the men who sat there. The girls sat down and Mangle settled back to watch the main act. The silver-sequined girl slid slowly down into the splits, her torso against the pole, and ran her hands wantonly up and down it.

Tazeem signalled to the waitress to refresh their drinks. Decker hadn't taken his eyes from the girl on the stage. Mangle picked up his glass and drank the last inch. The ice cubes clicked like dice as he replaced it.

The two girls walked back down into the main room. Mangle wasn't sure what kept drawing his attention back to them, until the girl wearing the turquoise bikini met his eye for a moment as she looked across the club.

'That's her,' he exclaimed, 'Decker, look.' He reached forward and tugged at Decker's shirt sleeve.

'What's who?' Decker said, irritably pulling his arm away.

'The girl from that job, that's one of the ones from the warehouse.'

Tazeem was all attention now. 'The last job you did?' he asked.

'Yes,' Mangle said, turning to him.

Decker squinted at the two girls. 'You can't be sure. It was over a week ago and the light in here is terrible.'

'Either way, I think we should go,' Tazeem said, getting to his feet.

A couple of women working the club glanced over at the sudden movement. The girl in turquoise stood rooted in the centre of the room, watching Mangle intently. Decker and Mangle got up and Tazeem led the way calmly but purposefully towards the stairs.

'I see you before.'

Mangle spun around to see that the girl had followed them. There was no trace of the fear he'd seen at the warehouse. The bruising and puffiness had faded from her face, but up close her eyes looked hazy and unfocused, like someone just roused from sleep.

'No, I don't think so,' he said, and turned away.

Men from the shaded area had begun to pay attention now and two of them stood up. Tazeem opened the door and walked quickly down the stairs.

'Will you help me?' the girl asked, and grabbed for Mangle's arm, but Decker was already pushing him through the doorway.

Mangle's heart was racing. He was in no doubt that it was the same girl. Decker smiled at the doormen and all three walked out into the cold night air. The ground soaked from a heavy rain that continued to fall.

'Keep going,' Tazeem said evenly from a few paces ahead of them. He ducked into an alley and broke into a run. Seconds later, loud voices could be heard behind them from the direction of the club. Decker and Mangle kept up with Tazeem as he ran this way and that down a rabbit warren of back streets.

'Did you recognise anyone else in there?' Tazeem asked, bent over with his hands on his thighs and breathing heavily when he came to a halt a few moments later.

'No, just her. The guys at the top table seemed to have some authority, but I couldn't see their faces. It's possible one or more of them could have been at the warehouse,' Mangle said.

'The way they all chased after us, I think you must be right,' Decker said, and glanced back up the alley to make sure no one was following.

'So what do we do?' Mangle asked.

'Nothing. We don't know anything for sure, but if you are right the last thing we want is to be identified. We take separate cabs and go home. I'll be in touch if I learn anything tomorrow.'

When the taxi pulled up outside Tazeem's house he paid the driver and got out, but instead of going into the house he climbed into his car. He knew he wouldn't be able to sleep. He ran a hand over his forehead, then smoothed down his wet hair. Events of the day circled inside his head, like the predatory women at the club. He knew he'd think clearer behind the wheel of his car than he would do lying in bed, staring at the ceiling.

Tazeem turned the key and his Mercedes purred awake. He breathed into his hand and sniffed. He was probably over the limit to drive, but not by much. He reversed out of the driveway and started down the street, keeping his speed down to avoid getting pulled over.

Tazeem thought Mangle and Decker had handled the unforeseen, dangerous situation they'd found themselves in on their last job very well. Mangle's fake phone call before entering had been a stroke of genius. The man couldn't bundle them into the back of a van if someone knew their location and was expecting their imminent return.

The contacts Tazeem used were usually reliable, but the very nature of the information he sought made it dangerous for them to question things too openly. He had been told with reasonable certainty that the warehouse was used to take delivery of stolen goods. That had seemed perfect, just the type of place they were after. Now it appeared that stolen goods hadn't been what they received there at all, and that made their current situation a lot more hazardous. If people were the trade, rather than goods, then the men behind it would be a lot more organised and a lot more dangerous.

Tazeem cursed his stupidity for accepting the passes from Sadiq. They were the only thing that linked them to South of Seven. He'd erased any trace of their connection to the electric company jobs, but for now it might be best for Decker and Mangle to avoid going into Latif's shop as well. He scrolled down to Latif's number in his phone, clicked it, and waited for him to pick up. It was after 1a.m. now, but after the busy opening night there was a chance he'd still be finishing up at the restaurant.

After five or six rings Latif connected the call. 'Tazeem, it's pretty late and I'm just about to head home. Can this wait until tomorrow?'

'I just need a few moments, my friend. Can I come and see you before you leave?'

'Alright, Tazeem. But hurry up, I want to get home and sleep.'

Tazeem promised he'd get there as soon as he could. A peal of thunder rumbled overhead as he turned onto the highway.

Thick sheets of rain fell as Tazeem pulled into an empty parking space opposite Mailsi. A jagged vein of lightning lit the sky a bright white as Tazeem climbed out of the car, before another roar of thunder like rolling boulders echoed over him. He put up a hand to shield his eyes and saw a hooded figure get out of a car directly outside the restaurant. The hands poking out from the long sleeves were almost luminously white in contrast to the black top the figure wore. Tazeem, recognising Latif's car parked two spaces further down, supposed it must be a staff member kept back to help out, and he began to cross the road.

Oddly, the hooded figure broke into a run, pulling something from his jacket pocket. Tazeem stopped in the middle of the road, unsure why he felt such trepidation as the man ran down the deserted street. When he reached the corner he turned, and looked back the way he'd come. His face, a ghostly white oval, appeared almost featureless from this distance. They stood watching each other, unmoving, for a moment longer before another crash of thunder spurred the man into action.

The blast of hot air lifted Tazeem from his feet and threw him onto his back in the road. He blinked up into the night sky; raindrops glowed orange as they fell towards the earth. With great effort he sat up and looked around dumbly. The car parked outside the restaurant had been reshaped, its metal skeleton taking on the crumpled appearance of balled-up paper. All of the windows and the driver's side door were gone, and the whole thing was engulfed in flames.

The front of the restaurant was a fiery mess. The windows had blown inward. Curtains, tables, in fact everything he could make out inside, was burning.

Tazeem hauled himself to his feet, walked past the flaming carcass of the car and kicked what was left of the restaurant door inward to gain entry. He couldn't hear anything, and when he reached up to touch his ears his fingers came away coated in blood. He stepped through the shattered frame, looking for any sign of life. He shouted Latif's name over and over, or thought he did: all Tazeem could hear was a muffled echo among the carnage around him.

Tazeem stepped in further, overturned a flaming table and tried to make out any signs of movement through the smoke. One of the curved beams fell from the ceiling and crashed to the floor in a cloud of sparks no more than 2 feet away. Tazeem recoiled instinctively, then again tried to move forward. He tore off a shirt sleeve and held it to his face in an effort to filter out the repressive toxic fumes. The smoke had begun to take effect. He felt dizzy and stumbled, reached out, putting a steadying hand against one of the booths, and cried out as his flesh made contact with the burning wood.

He cast a last forlorn look around the interior, but in vain. He could only pray that Latif hadn't been inside when the explosion happened. His hearing hadn't yet returned but no doubt sirens were marking the imminent arrival of the emergency services. Tazeem hurried back to his car and drove away.

A mile or so down the road he texted Decker and Mangle and told them to meet him at the lock-up immediately. When they arrived, Tazeem explained everything he'd seen.

'Someone must have recognised you at South of Seven, and they've made the connection between you and Latif. You both work at his store and you said there was someone from the stock-room with Sadiq at Mailsi tonight.'

'So they go and blow up his restaurant? Jesus! And what the fuck do we do now, live in here?' Decker said, toppling the chair backwards with sudden ferocity as he jumped to his feet, gesturing dramatically around the dingy interior.

'No, but you have to stay out of sight till we can work out what is going on.'

'You mean you aren't staying?' Mangle asked him.

'I'll be back, but I need to make sure Ermina is OK first. She'll be home alone, and if they have connected me with this as well, then she is in danger.'

Tazeem drove quickly back to his house. He couldn't believe he hadn't thought of Ermina sooner. He hadn't even checked on her when he'd arrived home earlier, just got straight into his car and drove away.

Everything looked undisturbed as he pulled up, a few houses further up the street. The porch and hallway lights glowed reassuringly. Tazeem let himself in after first checking that there were no signs of forced entry, and called Ermina's name once inside.

When she didn't reply, Tazeem went from room to room to make certain no one else was in the house. He climbed the stairs two at a time, knocked loudly on her bedroom door, and when greeted only by silence he walked in. Ermina's bed hadn't been slept in and there were clothes haphazardly scattered across it. Both of the wardrobes were open and most of her clothes were gone.

'No,' Tazeem said, despairingly.

He searched upstairs and down for a note or any clue to her whereabouts. He dialled the number for her cell, but it was turned off. In desperation he even called Sadiq, but got no reply. Tazeem tried to gather himself. He splashed cold water onto his face then threw some of his own clothes into a bag. He knew it wouldn't be a good idea to return here for a while.

When Tazeem arrived back at the lock-up, Decker and Mangle sat silently in front of the old TV set nursing cracked mugs of coffee, watching Kasey Haugh present a live Channel 10 news report.

'Have you heard?' Decker asked as Tazeem went to pour himself a cup.

'Heard what?'

'They hit the computer shop as well, another car bomb. Daisycutter bombs, or something, the news reports are calling them,' Mangle said. He looked dazed by what he was hearing.

Tazeem sat down heavily, his head swimming. He gulped down some of the hot, bitter coffee and tried to gather his thoughts.

'It was at the same time as the restaurant. It's all over the news,' Mangle continued. 'Maybe it was intended as a warning and they didn't know he was still inside.'

'So they've found a body?' Tazeem asked.

Decker nodded. 'One body in the restaurant, but it hasn't been identified. Is Ermina OK?' he asked as an afterthought.

'She wasn't there. And her clothes and stuff are missing.'

'We should take this to the police,' Mangle said.

'No, I can't risk anything happening to her. Besides we have nothing but supposition, nothing to link it to Sadiq or anyone else. And you can guarantee the warehouse all this started in will be wiped clean.'

For the next few days all three stayed inside the lock-up as much as they could. Tazeem's calls to Ermina went straight to voicemail. The TV reported that Latif's body had been identified. At first the news channels were rife with speculation as to why a regular businessman had been targeted in such a way. But as no light was shed on the mystery, the coverage grew sparser before other disasters and the mayoral elections were deemed more worthy for public consumption and the two explosions were forgotten.

Tazeem had put out feelers on the street for any information, and on the third day he got a call from an informant. He arranged to meet him at a riverside cafe called Harley's at 1p.m. that afternoon, but arrived 20 minutes early.

Harley's was an old cafe that had seen better days. It used to service a nearby textile mill before its closure a few years earlier.

These days it captured little passing trade, but many of the factory workers would return from time to time to drink cups of tea and reminisce with the owner. The floors were unmopped and the windows were milky, covered by handprints and a film of cooking grease.

Tazeem walked in, ordered a sandwich at the counter and sat in one of the many vacant booths. The man serving shared a joke with a customer sitting at the counter. He had a rasping laugh that sounded like splintering wood. Tazeem cleared his throat and checked his watch as his informant, Ferret, entered and sat down.

'What have you got for me?' Tazeem asked. He took a bite from his sandwich and pushed an envelope across the table.

Ferret had nervous eyes, copper hair and beard, and moved with sudden bursts of intent. He snatched up the envelope, and once certain that their conversation was of no interest to the men at the counter, he began to speak.

'I know a guy, Ben, works behind the bar at the club you mentioned.'

'South of Seven?' Tazeem asked. 'I want something on the explosions.'

'You gonna listen to what I have to say or not?'

'Alright, Ferret, get to your point, I'm listening.'

'He was in there the night of the bombs. Said three guys left the club, suddenly, and it caused a commotion. Said there was a lot of coming and going after that, management and people in the VIP section.'

'I know this already.'

'He overheard something. An Asian guy in a sharp suit and sparkles,' Ferret said, fluttering nicotine-stained fingers at Tazeem. 'Took a phone call then said, "Do both places. Get the point across."'

Sadiq. He must have been in the building or arrived there shortly after they left. This confirmed that Sadiq was behind the explosions, but gave them nothing new.

'What else did he say?'

'About the explosions? Nothing. He had more on the club, if you want that.'

Tazeem nodded but Ferret remained quiet and drummed his fingers on the table. Tazeem had anticipated this and reached for the second envelope. Ferret licked his lips, lizard-like, and grabbed it.

'He says the girls are coming and going real quick these days. They used to have a rotation of regulars working the place. But now there's a constant stream of new girls with accents, maybe Russian or somewhere like that. He says they show up all beautiful but kind of dopey-looking and it's made pretty clear that for the right price a lap dance can have a happy ending.'

Tazeem nodded and waited for Ferret to continue. He was obviously holding out for a third envelope but Tazeem didn't budge an inch and just returned his stare. Eventually, Ferret accepted that he'd milked the situation for all it was worth.

'He's heard there's another place.'

'Another lap dancing club? So what, they're all over the city.'

'This isn't a regular strip club. It's a real high-roller anything-goes type of place,' Ferret said. His eyes glittered as he reached across the table and touched Tazeem's arm. 'And I mean anything goes.'

'Lap dancers getting paid extra to fuck is nothing new. What's the big deal about this place?'

'It's not just fucking, aren't you listening to me? These girls learn the ropes at Seven and are moved on to the other place. More and more are coming through every day, man. How many fucking strippers does a place need, for Christ's sake?'

'Oh my God,' Tazeem said, as he began to understand, and thoughts of Ermina spiked in his stomach. 'Do you know where it is?'

Ferret took out a folded scrap of paper and passed it to him. 'My guy Ben doesn't know where the other club is, but the girls are being shipped in from here, a rehab centre in Newtonville.'

'Well, what's this other place called?' Tazeem asked as he slipped the scrap of paper into his pocket.

'The place is just known as The Club. But the behind-the-scenes bit that only the real big spenders get to see, there's no official name, 'cause officially it doesn't exist, that's called The Zombie Room.'

10

When Tatiana got back to the clinic she found Laura still awake, sitting and gazing out of the window onto the moonlit fields below. Her companion from the trip to the lap dancing club went to bed, and within moments was asleep. Tatiana pulled up a chair beside Laura.

'Can't sleep?' she asked. Laura shook her head.

'Are you thinking about home?'

Laura looked puzzled for a moment, before answering. 'No. That is not something I ever think of any more.' A slight smile played at her lips, her forehead smooth and unconcerned.

Tatiana didn't know what to make of that, as the memories of her life before her parents died were the only thing that kept her sane. But she had noticed a similar change in the other girls; they communicated very little any more, not just with Tatiana, but amongst themselves too, and any conversation that did germinate never involved what they had left behind, what they had lost.

'Do you think we will ever again be happy?' Tatiana asked after a few moments. Laura didn't answer. Tatiana wasn't sure if she had heard.

'What is happy?' Laura said quietly, after Tatiana had given up hope of a response. 'I think I would settle for being at rest.' She turned and faced Tatiana. 'Do you know what I mean?'

Tatiana nodded, although she wasn't sure that she did. 'I couldn't ever be at rest while the man responsible for killing my family walks free.'

Laura had turned to look back out of the window, then her eyes slipped out of focus. She was no longer listening.

The clinic had previously been the lavish home of a successful businessman. After his systematic fall from grace due to illness, and ostracization of remaining family, he donated the house and remaining land to a charity organisation that specialised in treatment of patients suffering from bipolar disorder, the only stipulation being, that it retain its name of The Walker Estate. When the charity fell on hard times it was finally placed on the market, but the reclusive location and lack of good farming opportunity saw The Walker Estate lie vacant for many years, during which time its existence had mostly faded from memory.

They parked about a mile away, and walked through scrubland and the occasional wooded copse. When they neared the fence Tazeem was surprised by the lack of security. It looked no different from any 3 foot fence surrounding regular farmland, designed to contain livestock. He began to question Ferret's information.

The main building was a few hundred yards to the west; a modest two-storey country house with creeping ivy, well-maintained gardens and suitably pruned hedgerows. Three single-storey outbuildings ringed the rear of the property. So far there'd been no sign of anyone.

'You sure this is where they keep the girls?' Mangle asked.

'Am I sure? No, but this is where Ferret said it was,' Tazeem answered.

'So you think that upwards of a dozen girls are kept in here, possibly Ermina among them, while they're brainwashed into being sex slaves?' Decker said dismissively, and turned to begin walking back to the car.

'We're here now, we may as well wait a while and see if we see anything.' Mangle said.

As he spoke, the sound of a buzzer emitted from the property. All three lay down in the grass and watched as a procession of five girls wearing shapeless sky-blue jumpsuits were led from an outbuilding toward the main house. A woman who looked older than the others walked with them. She wore the same outfit in beige. One man accompanied them, who stood watching, but made no movement to usher or hurry any of them along. From this distance they couldn't hear what, if anything, was being said, but he at least appeared to be unarmed.

A door opened and the girls began to file inside. The man scratched his chin and gazed off across the fields as the first three girls passed into the house and out of sight. Mangle, Decker and Tazeem watched silently from their vantage point as the second to last girl suddenly broke ranks and started to sprint across the grounds.

'Fucking hell, she's coming this way,' Decker said. 'How come the guy isn't chasing her?'

The attendant seemed unconcerned by the fleeing girl. No alarms sounded and still the solitary man by the house was the only witness. She got close enough for them to see a bright red welt on her left cheek, the size and shape of a hand print. She was 100 yards from the fence now. Glancing to her left, she saw the three lying in the grass and angled her run toward them.

'Shit, she's gonna get us noticed for sure,' Tazeem said.

'There's something around her neck,' Decker said, 'some kind of collar.'

'Start backing away from the fence,' Tazeem said. 'Someone's bound to come after her.'

She couldn't have been more than 50 yards from them when she collapsed onto the ground, convulsing and clawing at her neck. The door to the building had closed on the other girls. The attendant began to walk across to the runaway, who writhed and kicked her legs spasmodically. The woman in the beige jumpsuit stood sentinel by the door but made no move towards the flailing girl.

Decker and Mangle had retreated back to nearby trees and Tazeem ducked down beside them.

'You can hear it,' Mangle said, shushing them. 'Listen, you can hear the buzzing.'

Tazeem held his breath and sure enough could hear what sounded like an overloaded electrical socket. A steady buzzing was punctuated only by an occasional dull thump as one of the girl's limbs flopped onto the grass. A few more seconds, and the buzzing stopped. Other than the occasional twitch, the girl now lay still.

Presently, the man arrived where she lay. He hoisted her onto his back with practised efficiency and started back toward the main building.

'Fucking hell,' Decker said once he was sure the man was out of earshot. 'Least we know why they don't bother with fences now.'

'Yeah,' Mangle said, 'this is definitely the right place.'

Tazeem rented a small bungalow in a quiet residential district, a few miles north of the city. He left his easily identifiable Mercedes in the lock-up garage and they used the white VW to get around in. Ferret was now incommunicado and Tazeem spent the next few days trying to gather further information through his network of sources.

Mangle and Decker grew weary hiding out waiting for Tazeem to plan their next move, and decided on another reconnaissance visit to the clinic. They stationed themselves by the fence in an area of dense dogwood bushes. The first hour produced nothing but boredom and creeping damp patches on their clothes from lying on the ground.

When finally a buzzer sounded, both Mangle and Decker

expected the same routine as they'd previously witnessed, with a troop of girls being led from an outbuilding back to the house. This time, however, the door from the main building opened and eleven girls wearing the uniform sky-blue jumpsuits, led by the single woman in beige, made their way outside.

'What are they doing?' Decker asked after several moments.

'Not much of anything, it doesn't look like; just walking around.'

The girls appeared to wander aimlessly around the grounds. Again there was a single man stationed beside the house. He had brought out a chair and sat reading a book beside the doorway, paying virtually no attention to the girls.

'You recognise any from Seven? Or from the warehouse?' Decker asked.

'No, not from here anyway. None that look like they could be Ermina either.'

One girl followed an angular path around the flower beds, slowly gravitating further away from the building. Mangle kept low and watched for any sign of interest from the attendant. She never cast a glance back over her shoulder and he didn't appear to look up.

'Is that the one from the warehouse?' Decker asked.

'I can't tell for sure while she has her head down like that,' Mangle said, squinting at the girl closest to them. 'But it doesn't look like she's wearing one of those collars, and the guy over there seems fine with her being so far from the house.'

He was right. The girl still followed the perimeter of one flower bed after another, maybe 200 yards from the house, and neither the attendant nor the woman in beige paid her any heed.

'She's humming,' Decker commented. 'What have they done to make them so sure the girls won't run off?'

Mangle didn't answer. He could hear the girl now as well. 'Hey,' he said, in a voice he hoped would carry to her. If she'd heard him she gave no indication.

Decker picked a small stone and tossed it towards her. It bounced in the grass a few feet in front of her and she immediately stopped humming. The girl peered absently over towards the fence but looked less than curious at their presence. After a prolonged moment of staring, she resumed the tuneless humming and again walked the line around the flower bed.

'It's her,' Mangle said, with rising excitement in his voice. 'It's the same one.'

The woman in beige walked toward the girl but there was no urgency or suspicion in her movements. She linked arms with her, and turned back towards the clinic. 'Come on Tatty, time to go back inside and see Dr Chu.'

Back at the bungalow Tazeem still sat dejectedly at the table with his phone pressed to his ear. He looked older than Mangle had noticed before; the added worry of each passing day had aged him.

'OK, call me right away if you hear anything,' he said and ended the call.

Mangle sat down beside him and Decker went to fetch three beers from the fridge. By the time the beers had been drunk Tazeem had been brought up to speed about their trip back out to the clinic.

'So she was right out by the fence and didn't make a run for it?'

'No. She didn't even look like it had crossed her mind. And she wore no collar like the girl last time,' Mangle said.

'The attendant didn't seem concerned in the slightest. He barely looked up from his book. The girls were wandering around out there as if they didn't have a care in the world,' Decker added.

'I'm getting nowhere. It looks like the one person who can give us some answers is this Dr Chu.'

At just after 6 p.m. on Friday, Benjamin Chu was eager to begin his weekend of rest and relaxation. He climbed behind the wheel of his steel-grey Aston Martin, pressed the ignition button and waited as the seats, mirrors and steering wheel hummed into his pre-programmed position. He tossed his security pass onto the seat beside him, and followed the gravel driveway the mile towards the main gate. The evening had prematurely darkened and the gathering clouds began to shed a fine rain.

The Saturday night of unadulterated pleasure he had planned at The Club, inaugurating the new girls, was a tantalising prospect. The Club had priced itself out of the market for all but the most lavish and frivolous of patrons. The delays and disappointments he had faced at the clinic in achieving the ladies' cultural reform could be disheartening, but finally seeing them in their new environment, acting as he had instructed, was almost reward enough. The generous six-figure salary he collected in addition he considered to be a very welcome bonus. He smiled to himself as the gate opened allowing the car in front to proceed, and reached for his ID as he pulled into position at the security console.

'Please present identification,' a voice crackled through the speaker. Benjamin placed his hologramatic ID card with the neon green triangle against the scanner, and looked into the camera lens. These security measures were completely unnecessary in his opinion: considering the lengths he went to with the girls, there was zero risk of escape. Too much security might draw unwanted attention to the clinic from curious outsiders, but the ID scanner at the gate at least ensured there were no tourists.

'You may proceed,' the voice announced, and the gates parted for him to leave.

Benjamin withdrew his ID and drove through the gate. The job at the clinic was a result of furthering research his father had begun many years ago in China. This work was intended to create an alternative to life imprisonment or execution, for the most serious and habitual offenders. His father believed that by curing the behaviour patterns that led to extreme anti-social behaviour, you could regulate and rehabilitate the individual, enabling their release back into society.

The implications for other potential applications of his work were quickly realised. Benjamin's father had been a good man, and when the government took control of his work, he destroyed as much of the research as he could and fled the country. He settled in Garden Heights as a political refugee, took on a menial position, and married. After some years his father had written memoirs of his time working in China that he absolutely refused to have published, but was pleased when his son took such an interest and happily answered his questions. His father died when Benjamin was a teenager, and when he announced that he wanted to continue his father's work, initially his mother was delighted.

But to have such capabilities, and not exploit them ambitiously and financially, made no sense to Benjamin. His growing expertise took him outside the realms of general decency and beyond his university's tolerance for negative publicity, and he was subsequently expelled. His mother moved away, unable to tolerate the mistrust of the community after Benjamin was labelled a 'Psychological Frankenstein' in a newspaper exposé.

Without the university's resources Benjamin was left with a huge financial shortfall, and test subjects were hard to come by. He was in need of a sponsor. But the negative press from his research scandal had attracted the attention of an organisation capable of satiating his desires for wealth, power and, above all, knowledge.

The rain fell heavier and Benjamin's Aston Martin automatically increased its wiper speed. He chose to believe that his father would be proud of his accomplishments, whatever his mother had said. His father's research had been limited to psychological manipulation, and environmental control, but with the added chemical element that Benjamin had perfected, he believed that given time, there was nothing he couldn't coerce a patient into willingly doing.

A set of flashing hazard lights up ahead caused Benjamin to ease off the accelerator. Some idiot had broken down and left their car jutting out, blocking most of the road. Benjamin steered towards the grass verge, planning to drive onto it to pass by, but the stranded motorist was now walking towards his car waving their arms to flag him down. Great, he thought. A chunk of my weekend wasted already. But a quick phone call to roadside assistance and he'd be on his way. Five minutes he'd give, tops. His window purred down only a couple of inches to prevent any rainwater invading the interior, as the soaked motorist walked around to the driver's side.

'Hi, thanks for stopping. Could you help me get the car going?'

'I know nothing about cars, you should phone for assistance,' Benjamin said irritably, and looked forward again, indicating his desire to leave.

'It'll just take a moment, I'd really appreciate it.'

'If you don't have a phone, I'll make a call for you. Other than that you're on your own, friend,' Benjamin said impatiently and revved his engine.

The passenger side window exploded inward, showering Benjamin with shards of glass. He panicked and stamped on the accelerator, sending the Aston Martin skidding forwards on the greasy road surface. Through the rain-streaked glass of the car in front, he saw a head pop up in the driver's seat, and the car reversed into his path. The front of Benjamin's car crunched into the rear bumper of what was clearly not a broken-down car. The Aston Martin stalled. Whoever had smashed his window caught up and reached through the shattered pane, grabbing a fistful of Benjamin's jacket and screaming threats of violence if he tried to move the car again.

When the doctor refused to get out of the car and help, Mangle was at a loss. He hadn't contemplated somebody who wouldn't get out and help in a similar situation. He saw Decker sneak out and around the side of the doctor's car, and when Decker smashed the window, Mangle was almost as surprised as the doctor. Tazeem saw things weren't going to plan and slid over into the driver's seat of the Volkswagen. Mangle regained his senses and ran towards the cars. Decker was already ahead of him, yelling and attempting to haul the doctor from the Aston

Martin. He snatched away the doctor's cell phone before he could call for help.

'Throw him in the back,' Decker said, pulling the doctor through the shattered window.

He rushed around and restarted the doctor's car. They had picked the spot carefully and Decker drove towards a dense clump of fir trees and manoeuvred the car behind them. Running back to the road, Decker kicked away the broken glass, leaving no evidence of the collision.

Mangle hopped into the driver's seat of the Volkswagen and once Decker, Tazeem and their captive were all on board he accelerated away.

The lock-up wasn't the ideal location to interrogate someone, but their only other alternative was the bungalow, so it would have to do. Tazeem pulled down the shutters and locked them. Decker dragged the terrified doctor to the chair they had prepared, and taped his arms in place. He didn't know how far they would have to go to get the information they needed.

'What do you want? I have money, I'll give you all I have,' the doctor said in a shrill voice.

'We don't want your money,' Tazeem said bitterly. 'I want to know where my cousin is.'

'What?' The doctor stammered.

'Is Ermina at the clinic?' Mangle demanded.

'I don't know the name of every girl there,' the doctor protested at what he considered to be an absurd notion.

'So how do we find out if she's there?' Tazeem asked. His voice raised an octave, and a note of pleading had crept in.

'It'll be in the records, if she's there now or if she's been there. They're in the office next to mine.'

'You can't think if we let him go he'll just gonna call us up with what we want,' Decker said, as Tazeem looked to be contemplating the possibility. The doctor's immediate claim that that's exactly what he'd do if they freed him went unheeded.

'You'll have to get us in there,' Tazeem stated.

'That's ridiculous. You can't just walk into the clinic, they have security.'

'How many guards are on duty at the weekend?' Tazeem persisted.

'Right now, just one. This is a very busy weekend, a lot of the girls are being moved into the club environment,' the doctor said, pride evident in his voice. It made Tazeem feel sick.

'Will he be armed?'

'Yes, the security staff are always armed. But the attendants aren't armed as they chaperone the girls between sessions, in case anyone sees them.'

'We're going back there now. No one will know he's missing yet. This will be our best chance to get inside,' Tazeem said.

Mangle and Decker exchanged looks but said nothing. The doctor protested enough for them both. Tazeem peeled off the tape holding the doctor's arms to the chair and ushered him back toward the car, pushed him into the back seat and slammed the door.

'Are you sure about this?' Decker asked.

'No, but what else am I left with? There's been no word from Ermina in over a week. I have to know if she's been forced onto this … conveyor belt of sex slavery,' Tazeem said, shaking his head as he reached for the right words. 'If there's even a possibility of her being there, I have to try. I appreciate all the help you've both given, but you shouldn't come with me. We don't know if anything he said is true; there could be a dozen guys back there. Get a cab back to the house and if I can I'll meet you there later.'

'After seeing that girl in the club, the way she looked at me and not being able to help her, I'd rather come too,' Mangle said.

'What about you, Decker?'

'Alright, let's go. But you both owe me way big after getting messed up with all this shit. I'd have had a safer life if I'd gone into dealing drugs.'

The plan was for the doctor to drive his Aston Martin through the gates as they crouched down out of sight. They'd keep both front windows down so there'd be no evidence of the smashed passenger side, and the doctor could use the prang on the front of the car as an excuse for returning if the security guard mentioned it. Although they had no firearms, all three picked up sharp implements from around the garage that would act as makeshift weapons if necessary.

The doctor's car was parked behind the trees where Decker had left it. They pulled the Volkswagen alongside and transferred over.

'This screwdriver is up against the back of your seat,' Decker warned after tunnelling through the padding, 'and if you try to alert the guard, I promise you I'll ram it into your spine.'

Benjamin nodded and swallowed, but said nothing. He looked pale and his hands shook slightly as they gripped the steering wheel.

The rain subsided as they drove the few miles to the clinic in silence. The doctor picked his ID card off the floor where it had fallen after the collision, and held it as he drove up to the scanner outside the gates.

'Please present identification,' a disinterested voice announced after a few moments. Benjamin held his card to the scanner and waited.

'Hello, Dr Chu. I wasn't expecting you back tonight.'

'Hi, Tom, I forgot some files I need to look at over the weekend,' he said, and smiled thinly. Decker pushed the screwdriver through the fabric and Benjamin could feel the steel tip pressing against his lower back.

'OK, Dr Chu, you may proceed.'

Benjamin dropped the card onto his lap and drove through the gates. The gravel grumbled beneath the Aston Martin's tyres as the doctor navigated the driveway, unfurling through a thick stand of pine trees. The road was unlit; the only illumination came from the one remaining headlight on the Aston Martin.

Benjamin kept the car at a sedate speed and after several moments the clinic came into view.

'Where do you normally park?' Tazeem asked, peering above the dashboard.

'Over there,' Benjamin said, indicating an empty patch of gravel 50 yards from the main entrance, with room to park around a dozen cars.

Tazeem scanned the area. A security camera protruded from the second storey on a metal arm, perusing its automated arc.

'Park under the camera,' he instructed.

Benjamin pulled up where he was told and killed the engine.

'Will we pass by anyone on the way to the office?'

'No. The guard's station is on the south side of the building next to the girls' living quarters. The offices are in the other direction.'

'What about cameras?' Decker asked.

'There's one on the main door. That's the only door that can be opened from outside.'

'How are we to get past without the guard seeing us then?' Mangle asked.

'You'll have to find something for him to do that will distract him for a few minutes. Just enough time to get us through.'

'Well?' Decker said, leaning forward towards the doctor. 'Think quick.' And again he pressed the sharp point of the screwdriver into his back.

'Alright … we have had some issues with one of the girls. She's in one of the isolation units. I could ask him to make an extra trip down there.'

'Isolation unit? Jesus, it's worse than prison,' Decker said.

'Is that anywhere near the offices?' Tazeem asked.

'No, it's close to the guard's station so he would only be away a few minutes.'

'OK, do it,' Tazeem ordered, and handed back the doctor's phone.

He watched carefully as Benjamin scrolled through the phone's contact list and highlighted 'Clinic Security'.

'Tom?' Benjamin said into the phone after it rang a few times. 'Could you go and check on the girl we have in L2? … That's great, but if you'd just have another look I'd feel a lot better … No, just call if there are any problems. I'll be in and out in just a few minutes … OK, Tom, I'll see you Monday.'

Tazeem took the phone back and counted to 60, which he hoped was long enough for the guard to have moved away from his post by the monitors.

'OK, let's go,' he said, and got out of the car.

Benjamin, Mangle and Decker got out and followed him to the entrance. Benjamin tapped in the five-digit access code, a beep sounded, then a green light flashed announcing that the door was unlocked.

'It's along the hall to the right,' Benjamin said, walking through the dimly lit reception area. He turned right and passed by six identical wooden doors before stopping outside the seventh. He reached into a pocket, withdrew a key ring and unlocked the door.

The room was dark. Mangle pressed the light switch and four fluorescent tubes flickered into life, casting the room in a cold blue glare. Filing cabinets were lined up along two of the walls, and the windows were obscured by closed venetian blinds.

The doctor handed the key ring to Tazeem. 'This key will unlock them,' he said. 'Take whatever information you want and then please leave.'

Tazeem unlocked the first cabinet and began flipping through the folders inside. 'There must have been hundreds of girls through this place,' he said, disbelievingly.

Decker stepped forward and pulled out a folder at random. A photo of a dispirited girl in her early twenties looked back at him when he opened it. Name: Alenka, and a reference number written in black marker.

'What are these numbers for?' he asked, flipping through the pages.

'The girls are rated,' the doctor said, taking a seat behind the desk.

'Rated for what?' Mangle asked.

'Lots of things: receptiveness, obedience, ability.'

'That's disgusting.'

'It's just organisation. A way of finding which girls are better suited to which tasks.'

'There's no mention of her so far,' Tazeem said and moved onto one of two remaining cabinets.

Mangle opened the last one. 'What do you do to them to make them so subservient?' he asked.

'We work with what is known as the BITE method: "Behaviour, Information, Thought and Emotion". A dependency is created by controlling stimulus through all channels. We strip away all distractions and begin their thought reform from scratch. The process can be both invigorating and rewarding for the patient.'

'What do you mean by strip away?'

'We take away their identity, their individuality. Keep a tight grip on information, no outside influences. Show them that independent thought is responsible for the bad situations they found themselves in, in the past; that by following the programme they are positively moving towards a new life for themselves and all the rewards that it can hold.'

'You make it sound like a liberating experience,' Mangle said bitterly as he continued flipping through countless profile folders. 'These girls are sex slaves. Their lives are worthless after you're done with them.'

'The reconditioning helps them get past any moral or societal boundaries imposed upon them during their upbringing. Sure, some of the girls work in the sex trade for a while to pay for the treatment; this is a very expensive business. But afterwards, they move on to new lives and leave their past behind them.'

'This guy's insane. He's trying to convince us this is a service they're providing and not exploitation,' Decker said, cracking his knuckles.

Tazeem closed the filing cabinet he'd been searching. 'Mangle, have you found anything on Ermina?'

'No,' he said holding onto a folder and closing the last cabinet. 'She isn't in here, but I found the girl from the warehouse that we saw here and in Seven.'

Mangle turned to the doctor and started to say something but the words fell silently from his lips and he stood still. Tazeem and Decker whirled around to see what had startled him and saw Benjamin sitting back in a chair with a black pistol levelled at them.

'I protested against a lot of the security measures, as I considered them ridiculously heavy-handed. Who'd have thought I would be the one to benefit from them? The security guard isn't called Tom. "Tom" is the code word for entry under duress. The gun fixed to the underside of the desk another touch that came in rather handy.'

'You son of a bitch, I'm just trying to save my cousin,' Tazeem protested.

The door handle turned and a security guard stepped into the room, armed with a handgun of his own.

'I made the call. They should be here within a half hour,' he informed the doctor.

'OK, great,' Benjamin said. All trace of fear was gone, leaving only a look of irritation at the position he had been placed in. 'Do you know how close you came to destroying everything I have worked for? If these files got out and compromised my research, the clinic would be finished. Put that folder down on the desk please,' he said to Mangle.

'No,' Mangle said, looking from the doctor to the security guard, then back again.

The tension in the air heightened. Mangle looked worried and Decker took a step back towards the wall.

'Take that file off him,' Benjamin said to the guard.

The guard shuffled uncomfortably before stepping forward. He repeated the command to put down the file but Mangle remained defiant.

'I have a gun on him, just walk over and take it,' Benjamin said impatiently.

The guard took two more steps, past Decker and within a few feet of Mangle. This was clearly more than he had anticipated from the job and he looked as if he wished he were somewhere else.

'Just take it, he isn't armed!' Benjamin shouted at the reluctant guard.

He looked nervously at the doctor and then as he stepped towards Mangle, Decker lunged forward and grabbed his gun arm. The guard threw himself back into Decker and they both fell heavily against the wall. Benjamin jumped to his feet, his arm outstretched, trying to get a clear shot at Decker. Decker struggled with the guard, both of them fighting for control of his weapon, the guard's arm waving frantically in front of him.

The sound of the shot was impossibly loud in the small room. Mangle and Tazeem backed up, unsure which gun had been fired. Benjamin saw the large-calibre bullet hole in the plaster, mere inches from his head. He panicked and squeezed off three successive shots.

The guard looked blearily down at the scarlet bloodstains blooming on his chest. He appeared to think of something that he needed to say, but as his lips began to form the words his knees gave up the strain of supporting his ruined bulk. He collapsed to the floor, his throat issuing a final sound like a bubbling casserole.

Decker quickly patted himself for wounds, but two of the bullets had hit the guard and one the wall behind. Benjamin looked surprised by the result of his actions, but quickly regained his composure and raised the weapon again.

'Enough of this shit,' he cried at them. 'All three of you back up against that wall.'

They obeyed, eager to avoid provoking him. The doctor stepped forward and retrieved the guard's gun.

'The others will be here soon, and I'm not taking any more chances. I'm locking you in here. And don't bother thinking about going through the window. That glass is two inches thick.'

Benjamin reached behind him, turned the door handle and stepped through the door. There was a sudden blur of movement from the corridor as a pair of balled fists were brought down against the back of his neck. He gave a startled 'Ohh', as if somebody had highlighted a point in debate that he hadn't considered.

Decker seized the opportunity, quickly strode forward and kicked the doctor in the side of the head. He picked up the pistol and shoved it into his waistband.

'We have to get out of here now,' the trembling voice of the woman in the beige jumpsuit said.

'Who the hell are you?' Mangle asked, struggling to accept their turn of fate.

'I don't know any more,' she said. Her eyes were misty and seemed to focus on a point far behind them. 'I just know I need to go.'

11

'You said you don't know who you are,' Mangle spoke tentatively as he looked over his shoulder at the woman in the back seat.

They'd parked the Aston Martin under cover of the fir trees and climbed back into the Volkswagen and were waiting for whoever the guard had called to pass by on the road.

'They call me Laura.'

'But that's not your real name?'

She shrugged. 'I don't think so, I don't know.'

Decker and Mangle exchanged a look. Tazeem shifted uncomfortably in the back seat.

'Do you know how old you are?' Tazeem asked. 'Or how long you've been there for?'

Laura shook her head. She moved a hand up suddenly and touched the side of her neck. There was a noticeable tremor.

'There are headlights coming on the road,' Decker said. They fell silent and listened as two cars whispered past.

Mangle waited a few seconds before starting the engine. He backed out without turning on any lights and drove away.

When he felt they'd put enough distance between themselves and the clinic, he turned on the headlights and asked Laura,

'How many girls have been through the clinic since you've been there?'

'I don't know the answers to any of your questions. That is how they control us. I remember what I had for breakfast this morning, and I'm sure I had breakfast yesterday, although I don't know what. Before that I have no idea. I could have been here for three weeks or three years, I just don't know.' Her voice cracked as she succumbed to the tide of suppressed emotion, and she began to sob uncontrollably into trembling hands. 'I just don't know.'

Tazeem reached over and awkwardly tried to comfort her. One thing was clear: she'd been afforded a certain responsibility so she must have been there for quite a while.

Tazeem led the way into the bungalow and drew the curtains in every room. Laura sat in a straight-backed chair in a corner of the living-room, furthest away from the other seats and with the door in her field of vision. She pulled her feet up and hugged her arms around her shins. The trembling that had affected her hands had gotten worse and was now evident in her arms and legs.

'Are you cold?' Decker asked. The property was centrally heated and none of the others felt a chill.

'No,' she said, attempting a smile. 'This is from missing my medication. That's where I was going when I heard the commotion in the office. I went looking for the guard to open the medical locker. They let me give my own shots.'

'Do all the girls receive this medication?' Mangle asked.

Laura nodded. Her shoulders were hunched with what appeared to be anxiety. 'Every day we get two medication shots and one session in the Audiology Suite. It keeps us well.'

'Audiology is the treatment of hearing disorders. You aren't all there for ear defects,' Mangle said, bewildered.

'I'm starting to feel a little strange,' Laura said. Her physical symptoms of medication withdrawal were visibly heightening by the minute.

'You can sleep in my room,' Mangle said. He walked into the hallway and pointed to one of the bedrooms. Laura walked past and nodded her thanks. Her teeth had begun to chatter.

Mangle slept on the couch and was the first to wake the following day. He rummaged through the cupboard to find something for Laura to eat. Hopefully, he thought, she'd feel better after resting and maybe they could get her to a doctor. Tazeem and Decker joined him in the kitchen shortly afterwards and the three ate toast and drank coffee while waiting for Laura to rise.

'You should go knock on the door, Mangle,' Decker said after a while.

They'd talked things over and decided their next move should be to locate Sadiq and get him alone to question over Ermina's disappearance. Tazeem was eager to leave and had frequently checked his watch while they sat eating breakfast.

Mangle went to the bedroom door and knocked, softly at first, and then louder after Laura failed to answer.

'Laura?' he said again. 'I'm coming in.'

Mangle turned the handle and walked in. The bed sheets were tousled, as if after passionate sex or an uneasy night's rest. The door into the en-suite bathroom stood ajar and he could hear running water. Mangle again said her name as he walked towards the bathroom. He pushed the door an inch and saw Laura's pale foot on the tiles. He stepped in and was stunned by the sight of the stark red puddle of blood that covered much of the floor. Laura's eyes were wide and startled. Her face was milk-white and her lips thin and grey.

Mangle knelt down next to her but could clearly see there was nothing he could do. He cupped her forearm around six inches below the wrist that bore the fatal laceration she'd bled out from. Her skin was cool to the touch. She'd broken out from the clinic, but he wondered how long she'd been able to hold out before taking her own life had been her only real way of escape.

'Fucking hell!' Decker exclaimed. He and Tazeem stood in the doorway behind Mangle.

'What the hell do we do now?' Tazeem said.

'Shouldn't we call the police?' Mangle asked, looking back at them.

'I'm a murderer out on licence. You think I'll be able to explain this away?'

'And I might have been spotted right before Latif's restaurant went up. We have to hide her,' Tazeem said. 'There's a storage space under the house.'

Decker walked into the living-room, pulled the coffee table to one side and rolled up the rug. He carried it to the bathroom and dropped it beside Laura's stiffening body.

Dan's clothing store sold a range of casually fashionable lines and was popular enough that parking bays outside were never vacant for more than a few minutes at a time during business hours. The stairwell to Sadiq's apartment had an adjoining doorway. Tazeem, Mangle and Decker parked almost a block further up and waited for any sign of Sadiq.

Tazeem sat wiping at his hands with his shirt tail and muttering to himself.

'Having something of a Lady Macbeth moment are we, Tazeem?' Mangle said flatly from the back seat. There was no humour in his voice, he just wanted to elevate the mood in the car.

'I don't know what the fuck that means,' Tazeem said, continuing to scrub. 'But I'm sure I still have some of her blood on me.'

They'd moved Laura's body in the rolled-up rug and washed out the bathroom with a strong solution of bleach. They all took showers and changed their clothes, but despite this, Mangle was pretty sure they all shared Tazeem's frame of mind.

After just over 20 minutes, Sadiq came out of the entrance to his apartment and walked to the kerb. Tazeem spotted him and immediately made to get out of the car, but Decker grabbed him by the arm.

'Wait. There's more of them coming out.'

Two more men they didn't recognise filed out of the building, and following them was Ermina and another man.

'Fucking hell, there she is,' Tazeem exclaimed, and attempted to throw off Decker's grip and get out of the car.

'Jesus! You see who the last one is?' Mangle said.

As the large man turned, the mid-morning sunlight caught on the shiny pink scar tissue across his face, making it look like melting ice-cream.

'That's the guy we saw at the warehouse, the one who was in charge,' Decker confirmed. 'Taz, you can't help her right now, but at least we know she's OK.'

Tazeem watched them, frustrated by his inability to help his cousin. She was arguing with Sadiq. They were too far away to catch what was said, but her body language was clear. Ermina slapped Sadiq as hard as she could across the face, turned and climbed into the back of a black Mercedes that had pulled up at the kerb. Sadiq clutched his face but didn't retaliate.

The other three men, visibly amused by her tirade, climbed into the car, leaving Sadiq standing watching as they drove away. After a moment he turned and walked back into the building. Tazeem shook off Decker's grip on his arm and bolted up the street as fast as he could.

'Shit,' Mangle said, as he and Decker threw open the car doors and went after him.

Sadiq had already vanished inside the stairwell and the auto-closer was slowly pulling the entrance door shut behind him. A red light had gridlocked traffic back along the street, and a delivery truck wheezed to a halt outside the building as Tazeem reached the door with only a few inches left before it locked. He grabbed the handle and pulled it open wide. Within seconds, Mangle and Decker caught up and they ran into the building together. Tazeem took the stairs three at a time, hauling himself up with the wooden handrail and peering up to see if Sadiq was still in the stairwell.

They reached the fourth floor and Tazeem stopped outside one of four doors on the landing. He nodded at Decker who took two steps towards the door and rammed the sole of his boot against the lock. The frame gave a crack and the wood groaned in protest but the door remained in place. He stepped back and kicked it again. This time the door crashed inwards, revealing the startled face of Sadiq halfway down his hallway. Splintered shards of door frame littered the carpet within. Tazeem charged inside and grabbed him by the throat.

'What did you do with my cousin?' he snarled into Sadiq's incredulous face.

'I didn't do nothing to her, yeah? The bitch just slapped *me*. She's fuckin' crazy,' he said, tapping the side of his head.

Tazeem drew back an arm and punched Sadiq in the mouth. He fell to the ground and Tazeem knelt on his chest, grabbing a handful of his shirt.

'What the fuck you doing man? You're as crazy as she is,' Sadiq said glaring up at Tazeem. He turned to the side and spat a thick wad of blood and saliva onto the floor.

'You best start talking or there'll be a lot worse than that still to come,' Decker said, looming over him.

'I don't even go out with her no more. Soon as a chance at something better came along she dropped me and got with that Jupiter guy, yeah?'

'Who's Jupiter?' Tazeem demanded.

'The big ugly guy with the fucked-up scars on his face. She just left with him.'

'You're saying Ermina is with him, like as his girlfriend?' Tazeem asked.

'That's exactly what I'm saying, yo. Now get the fuck off me.'

Tazeem stood and allowed Sadiq to get to his feet. He wiped the blood from his mouth and spat again.

'We know about the clinic, the club the girls are being taken to. What else have you got Ermina mixed up in?'

'You don't have a clue, Tazeem. I was doing fine with my properties and everything else. She was the one pushing me to expand. It was her idea to bring the girls in and get involved with Jupiter's crew. I had a scam going to bring guys into the country on tourist visas, and have them work for me as cheap labour. They were glad at a chance of making real money, man. They'd do anything I said. It was easy.'

'Jupiter heard about us. He sent a message and a meeting was set up. He told me what he wanted from me and what the rewards would be in return. I told Ermina about it but said I wasn't gonna get involved with them. She said I'd be crazy not to take the offer. Fuck, man, I was taking so much coke by then I'd have done whatever she said. After things kicked off with Jupiter she kept finding excuses to talk with him, you know, wait behind after I had to leave. Man, she planned this all along, I swear.'

'So if you claim that she got what she wanted, then why did she just slap you?' Mangle asked.

'I told them that I want out. I've had enough of all this shit, no matter how well it pays. I tried to get out before they blew up all of Latif's shit. We didn't always see eye to eye but we all grew up together, Tazeem. Once they'd connected the dots, they killed him 'cause he happened to know these two idiots,' he said, pointing at Decker and Mangle.

'That was the night Ermina went missing,' Tazeem said.

'She didn't go missing, man. She went off with Jupiter!'

Tazeem didn't want to believe what Sadiq was saying, but if Sadiq was lying there was no trace of it in the way he spoke or his body language. He seemed genuinely defeated. Vulnerability clung to him like a shroud and all his usual traits of boasting and self-edification were now gone.

Tazeem walked to the window and looked down onto the street below. How could Ermina have been involved with this all along, yet he had known nothing about it? Mangle and Decker continued to question Sadiq behind him, but Tazeem wasn't listening. So Jupiter had had Latif killed, not Sadiq? He would also have

Mangle and Decker killed for what they knew. And would Ermina carry enough influence to have him spared? After all, he knew as much about the organisation as they did. The only way any of them could be sure of safety was to bring down Jupiter, and everything along with him.

'We need to go to The Club,' Tazeem turned and said to the others.

'South of Seven?' Sadiq asked.

'No, the one where the girls are going –*The* Club, with The Zombie Room.'

'Are you fuckin' crazy? These guys don't mess around. If they see any of you there you're dead, no question.'

'The only way we can get out of this now is if we get some evidence of what's going on. I was seen outside the restaurant when it blew up; there's evidence linking those two to the computer shop, and a dead woman under our house. We're all on the run. Either Jupiter and his crew find us, or eventually we'll get picked up by the police.'

'A dead woman? What the fuck?' Sadiq blustered.

'Tazeem's right. All we have is Tatiana's folder from the clinic which doesn't prove anything,' Mangle said. 'Undoubtedly they'll have cleaned up there in case any police searches are forthcoming.'

'Right. And we don't even know which club The Zombie Room is in. We need you to take us there and get us inside,' Tazeem said.

Sadiq shook his head and looked anything but convinced.

'Aren't you listening?' Decker asked him. 'You don't get to say yes or no. You aren't in a bargaining position, and from what you've said, it looks like you're close to useless to them now as well.'

Sadiq looked from Decker down at the floor. He pulled a wrap of cocaine from his pocket and fumbled to unfold it.

'I can get us some IDs. We can alter our appearances to avoid being too obvious, but we still need you to get us in, Sadiq. You know how these people operate,' Tazeem said.

Sadiq nodded as he rolled up a note and snorted the remainder of the powder out of the wrap. 'I can't stay here, then,' he stated more than asked.

'No,' Tazeem confirmed. 'You'll have to come with us.' He turned back to the window and looked down at the street below. 'Get some things together. You might not be able to come back here for a while.'

Tazeem had barely finished speaking when the black Mercedes pulled up below and four men got out and ran toward the entrance.

'They're back,' Tazeem exclaimed to the others. 'Four of them just got out of that car. We have to go.'

The intercom buzzed, announcing their arrival downstairs.

'They won't be able to break through the door down there in broad daylight,' Mangle said. 'There's too many people around. Just don't answer it.'

'An old woman downstairs, Mrs Altrecht, she always opens the door if someone buzzes her.'

'Is there another way out?' Decker asked.

'There's a fire escape,' Sadiq said. 'But the windows onto it are all painted shut.'

The sound of heavy footsteps running into the stairwell alerted Decker. He withdrew Dr Chu's pistol from the waistband of his pants.

'Make your way down there,' he shouted to the others. 'I'll slow them down and meet you outside.'

Tazeem looked around the kitchen for something to aid their escape. He snatched up a small aluminium trash can from under the counter and hurled it at the window. The windowpane burst outwards showering glass fragments, fast food containers and empty beer cans onto the fire escape. Mangle picked up a dirty plate from the sink and began knocking out the remaining shards that clung to the window frame.

A shot rang out from along the hallway, and Tazeem, Mangle and Sadiq looked to see Decker leaning over the railing and firing off another.

'Hurry up,' he shouted to them, 'they're only two floors down.'

Tazeem swept away the broken glass scattered on the countertop with a brush of his hand, and climbed out onto the fire escape. Sadiq followed as more gunfire rang out from the stairwell. Mangle climbed up to slide out after them.

Decker was halfway back along the hall. 'Get out,' he yelled, 'they're nearly here.'

Mangle climbed out of the broken window as a shot sliced the air beside his ear. Decker spun and fired back towards the door. Their assailant ducked outside and took cover.

Crouching low, Decker walked backwards, his eyes fixed on the entrance to the apartment. Two guns angled around the door frame and unloaded blindly in Decker's direction. He heard the zip and crash of bullets and shattering crockery all around him. Making use of the time they needed to reload, Decker vaulted up onto the counter and slid his legs outside. The two assailants stepped into the hallway and fired.

Mangle and Tazeem grabbed Decker's legs and hauled him through the window and onto the fire escape. Instead of righting himself once outside, Decker fell into a crumpled heap. Mangle tried to put his arms around Decker to prevent his fall and they came away slick with blood.

'Fuck, no, they shot him,' Mangle cried.

Decker, who was still conscious, reached into his pocket and began to reload the pistol.

'Go on, I'll hold them up.'

'Don't be an idiot,' Tazeem said and tried to haul the bigger man to his feet, the expanding bloodstain beginning to dominate the side of Decker's shirt. Tazeem looked him in the eye and saw his friend's acceptance of the situation.

'Latif was a good guy. He really had faith in me, man. You have to make sure they pay for what they did.'

'Come on,' Sadiq hissed as he began to descend the zigzagging metal stairway.

Tazeem and Mangle were forced to face the futility of trying to help Decker escape. Mangle began to say something but Decker silenced him by raising the pistol and firing a shot through the broken kitchen window.

'I'm sorry, Decker,' Mangle said and followed the hastily retreating Sadiq.

Tazeem bit back his grief and fury and squeezed Decker's shoulder. He nodded without taking his eyes from the window.

Two single shots came from above as Tazeem reached the second floor. He looked up but couldn't see if anyone had been hit. He continued down to the bottom, where Mangle and Sadiq were waiting. Repetitive gunfire sounded from multiple weapons. They fled down an alleyway and into the backstreets of the city.

12

Once satisfied that they weren't being followed, Tazeem directed and Sadiq drove the car he'd just appropriated back to the bungalow. Mangle had sat despondent in the back seat the whole way, and now lay on the couch watching updates on Channel 10 News.

Tazeem and Sadiq sat at the table, Tazeem asking Sadiq everything he could think of about The Zombie Room. He shared Mangle's pain at the loss of their friend, but he knew he had to press on if there was to be any hope of bringing down the people who had killed him. He wanted to know the location, layout, number and placement of security guards, number of girls there, when it was open, and any escape routes. Sadiq, who twice stopped for hits of cocaine from another wrap he'd taken out of his pocket, seemed forthcoming, but the information he was able to provide didn't satisfy Tazeem that they would be able to pull this off. He knew that whatever happened, they'd be relying on a huge slice of good luck.

They left Mangle in the house, and went to ditch the stolen car and collect Tazeem's Mercedes from the lock-up. Tazeem stopped outside a pharmacy and Sadiq was sent in to buy hair dye, clippers, razors and scissors. Tazeem was determined to give them the best possible chance of success, and that meant a change in appearance, so made another stop to purchase some new clothes.

'You just missed a Kasey Haugh news report on what happened,' Mangle informed them on their return. 'She said it was someone staying in the building who went nuts and started shooting people at random. There are three people dead but they haven't released any names.'

'At least Decker managed to take out two of the bastards,' Tazeem said. 'Whatever the police may or may not know, we still can't count on their help.'

'Was there any mention of the rest of us?' Sadiq asked.

'No. The neighbours reported seeing an Asian man living there, but the name they gave wasn't yours.'

'Didn't keep it in my name, yeah? I like to keep an information buffer in case anyone comes looking for me,' Sadiq said, looking pleased with himself.

Over the next hour Sadiq shaved off his neatly cropped stubble, cut his hair shorter and removed his tell-tale jewellery. Mangle's hair was cut short and bleached blonde, and Tazeem, who had accrued a few days' beard growth, left that untouched but used the clippers to shave his head. It was far from foolproof but it did offer a discernable difference in their appearance.

It was past 1 a.m. when Tazeem cautiously drove his silver Mercedes along the back roads towards the docks. He kept to a sedate speed. It had been raining and the roads were greasy.

When they got close, Tazeem made two circuits of the immediate area while Sadiq filled them in further on what he knew. The Club was well out of the way. The Langdown Meat Packing Plant had been closed for purpose ten years earlier. The whole area had suffered from decades of steady decline, and Langdown was just one of many hulking slabs of dead real estate that no one, other than rats and pigeons, had showed much interest in for years. He reckoned a half mile of land, and all of the buildings on it had been bought as a package deal by an investor, but other than a modest casino and night club renovation inside Langdown, the other buildings remained untouched. A ghost town esplanade of boarded-up shops fringed the curve of the river, punctuated by empty parking lots and billboards advertising redundant products. An ebbing flock of seagulls were the only spectators to the desolation.

The ground-floor windows of the red-brick packaging plant had been bricked up, and all higher windows were sealed by steel plates. One thing was clear, nothing got in or out without express authorisation. There was an underground car parking lot, but Tazeem chose to park in the cover of a nearby derelict warehouse.

They slipped through a hole in the chain-link fence. Mangle pulled at the collar of his hastily-bought suit, which was irritating his neck. Tazeem and Sadiq looked more self-assured in their new attire than he felt, but undoubtedly it was nerves over exactly what they may face, rather than the quality of his clothing, that caused his discomfort.

After traversing the perimeter, Sadiq strode confidently toward the doorway of The Club, which would once have been a loading bay for trucks and their cargo of meat. No lights shone outside other than a single halogen bulb dimly illuminating a dusky blue oval at the entrance. No grandiose sign announced the name of The Club. No velvet rope. No red carpet. Nothing.

Sadiq nodded at the doormen and all three walked inside, up a flight of wrought iron stairs, and pulled on the aluminium bar of a fire exit style door. It opened outwards, allowing entry into The Club.

It looked completely different to any club Mangle had been in before. The floors, tables, bar and square support columns throughout The Club were black, either marble or an expensive wood, polished so intensely that they shone as if wet. It was very loud and very dark, and the casino was part of the same large room. An indirect soft green glow came from lamps mounted on the columns and along the walls. The same undulating green light shone from spotlights and lasers mounted at three points on the ceiling.

A thick white mist hugged the centre of the floor, around a foot deep. Laser canons would periodically break off from their pulsating display forming a perfect rotating isosceles triangle that floated upon the bed of smoke. The bar staff and croupiers all wore black with the same green triangle logo emblazoned on their shirts, and contact lenses which made their eyes shine an eerie vibrant green.

Nine or ten middle-aged men sat at a large S-shaped bar on the right-hand side of the room. On the left-hand side were the gaming tables: black jack, roulette, craps and poker. Maybe 20 or so men sat there, Mangle guessed, and he counted only four women in attendance.

They walked to the bar and Sadiq ordered whisky and cokes. The bar optics glowed with the same green light, the intensity of which was linked into the music. As the bartender walked away to fetch the drinks, a breakdown in the techno track commenced and the bottles began to palpitate. The bartender's eyes glowed with a hallucinatory felinity that made Mangle feel nervous.

'What do we do now we're inside?' Mangle asked Sadiq.

'We wait, and we pray Tazeem's cards check out OK,' he replied, running a hand over his freshly shaved chin.

They picked up the drinks and moved to a table at the rear of the room.

'After we've had a few drinks and can be sure your credit cards are holding up, I'll ask about getting us some extra entertainment,' Sadiq said, taking a sip from his glass. 'But we're gonna have to gamble for a while so they see we're serious about spending.'

'How much do we have on the cards?' Mangle asked Tazeem.

'Maybe fifty K. It's everything that we made through the utility scam. I linked the cash to the IDs I generated for us with a couple of layers of authenticity. If someone really goes digging they'll see through them, but they should pass a reasonable degree of scrutiny.'

'Right, we hit the tables, yeah?' Sadiq said.

'You know much about gambling?' Tazeem asked Mangle.

'Other than a little poker, the only gambling I ever did was driving home after a night out and hoping not to get breathalysed.'

'Great,' Tazeem muttered. 'You stick with that, but don't let the stakes get too high.'

They went and sat down at the gaming tables, Tazeem and Sadiq at roulette, Mangle at poker.

There were three other players at Mangle's table. There was no conversation and they eyed him suspiciously as he took his seat. Mangle gave his card to the dealer who swiped it and gave him the table minimum of 5K in chips. The table was covered with black felt and a green spotlight fired directly onto it from above. The surface of the cards appeared iridescent as the quick-fingered dealer slid them effortlessly across the cloth.

He folded the first two hands before the flop, losing few chips. The next four or five hands were kind. After a half-hour Mangle decided to take a break and see how Tazeem and Sadiq were getting on. He gathered up his chips and accepted the dealer's offer of a carry case.

Sadiq's eyes were wide and glittered unnaturally. Mangle guessed his whisky had been topped up with a cocaine chaser. Tazeem hunched over expectantly at the table and then slumped back into his seat as the roulette ball fell into place.

'Have you had any luck?' Mangle asked.

'Sadiq wiped out and I'm down about 10k,' Tazeem informed him. Sadiq sniffed and shrugged his shoulders. 'How much you got in there?' he asked nodding at the case.

Mangle put it down beside Tazeem who rifled through the chips.

'There must be almost eighty thousand,' Tazeem exclaimed. 'If we're gonna get anywhere here tonight we're gonna have to put our resources behind you, Mangle.'

'Steady on,' he protested. 'I had a lucky run but that's not to say I still won't lose the lot.

'We can't come back and try another time, hoping for more luck. You're just gonna have to do the best you can.'

Sadiq got up and walked back towards the bar. Tazeem turned back to the table and slid a stack of chips onto the board. Mangle knew his poker skill wouldn't win out, but maybe if he lost spectacularly enough then that may be enough to highlight them as big spenders and get them further access to The Zombie Room.He returned to the same seat at the poker table and took his chips out of the carry case.

'You've decided to lose them after all?' the man opposite asked with a wry smile. He looked to be in his fifties, had a full head of hair, as white as cotton, brushed neatly behind his ears. His eyes were shrewd and observant and he wore a dark grey suit that was elegant yet conservative, with a dark blue cravat.

'No, I just decided I hadn't won enough yet for tonight,' Mangle said, and hoped the cocky smile he attempted looked more natural than it felt.

The man laughed and Mangle relaxed a little. Maybe he would be able to pull this off after all.

'Dyson Steiger,' the white haired man said and extended his perfectly manicured hand to Mangle.

'Eric Lowell,' Mangle lied, using the name on his fake ID and credit card, and shook the proffered hand.

'Alright, enough chat, Eric Lowell, let us play.'

Mangle managed to accrue another pile of chips over the following dozen hands. The other two players at the table were becoming a little worse for wear, and their chips were going down as fast as their blood alcohol level went up. Steiger appeared equally as aware of this, and also harvested his fair share of the spoils. A few hands more and one of them decided to go all in, and made a magnanimous gesture of pushing his remaining chips into the centre of the table. Mangle was holding nothing worthwhile so folded. Steiger took a few moments to assess, but his eyes were focused more on Mangle than on his opponent, and Mangle was feeling uncomfortable.

'Call,' he announced and pushed his own chips forward.

The last player folded and the cards were turned. Steiger held the better hand by some margin, and didn't look at all surprised to discover so.The bankrupted player offered up a few empty clichés as he withdrew from the table and walked unsteadily back to the bar.

Both sides of The Club had filled up now. There was a queue to be served at the bar and a few women were dancing in the smoky centre of the room. A couple of times Tazeem had pumped the air with his fist, apparently jubilant at a win, but that hadn't happened for a while and now he was even more slouched in his seat than earlier. The remaining player next to Steiger had an elbow on the table and his chin cupped in the palm of his hand. His eyes were heavily hooded.

'I hope we aren't keeping you from something important,' Steiger said to him.

After a few seconds the man realised he was being addressed and turned to face Steiger.

'What?'

'You seem barely able to contain your excitement, friend. Positively brimming with kinetic energy.'

'Hmmph,' the man remarked, unable to think up a witty comeback of his own when he realised this was an attempt by Steiger to rattle him.

The next hand was dealt, and after less than a moment's contemplation the other player went all in, leaned back on his chair and folded his arms. Mangle looked at his own cards again. He had a strong hand. Steiger watched and studied every movement of hand and eye Mangle made.

'Call,' Mangle announced, consciously stopping himself from wiping his brow.

Steiger chuckled. He looked completely at ease. Not a trace of concern marred his cool demeanour.

'I'll let you play this one out, Eric Lowell,' he said and folded his own cards.

The dealer turned the remaining card on the board. It made no difference. The man had made a crazy bet, hoping his opponents would fold, but it had failed. He shook Mangle's hand in silence and walked to the exit. Another two men made to sit but Steiger held up a hand.

'We'll play this one out, friends. Choose another table,' Steiger said, continuing to smile.

The potential players looked slightly nonplussed but moved away. Tazeem and Sadiq came over from the roulette, their body language suggesting their earlier lack of fortune had not changed.

'Shit, that has to be around a hundred and fifty K,' Tazeem said as he stood behind Mangle.

'Your friend has done very well,' Steiger confirmed. 'Have you played here before?'

'It's our first time,' Mangle said. 'To be honest, we were hoping to get a full membership.'

If Steiger had heard, he didn't offer a response. The dealer spun each of their two hole cards across the felt. Mangle looked at his: King of Spades and Four of Diamonds.

Steiger bet 30 thousand. Mangle called. The dealer turned the flop on the board.

'Queen of Diamonds. Four of Hearts. King of Clubs.'

Mangle had flopped two pairs and knew he was in a strong position. Steiger bet another 30 thousand. Again Mangle called. He didn't want to scare his opponent away with a strong bet too early in the hand. The dealer revealed the turn card. Seven of Diamonds. That made no difference to Mangle's hand or the board at large. Steiger waited and studied him.

'I'm going to play all in, my friend,' Steiger said, with the air of one revealing the much anticipated punchline of a good joke.

'Holy shit,' Tazeem exclaimed. 'If you call, that'll make it around 300k in play.'

'Three hundred and twenty-eight thousand, I believe,' Steiger said as if it were nothing.

'Call,' Mangle said.

A soft 'Ohh' eminated from the burgeoning crowd of spectators. Mangle turned his head. He hadn't realised the amount of attention their game had gathered.

'Turn your cards please,' the dealer said. 'Two pairs, Kings over Fours,' he announced after Mangle revealed his hand.

Steiger turned his first card: Queen of Hearts. He turned the second: Queen of Spades.

'Three Queens,' the dealer said. 'Mr Steiger has the advantage. The river card still to play.'

'A Four or a King will give us a full house and a win, yeah?' Sadiq said.

'Only the King. The Four would give that guy a higher full house and we'd still lose,' Tazeem corrected him. 'So the other two Kings are the only cards left in the entire pack that can help.'

The dealer was obviously used to this type of situation and milked every ounce of tension that he could from the crowd. 'The river card,' he said, 'is … the King of Hearts. Mr Lowell wins with a full house, Kings over Fours.'

Steiger chuckled and again reached for Mangle's hand. 'Well played, my friend. And dare I say perhaps a tad fortunate.'

Mangle shook his hand and thanked him. The dealer counted up and took Mangle's card to credit with his chip total.

'When will I have the opportunity to win back some of my money?' Steiger asked, getting up from his seat.

'I'm not sure,' Mangle said to Steiger once they were away from the still chattering crowd at the table. 'Like I say, my friends and I were hoping for a little more action than just some gambling.'

Steiger nodded and beckoned to an attendant beside the bar. 'These gentlemen would like to become full members. I will vouch for them.'

'Very well, Mr Steiger,' the man said, and retreated.

'Go with this man, he will take care of it for you. Maybe next time the gods will smile on me, Mr Lowell.'

Mangle, Tazeem and Sadiq followed the attendant through a black door to the side of the bar, and into a waiting room. A black velvet couch, two chairs and a wooden table, with a cushioned lip that matched the upholstery, were the only furniture in the dimly lit room. A large mirror ran the length of the wall opposite.

'I'll be just a few moments, gentlemen,' the attendant told them, and disappeared through an identical door to the rear of the room.

The three sat down and waited uncomfortably for his return. Sadiq began to speak but was silenced by Tazeem before he got out more than a few words. He didn't want to risk anything being said by his cocaine-laced companion that may jeopardise things now they were so close. After a few moments in the prison-like waiting room, the attendant returned, carrying what looked like some kind of medical device.

'The credit checks have gone through, now I just need to implant your membership chips and you'll all be signed up.'

'Membership what?' Tazeem asked.

'Oh, I presumed you would be aware of the procedure, having been vouched for by Mr Steiger. Your credit details and membership identification are stored on the chip, and it is implanted into your forearm. Don't worry, it is quite painless.'

'Quite painless? So is carrying a card,' Tazeem said, already rubbing his arm, as if in anticipation of the violation.

'I'm sure you're aware how exclusive our club here is, sir. No one is issued with a card or any other identification that could fall into the hands of an outsider. The chip is encrypted with a 256 bit algorithm. That simply means it can never be read by anything other than the scanners inside The Club. You never have to carry any identification or payment when you attend The Club. You're charged directly and it will show up on your bank statement as an innocent business expense, from any of a few dozen companies that in no way trace back to this establishment.'

'Sounds like you have it all worked out,' Tazeem said, reluctantly rolling up his sleeve to expose his right forearm.

'Not me, sir. I am merely here to carry out my instructions,' he said.

The attendant smiled warmly and placed three opaque containers and a box of surgical wipes onto the table. The containers were labelled with their aliases, and each held a small capsule that presumably housed the microchip.

Tazeem lay his exposed forearm on the table and the man moved the device into position. A transparent suction cup created a vacuum as he slowly pulled back a handle on the barrel of the device. An injection tube tipped with a tiny needle slid down against Tazeem's skin. The man picked up the relevant box, removed the capsule, and inserted it into a chamber in the barrel.

'Ready, sir?' he asked Tazeem, who nodded and turned his head away.

The attendant twisted the handle 90 degrees then depressed the trigger. The barrel was released and the microchip injected into Tazeem with clinical efficiency and a sound like a hand smoothing folded paper.

'That's it?' Tazeem asked as he turned to face the man again.

'Yes, sir. I hope it was less traumatic than you perhaps anticipated.'

Tazeem nodded, and rubbed his arm, which bore a circular indent from the suction cup. He inspected the point where the chip had gone in, using one of the surgical wipes to remove a small spot of blood.

The attendant changed the injection tube and Sadiq was next, the process quicker this time as the operator had to offer less reassurances. 'And lastly it is your turn, sir,' the operator said, again changing the injector and smiling at Mangle.

Mangle exposed his own forearm. He was less than overjoyed at the prospect of having this company's technology embedded under his skin. He watched the procedure intently. The man was right, it was relatively painless – although they had drunk a few whiskies over the course of the night. He rubbed the point of injection and was surprised to discover he felt no protrusion.

'So we're clear to go in now?' Mangle asked the attendant.

'No, sir, there is a waiting period of 24 hours while the membership chips are activated. Return any time after that and you can go right up.'

13

'How do we know we ain't gonna be walking into a trap when we turn up there again?' Sadiq asked when they were back at the house.

'I guess we don't, but what choice do we have?' Mangle said.

'If they know who we are they could have taken us tonight,' Tazeem added.

'But you said you didn't know if the identities would hold up if they looked deeper, yeah?'

Mangle said nothing but turned to look at Tazeem.

'I can't guarantee it, no.'

'But the longer we wait, the greater the chance of being discovered?' Mangle asked.

'I guess so. It'd take quite a lot of probing for them to be revealed as fakes.'

'Then we have to go back as soon as possible. It's the only thing that makes sense,' Mangle said. Sadiq nodded silently.

None of them got much sleep after the intensity of the night they'd had, so they slept much of the following afternoon in order to be fresh for that night. There'd seemed little point in discussing a plan, as they had no idea what to expect on arrival, or on their admittance to The Zombie Room. Sadiq had been able to supply only rudimentary, hearsay information about the place, and confessed he had never wanted to go in there himself. His trepidation about getting involved with these people had already manifested into dread and regret by the time he'd got close enough to be allowed admittance.

Tazeem drove, and parked in the same spot as the night before. Mangle checked his watch while they walked to the entrance. It was only 22 hours since the chips were implanted and he hoped the 24-hour thing wasn't to be taken literally. Hanging around inside for another two hours would be too much to bear. He felt nervous enough already, walking into the lion's den.

They were walking towards the entrance when Mangle caught a glint from one of Sadiq's diamond rings. 'Sadiq, you're gonna have to take them off. You look way too conspicuous with that lot on.'

'He's right, man. What were you thinking?' Tazeem asked.

Reluctantly, Sadiq slipped the diamond bracelet and rings into his pants pocket, muttering how he didn't feel right without them. Despite this, he sauntered past the two men on the door in his usual carefree manner, and Tazeem and Mangle followed. Either Sadiq had perfected the art of exuding confidence, or he was genuinely fearless, or he had taken a big hit from his coke supply before they left the house.

Mangle thought back to his own days of substance use and abuse, now behind him. Sometimes he missed the numbed, walking-underwater feel that the cocktail of narcotics used to give him. But if a situation went down in here then he was going to need all his wits to get out of it.

They entered The Club. Despite it only being just after midnight, there were already more customers inside. Mangle scanned the room as Sadiq walked up to the attendant beside the bar who had performed their membership induction the previous night. There was no sign of Dyson Steiger at either the gaming tables or the bar. He was pleased about that; the last thing Mangle wanted was another one-on-one battle that would almost certainly see their funds obliterated.

'We're clear to go in,' Sadiq said in a matter-of-fact tone when he returned a few moments later.

The attendant he'd spoken to was gone.

'So where do we go?' Tazeem asked.

'He'll come over and fetch us in a few minutes.'

Sure enough, shortly afterwards Mangle saw a door open up near the booth they had sat in the night before. The doorway wasn't evident before opening, just a featureless black wall panel. Mangle took a deep breath and followed Sadiq and Tazeem toward the door.

The attendant gently took Mangle's arm as he walked by.

'Mr Lowell,' he said. Mangle's heart leapt in his chest. 'Mr Steiger asked me to pass along a message, if I saw you. He requests the pleasure of your company at the tables later.' He smiled coolly before releasing his grip.

Mangle nodded. The attendant lowered his hand and they all continued inside to the bottom of a wide stairway that curled lazily to the left on its ascent. The lighting was the same green tinge as the previous room, and the decor of black floor, walls and ceiling continued throughout.

'Upstairs now, gentlemen,' the attendant instructed.

Another doorway stood at the top of the stairs, this one marked with the green triangle logo, with curtained cubicles arranged to either side on the landing.

'If you would each proceed into one of the cubicles, gentlemen. Remove all clothes and leave your belongings inside. There are robes and slippers for you to put on, and let me assure you, all of your things will be perfectly safe until you return.'

'Take our clothes off?' Tazeem asked, looking slightly bewildered.

'Yes, sir. We have to be absolutely sure that no devices that record either sound or pictures are taken inside. This, I'm sure you appreciate, is to protect the anonymity of both the venue and our clients.' The same cool smile slid across his face like an ice cube in an empty glass.

With no option other than to comply, they each went to a vacant cubicle and stripped. The robes and slippers were black terry cloth and adorned with the now familiar logo.

'There's just one thing I need to take with me,' Sadiq said, poking his head out to speak to the attendant.

'I'm afraid not, sir. Everything you need can be supplied inside.'

'Everything?' Sadiq asked.

'Yes, sir. Everything.'

They congregated back on the landing, wearing their matching robes and slippers. The attendant looked up and nodded at a camera above the doorway. A humming sound was followed by a click and the door was electronically unlocked.

Inside was a carpeted hallway, lined on either side by rows of booths with large black-tinted windows. Empty booths were brightly illuminated from within. Occupied booths had the lights dimmed for privacy and a spotlight from the hallway shone against the glass, reflecting back the incredulous faces of Mangle, Tazeem and Sadiq as they were led onward by the attendant.

'There are three empty rooms here,' he said in the manner of an air steward signalling a plane's emergency exits. 'If you'd follow me inside this one, I'll demonstrate the facilities.'

The room was fairly small and cube-shaped, perhaps a few metres between corners. A sturdy-looking square armchair sat in the centre with a touch screen attached to one side. Black floor tiles gleamed like the reflective bar surface downstairs.

'There is a mini-bar within each room for you to make use of,' the attendant gestured flamboyantly once they were all inside. 'The screen here is used to place your orders, whatever your heart desires. Simply follow the on-screen menus and touch whatever you would like.'

A kaleidoscope of beautiful women cascaded as his fingers danced nimbly over the screen. He then selected 'Merchandise' and a vast array of drugs, both prescription and narcotic, awaited selection.

'The small window on the arm of the chair is a scanner, to charge whatever product or service directly to your account. Just hold your arm above it after you have selected on screen,' he said, and indicated on his forearm roughly where they had had the chips implanted. 'An attendant will bring to the room whatever you have chosen. A camera in each room ensures the absolute safety of the client at all times. They are monitored but not recorded, and there is no audio transmission. Also, it has been known on occasion that a client may try to elicit a service from one of the girls without paying for it,' he chuckled. 'But of course we wouldn't expect such behaviour from esteemed gentlemen such as yourselves.'

Mangle and Tazeem shared a look, but neither spoke.

'When you decide to end your session, use the screen to signal an attendant. A shower room is available through the door to the rear for you to freshen up, and a fresh robe and slippers can be found in there if you require them. Unless you have any questions I will retire and allow you to enjoy your night.'

He waited for a moment and when no questions were forthcoming he withdrew from the room. 'One of you remain in here, the other two can take the rooms on either side. And just to reassure you, the rooms are soundproofed and very strong,' he said, tapping his knuckles against the wall. 'Nothing will get through here.'

Mangle walked to the mini-bar and poured himself a large glass of bourbon. Tazeem and Sadiq took that as their cue to leave with the attendant. The door was closed after them and the lighting dimmed suitably to ensure client privacy. Mangle laughed at the notion. Some privacy when there's a camera over your shoulder at all times.

He sat in the chair and swivelled the screen around to face him. 'Please select a partner' it said, in bold lettering. A green triangle steadily revolved in one corner. He touched the screen and three categories appeared: 'Pristine', 'Exercised' and 'Impaired'. Mangle selected the first and a multitude of headshots of beautiful women filled the screen. He tapped one at random. A complete body shot of the women standing naked appeared. The figure on screen began to move around, a five-second loop of her twisting and turning in a sultry manner. Her eyes looked hazy and she didn't attempt a smile. A price for the girl to be summoned to your room headed a list outlining some of the acts she could perform and the additional prices for them. There were more option buttons to go into greater depth of possibilities.

He pressed the 'Back' button twice, and this time selected 'Exercised' from the menu. Another deluge of faces lined up across the monitor. The others had looked fresh, not happy but detached. These girls had clearly experienced more of what The Club had to offer, and a faraway yet hunted look haunted their eyes. Scanning over the images, Mangle recognised the face of Tatiana, from the file they had taken from the clinic. He tapped the headshot and her naked figure filled the screen and began to move. It was the same girl. She was undoubtedly beautiful but her performance lacked fluency or grace. She appeared like a marionette, her movements forced and controlled by another. Patches of her skin shimmered slightly as she moved, as if the image had been altered after it had been recorded.

Without realising he was about to, Mangle tapped 'Order' on the screen and held his forearm over the scanner. An electronic beep sounded and an automated voice thanked him for his custom, and told him his purchase would be delivered shortly.

Mangle drank the contents of his glass and went to refill it again. He ran a hand across his face and sat back heavily into the chair. He had no idea what Tazeem hoped to achieve from this, what evidence he could possibly get that would expose what was going on at The Club, and who was involved in the deaths of Latif and Decker. He took another large swallow from the glass and hoped that when the girl arrived she wouldn't inadvertently give him away.

A few minutes later the door slid open and a different attendant, holding the girl's arm, ushered her into the room. She wore one of the custom robes and when the door closed behind her she let it slip to the floor. Underneath she wore a black bra and panties, but that wasn't what caught Mangle's attention. As she moved towards him, he could see the areas that had been doctored on her video. A large portion of her right thigh looked swollen and inflamed, although make-up had been applied over the top to conceal the damaged flesh.

'What would you like me do for you?' she asked in a dreamy voice.

Mangle was immensely conscious of the camera perched silently in the corner of the room. He had been told there was no audio – but was that really true? He leant forward, positioning himself between the girl and the camera lens.

'Do you recognise me?' he asked in a soft voice.

The girl blinked but didn't react, like a computer that had been given an instruction that wasn't in its program bank.

'What would you like me do for you?' she repeated in the same accented English.

Mangle beckoned and she moved toward him and knelt down.

'Look at me,' he said to the girl, and holding her face gently under the chin, tilted it so she looked directly into his eyes.

The girl began to repeat her opening line, but Mangle pressed his finger to her lips and silenced her. As she looked at him, really looked now, he thought he saw a flicker of recognition.

'You know who I am, don't you?' he said.

She gave a barely perceptible nod. Her eyes had grown wide.

'You don't have to be afraid of me,' he said, thinking he was the cause of her alarm.

'They watch all the time,' she said, her wide eyes swivelled up in the direction of the camera.

'But they can't hear us?'

'No. Have you come to rescue me?' she asked, although there was no trace of hope in her voice.

Mangle didn't know what to say. He turned back to the computer and began flicking through the options on her profile screen so that they didn't appear suspicious to anyone who may be watching. Next to 'Services' was an option for 'Extras'; he selected it.

'I saw you at the place they first held us, then at the other club, then at the clinic also, but you do not seem like the others. Do you work for them?'

'No I definitely do not work for them, far from it,' he said.

The screen filled up with a wealth of sex aids, toys and lubricants, each one priced. A lot were the kind of thing he'd been aware of, that girls bought at those female-only parties. But many looked at the least very uncomfortable, and others downright painful. Some were grossly oversized and others had spiked areas or coarse sections to irritate and embed into the girl's flesh.

She slid her hand inside Mangle's robe and up his thigh. Mangle shifted uncomfortably at the unexpected contact.

'If we do nothing I will get into trouble,' she said. His robe fell open and she began to massage his cock. 'And they will be suspicious of you.'

Mangle tried to concentrate despite her touch that caused lust to open up within him. Another option flashed at the bottom of the screen that read, 'Ultimate Extras'. Mangle pressed it. It wasn't more sex aids that flooded onto the screen now. Knives, clamps, Tasers, even tetro-dyazine – a muscle paralyser – and other weapons and instruments to deliver pain and suffering were proudly displayed next to their prohibitively expensive prices.

'Oh my God,' he said as the sadist merchandise was digitally proffered. The girl took his exclamation as a sign of pleasure and quickened the movement of her hand. 'No,' he said uncomfortably, and she resumed her previous pace.

Mangle ran a hand over his mouth as if pondering which items to select, as he again looked at the screen. 'We could get out. There are guns on here. Jesus.'

'You cannot,' Tatiana said sharply, 'if you order a gun there is only a single shot, and once delivered the doors are locked and will not open until it has been fired.

Mangle continued scrolling through the despicable array of potential destruction. One thing was evident; he couldn't leave this girl here. It was clear why the three categories of girls had been available. The cheaper end of the scale would no doubt have been brutalised over and over in every way imaginable, and would carry the scars to prove it.

'There must be another way out. Are the girls led in and out through the main doors?'

'No. Sometimes they need to bring in more girls while The Club is open. There is a locked door down below, near our living quarters.'

'How do we get to it?'

'You cannot. This door is unlocked only when an attendant delivers items. Besides even if you got out of here, if you try to get into a restricted area he would activate the alarm.'

'But what if he didn't … are there cameras in the corridors?'

'No, only in the rooms. The clients wouldn't believe cameras anywhere else were for their safety and they don't like to feel exposed.'

'I can understand why,' Mangle said as he struggled to formulate a plan of escape.

He looked around the room hopefully for anything that could be used to aid them.

'Is something wrong?' Tatiana asked him.

'What?' Mangle said. He followed the direction of her eyes. 'Oh.' He'd been so caught up with devising a way out that he'd lost his erection. 'No, nothing's wrong.'

He scrolled around the on-screen menus and began to place an order. He waved his forearm over the scanner and was thanked for his custom by the automated voice.

'The attendant will be here in a few moments,' Tatiana said, her eyes cast downward to the floor. 'I guess it is time for you to have your fun.'

Mangle got up and walked back over to the mini-bar. He refilled his glass and stood sipping the bourbon. He watched Tatiana. She had curled her legs under her and began to suck her thumb. Not in a provocative way, but like a defenceless child seeking the protection of its mother.

The electronic lock released and the attendant entered. It was like watching a hotel employee deliver room service. He carried a silver serving tray with a circular lid. Tatiana remained in her almost foetal position but she watched the attendant like a field mouse watches an owl.

'I'll put this on the table for you, sir.'

'Very well,' Mangle said, 'although, could you wait just a moment which I check everything is there?'

'Certainly, sir,' he replied and put down the tray.

Mangle walked over and removed the cover. Tatiana's eyes were pinned wide in trepidation. On the tray sat a hunting knife, a Taser gun, a syringe and a pistol. She uttered a low guttural moan and closed her eyes.

'Is everything satisfactory, sir?' the attendant enquired politely.

'Yes,' Mangle confirmed as he ran his fingers across the items.

The attendant turned to walk back out of the door. In one fluid motion, Mangle snatched up the syringe, spun around and stabbed the 3inch needle into the back of the man's neck before administering the full dosage of tetro-dyazine. Tatiana opened her eyes again and watched as the helpless body of the attendant crumpled to the floor. His head fell across the threshold, preventing the automatic closing of the door.

'What have you done?' she said, horrified.

Mangle didn't answer but grabbed another item off the tray. He aimed the Taser at the metal housing on the underside of the camera and pulled the trigger. Two barbed electrodes leaped from the gun and for several seconds unleashed their surge of power. A crackling sound like broken twigs came from within. Mangle hoped he had managed to fry the camera, and before someone had noticed his assault on the attendant.

'Get up,' he ordered. Tatiana got tentatively to her feet. 'And pick those up,' he told her, gesturing towards the tray.

Mangle wielded the Taser, which had two remaining shots to fire, snatched her hand and stepping over the prostate yet still twitching figure of the attendant, hurried out into the hallway.

He had feared an immediate alarm and confrontation from several security guards, but if the alarm had been triggered, then it was silent, and any security staff were yet to arrive. Mangle moved to the door at the next room. He had hoped for a switch or button to unlock the door automatically, but the faceplate was smooth and featureless. The attendant must have unlocked it remotely.

He took the large hunting knife from Tatiana. One side had a slightly curved, razor-sharp edge; the other, jagged serrated teeth. Firmly gripping the handle he brought the knife tip down in a stabbing motion onto the lock faceplate. The first blow dented it but bounced off, leaving only a small hole in the metal. He stabbed at the lock again, this time perforating its covering.

'You cannot chop your way into the rooms. Someone will come, someone will come,' she wailed, looking from left to right up and down the hallway.

Mangle took hold of the Taser and holding it only a few inches from the hole in the lock plate, he fired. The electrodes impregnated the lock with their ejaculation of voltage. A popping and fizzing came from the compromised lock followed by the acrid smell of burning plastic. A loud crack sounded, and to Mangle's delight, not only that door, but the doors to all of the other booths opened in unison along the hallway.

The incredulous face of Tazeem stared back at him. He was still robed, as was the misty-eyed girl in the room with him, who sat beside his chair with a drink in her hand.

'Get up! Come on we have to go,' Mangle barked and ran to Sadiq's room.

Sadiq lay robeless on the floor, writhing around with two naked girls, all of them unaware that the door had opened. A bag of white powder stood open, and three huge lines remained on the cocaine-dusted tray.

'You idiot! Either come now or you're staying here.'

Sadiq's eyelids fluttered open as he was roused from his narcotic, sexual fugue state. The girls continued kissing and licking his body.

'What's happening?' he slurred.

Mangle stepped in and slapped Sadiq across the face. He walked back out to the hallway. Either Sadiq would follow, or he wouldn't, but Mangle wasn't about to waste any more time on him.

'Which way?' he asked Tatiana.

She hurried ahead. Tazeem stood by the door to his booth but the girl who was with him wouldn't come out. Mangle and Tazeem followed Tatiana, all of them barefoot, along the hallway. Mangle caught a glimpse of a man standing at the doorway of the last booth on the row as they rushed past. A middle-aged man, fully naked, with blood streaked down both arms and legs and also over his penis. Mangle's stomach convulsed at the sight, but the feeling of recognition as their eyes briefly met stayed with him.

At the end of the hallway Tatiana turned left and rushed on. Tazeem looked back over his shoulder and saw Sadiq stagger out of the booth, trying to wrestle on his robe. Tatiana reached a double door, stopped and waited for the others to catch up.

'I hope this isn't locked or we have nowhere to go,' she said, and pushed against it. To their relief the door swung inwards and she stepped into a narrow metal stairwell. Sadiq was the last one through and they descended to the floor below. On the landing there were four doors: two to their left, one directly ahead and one to the right.

'Which one?' Mangle hissed.

Tatiana moved to the door to their right and pushed against it. 'It's locked!' she cried, looking back at them. 'This is our way out.'

'I don't know what it is but I have to check it out. I'll have Tom move them to a different booth whenever the fuck he decides to show himself,' a man said as he backed out of a doorway to their left.

Instinctively, Tatiana raised the pistol she clutched. Mangle, Tazeem and Sadiq tried to back out of his immediate line of sight.

'Don't fucking move,' she commanded him.

The startled technician spun around, saw the gun pointed at him, and then the other three people in the hallway, and froze.

'What is it, Bill?' a voice from inside the room asked.

Tatiana clutched the gun in trembling hands. Sweat beaded her forehead. Perhaps sensing her hesitancy, the technician half-spun to duck back inside the room. Tatiana discharged the weapon's solitary round. The technician wheezed and clawed at his chest for a moment before collapsing onto the floor.

'What the fuck?' the man inside the room shouted.

Mangle sprang forward wielding the hunting knife, and snatching the handle, threw the door open wide.

Computer consoles sat on desks, and the walls of the long rectangular room were lined with an array of security monitors. Some remained black but most displayed an image from one of the booths on the floor above. A seated technician at one of the desks stared back at him.

'Open that door back there,' Mangle snarled, and held out the knife menacingly in front of him.

At first Mangle thought the technician must be in shock, as he just blinked at him. But then he saw his hand snaking under the desk. He lunged for the man but it was too late. Flashing red lights pulsed around the room; the silent alarm had been triggered.

'You'll never get away,' the technician stammered.

'Maybe not, but how much damage do you think I can do with this before anybody gets here?' Mangle couldn't believe he was uttering such words, but he knew he had to sound convincing if they were to have any hope of escape.

'No … no,' the man whined. 'Don't do that, please.'

'You'd better open the door now, I won't ask again.'

The technician's shaking hands fumbled as he tapped on his keyboard.

'There, it's open.'

'I'll wait up here till one of them shouts that the door below is unlocked as well. That way I won't have to risk you trapping us in the stairwell.'

The man squeaked, jerked reflexively and immediately began pressing more keys.

'There, everything is unlocked. Just go and leave me be.'

Mangle turned away from him; he was reasonably sure the technician was telling the truth. He shouted to the others to go down and make sure they had a way out while he waited by the door of the control room. They filed through the door Tatiana had first tried. Sadiq waited and held it open. Mangle looked back at the technician to make sure the man wasn't about to try anything, but he had pushed his chair back from the console and was holding up his hands to show he posed them no threat.

'It's open, Mangle. Come on,' Tazeem yelled up.

Mangle was about to run for the door when he noticed a bank of DVD drives by the computer closest to him.

'That's nothing, they aren't even used,' the technician said, before Mangle had a chance to ask anything.

Mangle began randomly pushing buttons to eject the drives. After a few seconds, the plastic drawers began to slide out, each proffering a solitary disk. Mangle snatched five of them, and fled for the door Sadiq held open. They ran down the stairway, and the sound of shouting echoed from above as the door slowly closed after them.

'Hurry up, they won't be far behind,' Mangle urged, as he ran into the welcome embrace of the cold night air.

Tazeem needed no further encouragement, and bolted in the direction of the car, Sadiq only a few steps behind. Mangle took Tatiana's hand and they ran as well as they could over the cracked and uneven concrete.

They'd barely gone a few hundred yards and were wriggling through the holes in the chain-link fence, when voices from behind announced the pursuing security guards had spotted them. Three shots were fired, forcing Mangle's already accelerated heart rate up even further. Tatiana cried out. At first he thought she must have been hit, but then realised it was a cry of frustration as her hair had become entangled in the ragged fence.

'Don't let them catch me,' she pleaded as Mangle struggled to free her.

Tazeem and Sadiq ran ahead, and after a moment the sound of a car engine fired up. Mangle prayed they weren't being left behind, as he tugged the last of Tatiana's hair free from the fence. She let out a squeal as a clump was torn out at the roots. Two more shots rang out. One impacted a few feet from where they stood, scattering pieces of smashed asphalt.

Tazeem's Mercedes swung around the corner of the warehouse and accelerated towards them. Mangle risked a glance over his shoulder. The security men were almost upon them. He grabbed Tatiana and ran for the car as another bullet lacerated the air above his head. Sadiq threw open the back door of the car as it skidded to a halt, and they both bundled inside.

14

Tazeem sped away from The Club as fast as he dared. They couldn't risk attracting the attention of the authorities until they had enough evidence to indict the owners and operators. Being suspects in a murder investigation, and God knew what else by now, driving around with wires hanging down from the steering column where Sadiq had hot-wired the car wasn't a good look.

Tatiana shivered continually and clung to Mangle in the back seat. The shock of her ordeal and shooting the technician was taking hold. He wrapped his robe around them both as best he could, and tried to ignore the sensation of her thighs brushing up against his own as she wrapped her arms around his chest.

It was the early hours of the morning and there was very little traffic on the roads. Three men in a car wearing nothing but bathrobes and a girl in black lingerie made for an unusual spectacle, so Tazeem chose sleepy suburban roads as much as he could for the route back to the bungalow. He was certain no one had followed them back. He hadn't seen another car on the road for over ten minutes now and they were almost home.

'I'll leave the car a few streets away just on the off-chance it could be recognised,' Tazeem said.

He dropped the other three at the kerb and pulled away. Sadiq went around to the back where he improvised a way inside as quietly as he could. Mangle went to put some clothes on and Tatiana picked through his things for something suitable to wear. She took the clothes into the bathroom to change into after she'd taken a shower. The scent of bleach still hung thickly in the air.

Sadiq said he'd had enough for one day and was going to get some sleep. Mangle took the DVDs he'd appropriated into the lounge to see what was on them. He switched on the TV, inserted the first disk into the player and collapsed into an armchair. The picture flickered for several seconds, remaining mostly black with an occasional green or purple peppering of digital artifacts. Eventually, an image appeared. It was recorded footage from one of the booths at The Club, as Mangle had suspected. An attendant was walking around, spraying and wiping the surfaces. Then he walked off camera into the bathroom at the rear of the booth. A moment later the picture went black. Another brief scattering of purple squares and the picture returned. The same attendant walked back through the booth and exited at the front. The screen went black.

Mangle began to fast-forward through the footage. It was evident that the recording was motion-activated. A succession of clients came into the booth and performed various sex acts with different girls. So far there was no evidence of anything other than prostitution. He put in the next disk and scanned through it. A client got violent with one of the girls and began slapping her around. The girl stood it as best she could as the attack became more brutal, and the perpetrator's face grew darker and more twisted, as if he saw before him a physical manifestation of his own demons, rather than an innocent young woman. Mangle scanned through the next two disks.

Tatiana had dressed after her shower and lay down on the couch facing away from the screen. There was nothing the DVDs could reveal about the place that she didn't already know. Tazeem had returned and from the tinkle of crockery it sounded as if he was making something to eat in the kitchen.

The fourth disk, and one client used all three shots from a Taser gun on one of the girls. She was standing when the first shot hit but crashed to the floor as her body went into spasm. Barely waiting for her to stop convulsing from the first shot, he fired off another set of electrodes. The tendons in her neck stood out, taut as steel cables with the pressure from her grinding teeth. Mangle hit fast-forward again as the man fired the third. He'd seen enough.

He ejected the disk, feeling sick from the successive images of brutalisation and violence. Tazeem had poked his head around the door a few minutes earlier but withdrew back into the kitchen when he saw what was displayed on the TV screen.

Mangle called softly to Tatiana a couple of times to see if she was alright, and ask if she needed anything, but she didn't respond. Her breathing had deepened now, the adrenalin rush from their escape perhaps subsiding sufficiently to allow her to sleep. Her body trembled slightly as she lay there. Mangle hoped that if it was the onset of the medication withdrawal, she would be able to cope with it better than Laura.

He put the final disk into the player. The beginning showed the usual combination of drink, drugs and violent sex. Mangle skipped ahead. The next client to come into the room looked familiar but he kept his face turned away from the camera, so it was hard to be sure. There was a steadiness, an assuredness about his movements. The other men had been jittery and nervous, even manic, but this guy was cool and in control. He selected some items from the screen and walked casually around the room sipping from a large glass while waiting for the attendant. He expertly defied the camera by turning his face away from the lens.

The attendant arrived, carrying the type of tray Mangle had seen earlier, and a girl, who judging from her looks and flawless appearance, must be from the 'Pristine' list and therefore extortionately expensive. The attendant placed the tray down beside the chair and left the room.

The man returned to his seat as the girl disrobed and then removed her negligée. She knelt down between his legs, pulled open his robe and began to work on him with her hands. The man seemed content, and continued to sip from his glass as his erection grew. He leaned over and removed the lid from the tray. The arm of the chair obstructed the camera's view, and it could not pick up the contents.

The man relaxed back into the chair and Mangle saw the minimal light within the room gleam coldly on the curved edge of the knife he now held in his left hand. The man played with it, twisting the handle this way and that and watching the light dance along the blade. He seemed almost to have forgotten about the girl working below him, until she slid his fully erect member into her mouth. He looked down, slightly amused it seemed, and gently pushed her back onto her haunches. She looked up at him expectantly, awaiting his next command.

Reaching forward he took hold of her left arm, delicately, as if she were a work of fine art. The girl surrendered to his touch. He examined her perfect white skin, then slid his fingertips gently upwards from her elbow before cupping her wrist in his right palm.

He leaned forward, and drew the tip of the blade slowly and precisely around her arm, working downwards in concentric circles. He kept stopping to readjust his seating position and grip on the handle, before continuing on with his macabre geometry. The girl sat motionless, unresisting to the light grip he held on her supple wrist. Blood began to flow, at first cautiously, as if embarrassed by its appearance; a few thin red lines exploring the gravitational trajectory of its new terrain. Now it flowed faster, steadily staining her pale flesh a horrific red.

The girl's head had dropped but still she didn't resist. The man released her left arm, took hold of the right, and began the sickeningly precise procedure again. It was unthinkable to watch someone treated so inhumanely, but now Mangle had the evidence that they needed.

The man sat back in the chair as the girl's blood pooled on the floor between his legs. He coaxed her towards him. She shuffled uncomfortably and resettled herself in the blood. Raising her trembling hands she took hold of his swollen cock and guided it into her mouth. Blood dripped and smeared the inside of his thighs with the motion of her sucking.

He took a handful of her hair and forced her to increase both speed and depth, then threw his head back, enraptured at her performance. The camera, for the first time, had a clear view of his face, and Mangle realised he had seen the man before. It was the Mayor of Garden Heights, Carson Keaton. It was the man who Mangle had seen in the booth as they fled The Club. The escape had happened in a whirl of action and danger, perhaps accounting for his failure to identify him at the time, but there was now no denying the famous face on the screen before him.

This was the man who had been plastered over TV screens for months, with his electoral pledge to restore basic family values and root out the organised crime that had taken hold of the city. He was hugely popular with the voters and looked a certainty to be confirmed for a second term in office.

The girl's head bobbed up and down and Carson screwed up his face in pleasure. Blood smears covered his stomach, legs and cock. He reached over the side of the chair with his left hand. As she brought him to climax, the silent footage showed a rapturous Carson Keaton scream out in ecstasy. She swallowed and he pulled back her head from his softening member.

His left hand came back into view holding a large calibre pistol. She blinked at him stupidly for a few seconds as he lined up the weapon in front of her face. Mangle held his breath.The Mayor fired.

The muzzle flash flared on the TV screen and her head was destroyed as easily as a ripe watermelon. Fragments of skull with matted strands of hair clinging stubbornly, rained down inside the booth. Blood spray decorated everything within the room an instantly grotesque red, punctuated by chunks of brain matter. Some pieces that exploded outwards onto the window now began their nauseating race toward the ground.

Mangle gaped at the TV. He'd known the pain of losing family members to illness and old age, but this vivid reality of seeing someone's life extinguished before his eyes slammed into him, leaving him breathless and disorientated. He'd witnessed the guard being shot at the clinic, and the technician earlier that night at The Club, but the drive for self-preservation had anaesthetised his senses to their deaths. The cold-blooded horror of this killing was something completely different.

Tazeem walked back through the room, positioned himself by a chink in the curtains and looked out onto the street. He seemed unaware of Mangle's state of mind and didn't once glance at the TV.

Tatiana rubbed her eyes and then looked around as she sat up on the couch. 'What is going on?' she asked, but neither responded.

Sadiq walked into the room and crossed to where Tazeem stood.

'What is going on?' Tatiana asked again, this time more forcefully, as she looked from one to the other.

'There's a van pulled up outside,' Tazeem said, turning back to face them.

'Nobody followed us,' Mangle said, trying to shake off the trauma of what he'd just witnessed.

'It's too early for workmen to be starting their shift,' Sadiq said. 'Everybody grab your shit.'

Mangle sprang forward and ejected the DVD from the player. He swiftly pocketed it, along with the other four disks. Tatiana was up off the couch and looked to Mangle, waiting for the order to flee.

'There's some guys getting out,' Tazeem said. 'Come on, out the back.'

Mangle grabbed Tatiana's hand and ran out into the hall.

Tazeem and Sadiq were through the kitchen and out of the back door, Sadiq grabbing Dr Chu's pistol off the counter as he passed. He shoved it into his pants pocket and began scaling the fence. Although Tatiana was fully clothed now she still had no shoes, but didn't protest as Mangle roughly helped her up and over the fence into a neighbouring garden. Tazeem led the retreat through some azalea bushes, down a path and out into the street.

They heard a bang and the splintering crack of a wooden door being forced in. There had been no shouts or warning of any kind. Whoever had arrived in the van, they definitely weren't the police.

'Shit,' Sadiq exclaimed, patting the sides of his pants. 'I dropped the gun.'

Tazeem snatched a glance over his shoulder to ensure the others were keeping up. 'We have no time for that now,' he hissed, and again began to run down the length of the neighbouring road, past rows of identical houses whose sleeping residents were yet to awaken to the joys of a new day. He crossed over and rounded a corner. Mangle felt Tatiana's grip on his hand become tighter the further they ran.

Tazeem and Sadiq climbed into the front of the Mercedes. Tazeem started the engine using his spare set of keys. Mangle and Tatiana got in the back. There was no sign of anyone else; so far they had eluded their pursuers.

Tazeem accelerated slowly to avoid attracting any attention, and navigated the succession of twists and turns to leave the slumbering estate.

'How the hell did they find us?' Tazeem asked no one in particular, when they were a comfortable distance from the house.

'We would have seen if anyone tailed us from the club,' Sadiq offered. 'Maybe a tracker in the robes?'

'They're nice robes but I wouldn't have thought they'd require that level of security,' Mangle said, attempting humour that he really didn't feel.

'The robes are easily discarded,' Tazeem said.

'So it's the car then, yeah?' Sadiq concluded.

'The car was parked two streets away and they came right to our door,' Tazeem retorted.

They drove in silence for a while. Tazeem took the turning for the highway and kept the car at a steady 60 mph.

'What about the chips?' Mangle asked.

'The membership shit?' Sadiq said, looking back at Mangle and pointing down at his arm.

'Yeah,' he said. 'Is that even possible?'

'That was just for identification and finance,' Tazeem said. 'It makes sense they wouldn't want a card or something that could be stolen from someone's wallet or intercepted by the authorities.'

Mangle rubbed the area on his forearm where the chip had been implanted. Other than a small red spot, there was no trace that the procedure had ever taken place.

'It leaves no mark,' Tatiana said, pulling up the sleeve on her sweatshirt and rubbing the same place on her arm.

'You have a chip as well?' Mangle asked her.

'They put in my arm, yes,' she nodded.

'Fucking hell, that's it then, yeah?' Sadiq said. 'Shit.'

'The only reason for chipping the girls would be for tracking in case they escaped,' Tazeem said.

'But why would they want to be able to locate the very people who are paying them huge sums of money?' Mangle asked.

'They said there was no recording, but you have the disks there to prove otherwise,' Tazeem said. 'I wonder how much they would be worth to the clients to prevent them ending up with the media, or the police.'

'That has to be it,' Mangle said. 'Even with the resources they obviously have access to, they couldn't hope to keep The Zombie Room running indefinitely. We might have had a lot of luck, but we managed to breach the security in one night. The whole thing must be an elaborate sting to get blackmail evidence that would effectively control the most corrupt yet powerful members of society.'

'Jesus, with that amount of power there's no telling what the guy pulling the strings would be able to achieve,' Tazeem exclaimed.

'But how do we get these chips out of our arms?' Mangle asked. 'As soon as we stop somewhere they'll be able to find us. That's if they aren't already trying to pin us down now.'

'For now we have to stay on the move,' Tazeem said, taking a turning onto a different road. 'When it starts to get light we'll have to find a doctor that can dig them out. Those things they planted in there weren't exactly microscopic, and like you say there isn't even a hint of a bump so they must be in pretty deep.'

'I know a guy,' Sadiq interjected. 'He isn't a doctor though.'

'What the hell is he then?' Tazeem asked. 'A fucking librarian?'

'Yeah, funny. He's a veterinarian. But we're tight. We can trust this guy to say nothing.'

'Unless anyone has a better plan …' Mangle said.

'Alright, we'll drive for now then go and see this guy first thing. We'll need to get new cell phones as well in case we get split up.'

Mangle settled back onto the seat. Tatiana had been perched forward as well, intently observing what was being said. She looked worried and her teeth had begun to chatter. Mangle reached over and gave her hand a reassuring squeeze. Into his mind flashed an image of Laura lying dead on the bathroom floor.

'Do you think we will manage to get away from it all?' she asked with a slight stutter.

'I'm sure we will,' he said.

'I would rather die than go back there,' she said softly, and shuddered. 'Why did you come for me?'

'After I saw you in South of Seven and you asked me to help you, I couldn't get you out of my head. I knew if there was a way to help then I had to do it. And then when I saw what was happening in there ...'

'Thank you,' Tatiana said, interrupting him, and squeezed his hand in return.

'The doctor told us that the girls were being given a new start, a chance to make a future for themselves.'

Tatiana laughed, a cold sound like old machinery. 'That is what they tell us, but when we get here it is not the case.'

'The other girls, back at The Club,' Mangle said. 'They had the chance of escape but they didn't come. What made you come with us if they refused to?'

'They were not in control of their minds,' Tatiana said. 'Back at the clinic, they would degrade us, make us wear headphones and sit in viewing room for hours and hours. It changed them.'

'We heard about something they were calling Audiology treatment,' Mangle said, not wanting to bring up Laura's name. 'It was some kind of hypnosis?'

'I don't know. After these sessions the others started to seem different. Perhaps they lost the memories of themselves and their fear. Or maybe the memories just became less important to them. Something they were aware of, yet they no longer cared.'

'So how weren't you affected in the same way?'

'Before I was brought here, my family was killed in an explosion.'

'Shit,' Sadiq said from the front seat.

'It was a bomb, an assassination attempt on the President of my country.'

'That's truly awful, but how is this anything to do with what happened to you here?' Mangle asked as sympathetically as he could.

'When the bomb went off I was injured as well, but in time almost all of my injuries healed.'

'Almost all?'

'Yes,' Tatiana nodded. 'Ever since that day, I have been completely deaf.'

Sadiq turned in his seat and looked back at Tatiana. 'So when they put these headphones on you, you just couldn't hear the shit coming out of them?' he asked.

'That is all I can think, yes,' Tatiana said and shrugged.

'So you only read lips, to hear the stuff people say, yeah?'

'Yes. I met some friends who helped me. I learned to read lips,' Tatiana said, and rubbed her hands on her face as she felt the onset of welling tears. 'Without my family I had nothing, so when the opportunity to come here arose I thought this may be my chance to start over. A new life for myself.'

'Shit. You definitely got a new life alright,' Sadiq said and turned to face front.

Tazeem had continued taking various turnings and doubling back on stretches of highway to keep their route unpredictable. The orange tinge of sunrise began to creep over the horizon ahead of them.

'There's a store by the airport that stocks disposable cell phones. It should be open at this time,' Tazeem said. 'Sadiq, I'll drop you at the door then I'll drive around while you're inside. We can't afford to all wait in the same spot for them to pinpoint us. Be as quick as you can and I'll pull back up outside when you're done.'

'Yeah, whatever,' Sadiq said, sounding far from pleased at being selected for the job. 'Man, I could use a line right now.'

Tazeem turned off the highway, pulled across two lanes of light traffic and around a corner, then stopped at the kerb outside the store. Sadiq, having rifled through his pockets, determined that he had enough for the purchase, jumped out of the car and went inside. Tazeem pulled out and drove away.

'Do you know who this vet is he's taking us to?' Mangle leaned forward and asked Tazeem.

'No, and no I don't feel comfortable about it either, but what else can we do? We have to get these things out of our arms.'

Mangle sat back again. There was no point in arguing, no matter how he felt, as Tazeem was right. If they didn't have the chips removed, they would be located again, and next time their assailants wouldn't be so carefree in their approach.

Tazeem indicated and turned onto a ring road that looped around the airport. A few minutes later they pulled up again outside the store. Sadiq stood uneasily in the doorway clutching a plastic bag. He jumped in and tossed it to Mangle.

'Let's get these things out then, yeah?'

Sadiq gave directions to Tazeem while Mangle set up the three new phones. He stored their numbers in all of the phones, and handed one each to Sadiq and Tazeem.

Tatiana edged along the back seat. She lay against Mangle and curled her legs up underneath her, trembling from the relentless gnawing of chemical dependency.

Tazeem took the next turning as Sadiq instructed and pulled into a central car park, flanked by shops and a truck stop diner that linked to its sister store on the other side of the highway by an enclosed footbridge.

'That's his place down on the left,' Sadiq said, pointing across the mostly deserted parking lot to a store that read 'Hamilton's Veterinarians'.

'How do you know him, Sadiq?' Mangle asked, suspiciously. Sadiq didn't much seem the type who'd be an animal lover.

'We used to buy ketamine and some other stuff off of him,' Sadiq said, and looked around at the worry-etched faces of the others. 'He does patch-up work as well, for people injured during robberies and shit. Ted's a good guy.'

This ringing endorsement did little to reassure the others in the car, who would soon be allowing this drug-dealing animal doctor to cut into their flesh.

'Sadiq, you go, and take Tatiana,' Tazeem instructed, turning fully in his seat so that she would be able to see what he said. 'Mangle can go in after you are both done. I'll go last. Call when he's finished, and then go wait in the diner, or somewhere with good visibility of the exits, and watch everyone who comes in. Listen for your phones. If anything happens, get away as best you can.'

Sadiq got out of the car. Tatiana followed reluctantly, casting nervous glances back towards Mangle as they walked across the lot. Tazeem backed up the car and pulled out onto the highway. Mangle watched out of the rear window as a blue Ford sedan that had just turned off the highway continued down the slip road and turned back onto it.

'The car behind might be them,' Mangle said. 'I can't see who's inside.'

'I'm watching it,' Tazeem said, snatching glances at his rear-view mirror every few seconds. He accelerated and pulled into a faster moving lane of traffic. The blue sedan was a few cars behind but it pulled out as well.

'Surely they can't be on us so quick,' Mangle exclaimed. 'It took a couple of hours for them to pinpoint us at the house.'

'Yeah, but they might have waited that long so we'd be asleep and easier for them to move on.'

Mangle hadn't thought of that. He swallowed and looked behind. The blue Ford wasn't attempting to close the gap but it was still back there. Tazeem veered across two lanes taking the turning off the highway as late as he could. A chorus of car horns voiced motorists' outrage at the manoeuvre. Mangle looked back anxiously, but whoever was driving the blue car hadn't attempted to follow.

'It mustn't have been them,' he said.

'The sooner we get these things out of our arms, the sooner we can stop jumping at shadows,' Tazeem said wearily.

He took the overpass and started back up the highway.

15

Sadiq introduced himself as a friend of Ted, to a sleepy looking receptionist who seemed barely old enough to be out of school. She put down her coffee and went through a door behind the counter to find him. The surgery had only been open for a few minutes when they arrived and the waiting room was still empty. A moment later the door opened again, fractionally, and Ted Hamilton poked his face around the edge. His initial smile melted when he saw who was waiting.

'What are you doing here?' he hissed at Sadiq, and looked nervously around in case someone might witness them together.

'I need a favour, yeah?'

Ted beckoned and disappeared behind the door. Sadiq and Tatiana followed along a narrow corridor and into a vacant treatment room at the back of the building. Ted closed the door after risking another nervous glance down the hallway.

'What do you want?' he snapped, tightly folding his arms.

Sadiq rolled up his shirt sleeve, and pointing at his forearm did his best to explain what he needed doing, without giving too much information. Understandably, the veterinarian was sceptical, thinking Sadiq was either whacked out of his mind on a cocktail of drugs, or had simply tipped over the precipice of insanity. Tatiana chipped in a couple of times to try and reinforce the believability of what Sadiq said, but he was talking so fast, it was hard for her to keep up with exactly what was being said.

'So you turn up unannounced, and want me to cut into your arm to retrieve a microchip – just like that.'

'No,' Sadiq said, looking impatient, 'you do me, then her and then there'll be two others.'

Ted scratched his chin, pondering the easiest way to make the situation go away. Sadiq stood immoveable in front of him, and waited.

'Even if you don't believe us, please just do as we ask and I promise we will leave right after,' Tatiana said calmly, to try and influence his decision-making process.

Ted Hamilton left the room without informing them of his intent either way. Tatiana and Sadiq exchanged looks, but both remained and stayed silent. A few minutes later Ted returned.

'I've told the receptionist to take the morning off and I've locked the front door,' he said, and began scrubbing his hands at a sink in the corner. 'Once I've confirmed this delusion by showing you there's nothing in there, I expect you both to leave, and tell whatever idiot friends you have coming here to turn right around as well.'

Sadiq nodded. There was no point arguing; he would see soon enough that they were telling the truth. The veterinarian dropped a tray of hastily gathered instruments onto the table beside two glass bottles. He pulled across an overhead Amsco light and clicked it on, flooding the room with its brilliant white glare. Sadiq sat on a chair and presented his arm to Ted who swabbed the area with a cotton ball and medicinal alcohol from one of the bottles. He then took a small syringe, filled it from the other bottle and injected the liquid into Sadiq's arm.

'What's that for?' Sadiq asked.

'It's a local anaesthetic. You may feel sensations of movement after I make the incision but there should be no pain.'

'Should be?' he stammered.

'I'm a veterinarian. I spend my time with cats and dogs and gerbils. I don't generally work with patients this large that wear clothes, so I'm sure you'll understand there is a margin for error.'

Sadiq averted his gaze and unconsciously gritted his teeth as he saw Ted pick up the scalpel.

'Pick up the clamp and gauze and wipe away the blood,' Ted told Tatiana. Sadiq repeated the instruction while looking right at her.

'Right here?' Ted asked as he held the blade over the small red blemish on Sadiq's arm. Sadiq nodded.

Tatiana's attention was rapidly switching between Ted's now cold and professional demeanour, and the flashing surgical steel held in his hand. Ted made a small incision and put down the scalpel. Using forceps he pulled apart the wound and peered inside.

'There's actually something in there,' he said incredulously, and bent over to get a closer look. Taking a pair of surgical tweezers, Ted removed the small capsule from within Sadiq's arm. 'What is it?' he asked, holding it up to the light for closer inspection.

'Never mind that,' Sadiq said. 'Stitch me up and then do her. The others will be here soon.'

Ted carefully placed the capsule into a small glass dish and sewed up the incision on Sadiq's arm. Before he had finished, Sadiq was already calling Tazeem to tell him to head back.

Ted was finishing the sutures after Tatiana's procedure when they heard banging on the glass door at the front of the surgery. Sadiq went cautiously to investigate and saw Mangle, hands cupped to shield the reflection from the morning sun, peering inside.

'Where's Tazeem?' Sadiq asked as he opened the door and looked past him.

'He's going to drive around for a few more minutes and then double back. He sent me in to get done first.'

'OK, go through to the back.'

Mangle went through the door behind reception and followed the sound of Tatiana's voice. Sadiq stayed in the waiting area watching for Tazeem.

Tatiana rubbed at the bandaged, numbed area on her arm as the veterinarian performed the removal procedure for the third time. Mangle watched as Ted used the tweezers and dropped another of the capsules beside the first two. A thin film of blood pooled under them in the small dish.

'I suppose you will tell me as little as your friend,' Ted said, looking up at Mangle. He shrugged and said nothing.

Alan Bryson mumbled his thanks to the floral-scented woman who held the door open for him as he left the dry-cleaning store. The bright morning sunshine had done little to elevate his mood; he squinted through it, unimpressed, as he paced back towards his car. This wasn't supposed to be how his life turned out, not the way he'd imagined his future as a youthful and optimistic cadet. He thought back along his timeline, trying to work out exactly when things started going bad. Had it been one wrong decision that changed everything, or a series of random events that led him to where he found himself today?

His wife did nothing to mask her feelings on his failure to satisfy in his role as provider and husband, and he more than half suspected her of cheating on him. Even when he started to bring in more money she still wasn't happy, and spent it as quickly as he brought it home. Her upbringing had a lot to answer for. Her father had spoilt her relentlessly as a child and even now at 42 she acted like a teenage princess when she wanted her own way.

Bryson's focus had switched, though, and he no longer cared what she thought and what she did, or who she did it with. He didn't even care about his job, and didn't put in the extra hours to strive for promotion like he once had. He'd begun to squirrel away money for his own future, one that would not include her, and for the time being he tolerated the relentless shit storm that was his life. Still, he thought, it would be nice if he could catch a break once in a while.

He unlocked the car door and crammed the dry cleaning receipt into his pocket, looking disinterestedly around the sparsely occupied parking lot before he got in. If he hadn't paused to light a cigarette he may not have noticed the silver Mercedes pull in just across from him, or had time to realise that the licence plate rang a bell. Bryson wound down his window a few inches and exhaled a cloud of smoke that was taken and dispersed by the wind. He tapped his lighter against the steering wheel thoughtfully, and willed his brain into higher gear. Bryson drank a lot of whisky at night, and cancelled it out with a lot of coffee during the day, but so far this morning his hangover fog hadn't been fed enough caffeine to lift.

Mangle went back through to reception and saw Sadiq still looking out of the window. A maroon SUV had parked up in front of the surgery, obscuring their view of much of the car park.

'He isn't back yet?' Mangle asked. 'Your veterinarian friend is getting pretty impatient back there. I think he's eager to get this over with.'

'I'll go and see if he's coming,' Sadiq said. He unbolted the door and went outside.

Tatiana and an agitated Ted Hamilton came back from the treatment room. He snapped on a fresh pair of surgical gloves in anticipation of the final procedure.

'What's taking so long?' he asked Mangle.

Mangle saw Sadiq approaching the surgery, so ignored the question, hoping that Sadiq had seen Tazeem arriving.

'He's gone,' Sadiq blustered.

'What do you mean, "gone"?' Mangle asked.

'His car is there, he isn't. So yeah, gone. He even left the keys in the ignition.'

Tatiana unconsciously covered her mouth with both hands, scrutinising the words described by their lips.

'Where the hell has he gone then?' Ted demanded. 'I can't wait around like this all day. I want you people out of here.'

'We need to go now, and get rid of those chips,' Mangle said.

'What about Taz?' Sadiq said, although he didn't look as if he believed hanging around would be a better idea. Waiting no more than a second for an answer, Sadiq ran back into the treatment room and snatched up the bloody chips. Ted held open the door with one arm, and flapped the other, urging them to make haste. 'Thanks Ted,' Sadiq said. The door closed and was locked immediately after they departed.

'What do we do, head out on foot?' Mangle asked.

'We take Tazeem's car,' Sadiq said, crouching behind the maroon SUV as he slid one of the chips as far up the exhaust pipe of the stationary vehicle as he could. Sadiq stood and hurried over to Tazeem's Mercedes. The door was unlocked, and after stealing a nervous glance around the parking lot, he got in and started the engine. Mangle and Tatiana got into the back of the car.

Sadiq wound down the driver's window, pulled forward, and dropped another of the chips into the back of a parked flat-bed truck.

'How long before they realise we managed to dispose of those things?' Tatiana asked Mangle.

'Probably not very long.'

'So where we go now?' Sadiq snapped from the front. The tension, combining with his cocaine comedown, wasn't doing his mood any favours.

'Tazeem's lock-up garage. Once we get rid of all of the chips it should be safe to go there, and we need to get Tatiana some clothes and shoes.'

Sadiq pulled out onto the highway, hung his arm out of the window and deftly tossed the last chip onto the back of a truck loaded with construction materials as it thundered past.

'OK then, which way?' he said.

*****

Mangle closed the door to the lock-up as Sadiq and Tatiana sat down in the office area, both looking as despondent as Mangle felt. As he walked over to sit in Tazeem's swivel chair, Sadiq's phone rang.

'Yeah?'

'I may have dialled the wrong phone. I'm looking for the one they call Mangle,' the voice said in clearly articulated English. Sadiq shrugged, his eyes narrowed as he passed the phone to Mangle.

'Hello?'

'Do you recognise my voice?'

It was familiar but Mangle couldn't immediately place it. The speaker didn't wait for him to connect the dots, and spoke again.

'You and your friends caused some trouble in my club last night,' he said, and now Mangle did recognise the voice. It was Dyson Steiger. So the man he'd played at cards was the owner of The Club. 'You have something that belongs to me, but now I also have something that belongs to you. In a situation such as this, I feel a trade would undoubtedly be mutually beneficial. Don't you agree?'

'You have Tazeem?'

'Astute as ever Mr – oh, I almost called you Mr Lowell, silly me, when of course your real name is actually Nicholas Garrett.'

'Let me speak to Tazeem,' he said, trying not to let the revelation that their true identities had been compromised shake him.

'Mangle, yeah I'm here,' Tazeem's voice said into the phone, then came a muffled sound, and Steiger was back on the line.

'There you are, Mr Garrett.'

'He'd better be OK,' Mangle said sternly, but Steiger didn't dignify this outburst with a response.

'You will bring the disks to The Club and your friend will be released to leave with you.'

'There's no way I'm going back into that place, I'd never walk out again.'

'You decide where it is to happen then, Mr Garrett, and call me back. This phone will remain turned on for the next ten minutes, but do not test my patience.'

The line went dead, leaving Mangle staring at the silent phone in his hand.

'What's the deal? They have Tazeem and want the disks in exchange?' Sadiq asked.

'That's pretty much it, yes,' Mangle confirmed. 'I have to call back within ten minutes.'

'Fuck, man, the pictures on those disks are priceless, we can't just hand them back. Besides, even if we do they'll still kill us.'

Mangle nodded dumbly. Ten minutes to think up a way of getting them all out of the situation in one piece. Mangle leant forward, put both elbows onto the desk and placed his forehead against his palms. The same phone began to ring again.

'No way, yeah? The guy said ten minutes,' Sadiq protested as Mangle connected the call.

'Yes?' he said, trying to retain the illusion of being in control.

'You don't know me but I just listened in on your call and felt I had to act quickly.'

'What? Who the hell is this?' Mangle stammered.

'I'm Detective Alan Bryson. We've had Dyson Steiger under surveillance for some time, but this could be the break we need to put him away for good.'

Mangle shook his head, trying not to get swept away by the complexity of the situation as it spiralled further from his comprehension.

'Are you still there?' Bryson asked.

Mangle nodded before recovering the power of speech. 'Yes … I'm here. What do you want me to do?'

'We have some of the same type of disks you got out of that place, blank ones. We want to switch them with the ones you have, and then use them to go through with the trade to get your friend back.

'Meet him in the quadrant to the south of The Club, near the fence beside the esplanade. He'll feel confident enough there to come in person, and there are no buildings nearby for him to hide any of his people and spring a trap. Tell him to take a car and meet you there, and that's where you'll trade the disks for your friend. We will have a squad ready to move in on The Club as soon as we have the evidence.'

'Why didn't you do this earlier if you knew what was happening?'

'We had to have proof. Those girls would never talk, and if we stormed the place to get it, by the time we got up to the control room everything would have already been destroyed. That place is like a fortress.'

'And you know what is on the disks we have?'

'No, but if Steiger is so determined to get them back, I can imagine it's pretty damning.'

'You're just a voice on the phone, Detective Bryson. How do I know I can trust you?'

'I guess you don't, but can you afford not take that chance right now? If you go through with the trade and we then try to recover the disks afterwards, Steiger may already have destroyed them. And if you go through with the trade with the real disks, what's to say he isn't going to double-cross you anyway? It's your call, Mr Garrett, but make it quickly while we still have options.'

'Alright. So where do I meet you?'

'There's an old bakery on the main approach to the esplanade. I'll wait behind it on my own and I'll have my badge so you know I'm legit. Call Steiger and tell him the exchange is in two hours. That'll give us plenty of time to meet first, but not so much that he'll have time to think up a way around the plan.'

'Alright,' Mangle said, and disconnected the call. He wasn't happy about an exchange with either Steiger or the detective, but with no alternatives he had no choice.

Sadiq knew that speaking out against the plan would win him no friends. Their concern was to secure Tazeem's release, and any monetary value the disks may hold was of no consequence.

But Sadiq had already lost too much. Ermina had insisted he invest more and more of his fortune into the growing deal with Jupiter, and now that had been taken away he had virtually nothing left. His frivolous lifestyle, and the respect he gained as a consequence, was dependent on having lavish sums of money to throw around. He'd even lost his diamonds when they fled from The Club. He felt exposed and vulnerable, and he didn't like it.

Carson Keaton was a hugely wealthy man, and he had everything to lose should those images be made public. Sadiq intended to make him pay to get them back. Once Mangle left he told Tatiana he was going outside to get some air. He rolled up the garage door and walked out into the bracing March air. The first call was to Mohammed. Sadiq believed he would remain loyal, despite the recent upheaval.

As soon as Mohammed connected the call, Sadiq worked quickly to fill him in on only as much as he needed to know. Sadiq wanted a phone number to contact the Mayor, the number of a call box they had used in a previous deal, and someone he could trust to collect the cash. Mohammed blustered a little at Sadiq's brush-offs to his questions of what the hell was going on, but he settled, got down to business and supplied what was asked from Sadiq within minutes. Mohammed was instructed to go nowhere and speak to no one; Sadiq would be back in touch with further instructions.

'The Mayor's office, how may I help you?' a nasal female voice whined down the line.

'I need to speak to Carson Keaton, it's of extreme urgency.'

'I'm sorry, the Mayor is very busy. How may I be of service?'

'You don't understand. This is something I must discuss with him personally.'

'I'm afraid the Mayor doesn't accept unsolicited phone calls or meetings. If you'd like to leave your name and number and reason for your call, I'll pass them along to his staff and I'm sure one of them will call you back.'

Damn it. Sadiq only had a small window of opportunity, and

any hope of success hinged on the Mayor playing along right from the start.

'There must be a member of his immediate staff that I can speak with now.'

'There's Mr Burgess, the Mayor's personal assistant. I'll see if he will take the call.'

Classical music chimed down the line as he was put on hold. Sadiq bit his lip and paced anxiously.

'This is Raymond Burgess, to whom am I speaking?' a voice asked stiffly.

'Raymond. This is someone who has something very valuable and very damaging to the Mayor,' Sadiq said, and grinned. He could feel the warmth of confidence returning to him now.

'What are you talking about? Who is this?'

'If you're the Mayor's right-hand man, I'm gonna presume you know some of the outside office hours' activities he gets up to, yeah? Maybe at a certain club down by the old esplanade?'

A deafening silence echoed down the line as Sadiq paused for effect. This was the confirmation he had hoped for.

'I have a recording from that establishment that is worth a whole lot to the Mayor. On the open market I know it would fetch a fuck-load more, but time is short so I only want two million.'

Sadiq heard some muttering followed by footsteps. The other staff members were presumably being asked to vacate the room.

'This is a very delicate time with the elections being so close, so I'm presuming this is just an extortionate attempt to smear the Mayor's reputation.'

'Whatever you have to tell yourself, Raymond, but you know what I'm saying is true.'

'Even if such a thing did exist, which I don't for a second believe it does, how would you propose to make such a trade?'

'You'll meet an associate of mine at a location I give you. You go alone. When you have given him the money he will hand you a phone and leave. I will call him exactly five minutes later on a specific land line. If he doesn't pick up I'll know you double-crossed me and the recording will go to the press.'

'You expect me to stand there with nothing but a phone after handing over a huge amount of cash?'

'This is an unusual situation, yeah? But as it's the only way this can go down, you're just gonna have to trust me. I'm not trying to make an enemy of the Mayor; after this happens you'll never hear from me again.'

'So in this farcical scenario you've concocted, what do you envisage happening next?'

'You stay put while my man leaves with the money. I call you after I know he's OK, with the location of the disks. You go there and collect. Everyone's a winner.'

Tatiana was cold and scared. Withdrawal lingered within her like disease and her whole body ached. Her escape from the torture and brutality of life at The Club was beginning to seem less liberating than she'd first anticipated. Tazeem had been taken, Mangle had left to try and save him, and despite his best efforts to convince her he would return safely, she knew just how dangerous and devious these people could be.

Being left alone with Sadiq in the cold, cramped lock-up garage made her skin crawl. Her conviction in the goodness of humanity had been shattered through her experiences, to the point that deceit and treachery now seemed inevitable. Sadiq had given her no reason to dislike him, but he'd given her no real reason to trust him either. Looking into Mangle's eyes, she believed he was a kind man who would do right by her. But the familiar detachment and absence of compassion she sensed when she looked at Sadiq added fuel to her already smouldering fire of anxiety. She felt a brief respite from her trepidation when Sadiq announced he was going out for fresh air. But this was short-lived, and suspicion stabbed sharply at her following his departure.

Tatiana stood and walked around the shadowed interior of the garage. She briefly saw Sadiq outside, but he was walking out of her line of sight. She crept around the parked camper van, and stepping over a leaking car battery she crouched as she approached the open garage door. Sadiq spun around and paced back the way he'd come. Tatiana shrank back, before realising that she wasn't the cause of his sudden change of direction. He was holding a phone and speaking into it in a tense manner. She couldn't lip-read every word as he paced back and forth, but by the time Sadiq got into the silver Mercedes and drove off, Tatiana had seen enough to know that she had to warn Mangle.

16

The city centre streets boasted a significant number of shoppers despite the temperature having dropped and the day rapidly growing dark. Each garish window display Mohammed hurried past promised bigger and better bargains than the last. He turned up his collar and looked nervously over his shoulder. The brown leather briefcase he gripped tightly knocked against his kneecap as he walked. He muttered protestations in vain at the task he'd been given, and carried on toward the meeting point.

Mohammed trusted Sadiq. He'd been his reason for hope during three years in jail. Their relationship didn't offer him rehabilitation, but liberation. A lot was being said about Sadiq; whisperings from lesser men that he was finished. They wouldn't have dared speak this way a month or two ago, and Mohammed believed that would be the case again. This job was surely evidence that his confidence in Sadiq was not misplaced. Those fools would quake when Sadiq again rose to power, and this time Mohammed would be right beside him – after all, he was the one who had been entrusted with this task. Mohammed smiled and shrugged off some of his earlier paranoia. This was his time.

He arrived at the coffee shop, and as instructed sat at a booth slightly away from the full-length windows. Mohammed ran a hand over his neatly trimmed beard and glanced around at the other occupied tables. A young mother was struggling to get a reluctant toddler strapped into a pushchair at the table beside him. The wailing of the child was caustic on his nerve endings. An old man sat statue still, a large cream cup nestled in his hand as he gazed out, unfixedly, at the passing shoppers. A group of students shared a humorous moment at the corner table, and a bray of obnoxious laughter drowned out all other background noise.

Mohammed, irritated, glanced over at them and scowled. He bit down onto the inside of his cheeks, a trick he'd learned in prison to help maintain focus when surrounded by distraction. The sharp pain drew his attention inward. The other customers ceased to matter.

An irritable-looking man in a sharp suit entered carrying a sports bag. He saw Mohammed, walked over and sat down in the seat opposite.

'Raymond Burgess?' Mohammed asked.

'If you attempt anything other than what has been agreed, you know we will find you, don't you?' the man said.

Mohammed nodded. Sadiq had warned him that the meeting would likely begin with a threat, and that he was to let it pass. He looked down under the table. Raymond slid the sports bag towards him with his foot. Sadiq pulled back the zipper, revealing the requested paper grocery bag inside. He began to take it out.

'What are you doing? Take the bag. You can see it's all in there.'

Again, as instructed, Mohammed didn't respond. He reached inside, thumbed through a stack of bills at random, and satisfied, folded the grocery bag closed. He flicked the briefcase clasps, releasing the nickel bar lock, and placed the bag inside.

'You needn't have bothered, there's no tracker,' Raymond sneered.

Mohammed snapped the case closed, spun the combination lock and stood up. 'In five minutes someone will call with the location,' he said, placing a disposable cell phone on the table.

Fury was evident on Raymond's face at his lack of control, but he could only sit and watch as Mohammed walked away from him and out onto the street.

Mohammed's fist clenched reflexively around the briefcase handle as Mohammed walked through a herd of teenagers. They converged again once he had passed without breaking stride. An unshaved man in a sheepskin coat busked outside of a shoe store, strumming an out-of-tune guitar. His eyes seemed to follow Mohammed who hurried across the plaza and into the nearby shopping mall. The clatter of shutters being pulled down outside an ice-cream parlour momentarily startled him. He bit down onto his cheeks again, hard enough for the bitter, metallic collusion of his own blood to pique the interest of his taste buds. He tried to relax a little, and snatched a look over his shoulder. No one was openly following him, but that didn't mean they weren't there.

He cut into an apartment store and almost knocked over an assistant who was refilling a rack of expensive-looking blouses. He mumbled an apology, quickly righted himself and resumed a quick pace. Then Mohammed forced himself to take a breath and slow a little. Getting picked up by a security guard mistaking him for a shoplifter was the last thing he needed. Mohammed jumped onto an escalator and walked through an electronics section. The flashing TV images and booming stereos made him feel less conspicuous. Again he looked back, but none of the faces around him appeared familiar.

He turned a corner, went down a short flight of stairs and followed a sign pointing towards the elevators and stairwell up to the parking garage. An attractive young woman wearing black stilettos and white earphones walked past, clumsily reciting something in Spanish. Mohammed forced another deep breath and pushed at the door to the stairwell. He stepped inside and collided with an old Sikh wearing a thick winter coat, a Santa-like white beard and a turban the shape and colour of a beehive.

'Watch where you're going, you old bastard,' Mohammed snapped, scrabbling to pick up the briefcase which he'd dropped in the collision. He started up the stairs.

The disquieting aroma of urine and disinfectant irritated him and he held his breath. At the next level he stopped by the door to the parking lot, and breathed again. Mohammed stole a glance at his watch, and then back at the pay phone he waited beside. Any second now, he told himself.

A good-looking couple in smart business attire, each holding the arm of a little girl in a frilly pink and white dress, who swung between them, walked past and out onto the parking lot. The woman had shoulder-length blonde hair worn conservatively in a bob. She stopped, released the girl's hand, and began to fish through her bags. The man had smoothly combed, glossy brown hair, like the 'after' shot in a commercial for hair dye. Mohammed watched the man for a moment as he patiently waited, then turned around and glanced back down the empty stairwell.

'Honey, you take Karen back to the car. I forgot to pick up the perfume,' the woman said, and handed over a set of keys.

Behind Mohammed the phone rang, a harsh sound that bounced off the enclosed brick walls. He snatched up the receiver.

'Yeah … yeah, I'm out OK. No worries. Make the call, I'll see you soon.'

He dropped the phone back onto its cradle, began to turn around and felt a sudden ice-cold furrow open up in his side. Strength drained from his legs, and a moment later he sank to his knees. There was warmth now that ran over the initial and persistent cold.

Mohammed was confused, and barely noticed the briefcase being removed from his grip. He heard the click of a cell phone opening, and a soft beeping as a number was dialled.

'The package is in my possession,' a female voice said and the phone clicked shut.

More warmth now, lots of it, this time spilling down his front. But by now everything had turned black.

Back in the car Sadiq dialled the number for the payphone which was answered abruptly after one ring. 'Mohammed? … Everything good? … OK, see you when you get back.'

He terminated the call and dialled the number for the phone given to Raymond Burgess. 'Here's my end of the deal,' he said as a tense voice answered the call, and informed him of a meeting to take place soon at a disused bakery.

After hanging up the call Sadiq pocketed his phone. Slowly, he peeled off the thick white beard, dropped it onto the floor beside him, and then removed the turban. He started the engine, smiled at himself in the rear-view mirror and patted the brown leather briefcase with nickel bar lock that sat on the passenger seat beside him.

Mangle, having foregone Tazeem's more noticeable Mercedes, chose to drive the compact red Nissan that was stored at the back of the garage. The Volkswagen they had been driving was still, he assumed, parked outside Sadiq's apartment, but going back there didn't seem a viable option.

Mangle wanted to retrieve the gun Sadiq had dropped during their escape from the bungalow the night before. He felt he should have something with him in case things turned nasty, so allowed himself enough time for the detour before his meeting with Bryson.

They'd agreed that Sadiq and Tatiana would travel independently. If Steiger had something else in mind – and undoubtedly he would – at least they would have a chance to escape. Mangle left the highway and its perceived security of blending in with other motorists and began what he hoped would be the final chapter of his ordeal, but hopefully not of his life.

The bungalow appeared to be empty as Mangle approached from the rear. An old man, two gardens down, caught sight of his unfamiliar face, and the eager snipping of his hedgerow's first pruning of the year fell silent. Mangle hunched down below the level of the greenery and hurried towards the fence. He plunged his hands into a thicket of small shrubs, and after a few seconds of scrabbling around they closed around the barrel of the gun. He tucked it into the waistband of his pants, stood up and walked briskly back out onto the street. A few seconds later a tentative snipping continued, but Mangle was already out of earshot and climbing back into the car.

The bakery was as Sadiq had told him it would be. A large sandstone building with boarded-over windows. An unrecognisable ghosted outline was all that remained of the bakery's wooden sign on the front. Decades of weather erosion had crumbled the sandstone below one corner of the heavy roof, which tilted down with the lack of support like a hat worn at a jaunty angle. Mangle drove the Nissan around the back to where he expected to find the detective.

A balding man with a middle-aged paunch stood beside a dark blue Subaru, greedily inhaling from a cigarette. He checked his watch as Mangle pulled up, and gave a cursory glance around the perimeter.

'Mr Garrett, I presume,' he said and flipped open a wallet displaying his detective's badge.

'You presume right,' Mangle said.

Bryson nodded. 'Let's have the disks, then. You don't want to keep Steiger waiting,' he said, putting away his wallet.

'First show me the blanks. If they aren't exactly the same you can forget it.'

Bryson laughed and reached inside his jacket. Mangle stiffened and had to restrain himself from grabbing for the 9mm Colt that lay in the pocket of the driver's door. He relaxed again when Bryson's hand withdrew nothing other than five DVDs in a clear plastic envelope. The detective tossed them into the car. Mangle took them out and inspected them one by one, flipped them over and held them up beside the originals. Both sets were black on either side and had the same green triangle logo. He could see no differences.

'How do I know he won't check them before he hands over Tazeem?'

Bryson chuckled again and shook his head. 'Where the hell would he think you had got more disks from? Do they look like something you could pick up in your local computer store?'

'No, but …'

'But nothing. Take the blanks and let's get this over with,' Bryson said impatiently, and flicked away his cigarette butt.

Mangle eyed detective Bryson with disdain. He realised time was of the essence, but should he really be speaking to someone about to go into a life-or-death situation in that manner? He turned the car around and drove away from the bakery. Bryson's reflection continued to watch him in the rear-view mirror.

He skirted the road on the perimeter of the grounds and started down the track to the southern quadrant as Bryson had instructed on the phone. What had seemed like a bad idea at the time now seemed ludicrous, and he couldn't believe he was going through with it; but now there was no alternative. If he drove off, then Tazeem would surely be killed, and for all he knew Steiger could have his own trap waiting to spring if Mangle attempted to back out of the deal.

He continued the slow approach, scanning around him for any evidence of vehicles or men with guns. It was useless, though: the deluge of abandoned properties meant that he could never conceivably know for certain if he were alone.

He pulled up at the end of the track. Mangle could see the logic in selecting this particular location amidst the morass of dejected real estate. The reinforced fence that had been erected to separate the esplanade from the industrial grounds was the only visible intervention against decline the area had seen in over a decade. It stood proudly at around fifteen feet and the original black paint still covered the majority of the steel. A cluster of buildings that had once housed restaurants and other small, tourist-attracting businesses lay a stone's throw away on the south side of the perimeter fence. There could be people waiting inside, but they couldn't get any closer without clearly being seen. Mangle checked his watch again. Steiger should be here already.

One more nervous glance around and he saw a car making its way along the track he'd driven down a few moments earlier. A black Mercedes with tinted windows crunched over the gravel and cracked asphalt on its lackadaisical approach.

Ermina turned in sharply and pulled up beside Bryson's Subaru. In one hand he held a forgotten cigarette that had burned down in a cylindrical line of ash, and in the other was a phone, pressed tightly against his ear. If anything had gone wrong it was her phone that would have rung, so Ermina knew it must be an unrelated call. She got out, squared her shoulders and walked towards him, waiting for his call to end before she spoke. Ermina knew how to be careful.

'I'm in the middle of something,' the detective said into his phone. He glanced nervously at his watch, briefly at Ermina and then turned away, listening to the voice on the other end of the line. 'I know you don't call unless it's urgent … A bit of a hole? What the hell does that mean? … Alright, look, I'll set off now. I'll be there as soon as I can.'

He turned back to face Ermina and held out the disks. She took them, watching Bryson for any hint of deception.

'Thank you, Detective.'

He nodded and climbed back into his car. 'I'll talk to Steiger another time to arrange payment.'

'Alright.'

'Duty calls,' he said stiffly, and drove off, his tyres scattering pebbles around her feet.

Feeling extremely pleased with herself, Ermina climbed back into her car. She'd hung around with that idiot Sadiq, waiting for an opportunity to elevate herself, and as soon as Jupiter arrived on the scene she knew she'd found it. But now, having been asked by his boss, Steiger, to perform tasks for him, Ermina felt she was on the rise again. Jupiter was just a stepping stone, as Sadiq had been before him. Ermina knew she was of higher quality, and therefore deserved – no, demanded – the highest quality in return. She smiled and started the engine, drove slowly around the bakery and began to turn back onto the deserted stretch of road.

The roar of another engine alerted Ermina a moment too late to the danger. The sudden impact, and the crash of broken glass all around her, the sound of buckling and twisting metal, were the last things Ermina heard before she blacked out.

'Grab the disks,' Raymond Burgess ordered as the back doors of the dark grey Humvee were flung open.

Even if Ermina were conscious, she wouldn't have recognised the man and woman from the parking garage who Mohammed had had the misfortune of meeting a short time earlier. The man quickly walked around, tugged open the passenger door and picked up the disks that had spilled onto the floor during the collision. The woman reached through the broken driver's side window and felt for a pulse.

'She's alive but out cold.'

'Get rid of her anyway,' Burgess said. 'No loose ends.'

The woman deftly removed a black carbon steel Remington 1911 from a holster inside her jacket, and fired two shots point-blank into the base of Ermina's skull. They climbed back into the waiting vehicle and sped away.

Steiger climbed out of the car, ended a phone call and walked towards the spot where Mangle stood waiting. The driver's window rolled down a few inches, revealing Jupiter's steely glare above the tinted glass.

'Mr Garrett. I'll forego the formality of a handshake.' Steiger's eyes flashed with the same confidence he'd exuded during their time playing poker, but the look didn't betray any sign of malevolence. Hope fluttered briefly within Mangle.

'Let's get this over with,' Mangle said. 'I want to see Tazeem.'

Steiger motioned to the car, the electronic lock was released and Tazeem stumbled cautiously out from the back seat.

'That's far enough,' Steiger said when Tazeem had crossed roughly half the distance between them. 'Toss over the disks.'

Mangle reached into his jacket, clutched the blanks and silently prayed the plan would work. Again his eyes flitted across the possible locations either Steiger's men or the police may be waiting to spring from. He threw the disks, which landed 6 feet from Steiger. Mangle waited but the man made no move to pick them up.

'Aren't you going to get them?' Mangle asked in what he hoped was a casually curious tone. Tazeem began to edge slowly over towards him.

'I know as well as you do that there's nothing on them, Mr Garrett.' He raised his hand to halt the stammering protestations. 'I needed something to lure you out of hiding. You more than rode your luck during our friendly game of poker, but I knew you wouldn't be so cavalier when your friend's life was at stake.'

Mangle tried to quieten the surging panic inside him. He scanned around him for any sign of assistance. Surely the police would sense the impending danger, especially if Bryson's involvement had been uncovered. They should be about to move in now.

'Detective Bryson is a man, much like myself, who enjoys to gamble,' Steiger went on. 'Unfortunately for him he doesn't know when to call it a night and subsequently fails to learn the ultimate lesson in gambling. Do you know what that might be, Mr Garrett?'

Mangle remained silent. The four of them were completely alone. He had the 9mm tucked into the back of his pants, but unquestionably Steiger and Jupiter would be carrying weapons, and be a lot more proficient at using them than he was.

'Eventually the house always wins,' Steiger said with a knowing smile.

That was why Mangle had detected no anger in the man when they'd first arrived. Why should he be angry, when he was in complete control? He'd written the script himself and knew exactly how the meeting would pan out. They were just playthings of which Steiger would grow tired and then dispose of.

A cloud of dust in the distance over Steiger's right shoulder grabbed Mangle's attention. A large van was coming towards them along the track. Steiger noticed his focus and casually cast a look over his shoulder. He and Jupiter glanced at each other uncertainly, but remained calm. If Bryson had never intended them to be saved by the police, and this wasn't part of Steiger's plan, Mangle wondered who the hell it could be.

Another moment and Mangle recognised the van. It was the camper that had been parked inside Tazeem's lock-up. Sure enough, once it drew closer he could make out the figure of Tatiana behind the steering wheel.

'What the hell is this, the cavalry?' Steiger asked, mockingly. 'The best she can hope for is to come back to work for me. The only other out is to die along with the rest of you.'

Jupiter climbed out of the black Mercedes and moved into position behind it. A firearm that dwarfed the one Mangle had brought along was clenched readily in his black-leather gloved hand.

The camper van pulled up alongside the red Nissan, against the perimeter fence. Tatiana climbed out of the cab, walked around and stood beside Mangle.

'Well, well,' said Steiger as Tatiana glared defiantly at him. 'Our little mockingbird has come home to roost.'

'I'd rather die than go back there,' she said, and spat on the ground.

The rumble of a car's engine from the south, beyond the perimeter fence, drew everyone's attention, momentarily shaking Steiger's air of control and second guessing Jupiter's resolute demeanour. An old Dodge sped over the mounds of grass-topped sandy earth as it careered towards the fence.

Jupiter braced his weapon against the roof and took aim. There were too many variables in play now even for Steiger, who retreated to a position beside him. Tatiana ushered Mangle and Tazeem behind her, one hand against the side of the camper van.

'There's no way out of here for you,' Steiger yelled from behind the shelter of his Mercedes. 'By now there are men in position by the top gate, under instructions to let no one out. Whatever you have planned you'd better forget it while you still have any chance to save yourselves.'

The rear door to the camper van was flung open and a cacophony of gunfire filled the air. Mangle and Tazeem crouched down with Tatiana behind the Nissan as spent shells tumbled to the ground around them. 'Wait for my signal, then follow me,' she shouted.

The car on the other side of the fence slid to a halt. Two men got out and began firing at the Mercedes, while there was a lull in the firing from inside the camper van.

'Now!' Tatiana shouted. She grabbed a thick piece of carpet from the cab of the camper and clambered onto the roof of the Nissan. From there she scrambled up onto the roof of the camper. Not waiting for a further invitation, Mangle and then, reluctantly, Tazeem began to follow.

'Decker?' Tazeem said, incredulously.

Mangle looked over his shoulder and saw the unbelievable sight of his friend climbing awkwardly out of the camper van, brandishing a large calibre revolver. A second man emerged, holding a machine pistol from which bullets sprayed with a roar.

Mangle tugged at Tazeem's shoulder and they continued their ascent onto the van's roof. Decker and his companion ducked down again to reload. Jupiter returned fire whenever the opportunity arose, but the ravaged, almost sieve-like appearance of the side of the Mercedes indicated he was completely outgunned.

More shots were fired from the Dodge as Tatiana threw the piece of carpet onto the razor wire. Using it to protect her body she vaulted over and landed onto the sandy earth on the opposite side. Unhurt, she dusted herself off and yelled for Mangle and Tazeem to follow. Tazeem needed no further encouragement and jumped the few feet of fence adorned with razor sharp barbs.

By now Jupiter had given up the cat-and-mouse game of returning fire and chose his targets more selectively. He resisted shooting as a yell sounded from one of the men at the support car to hurry it up, but when Mangle stood up to vault the fence a volley of bullets was sent in his direction. He thudded to the earth on the other side and gasped in pain. One of the bullets had whispered by so close that he thought his heart would stop with fright, but regaining his composure the only pain he felt was from his awkward landing. Tazeem and Tatiana scrambled over to the Dodge, but Mangle knew Decker, who was obviously still badly wounded from his last encounter with these men, would need assistance after he made the leap.

A cloud of dust rose in the distance as three support cars approached from behind Steiger's Mercedes. Once they arrived the odds would be stacked heavily against them, and any chance of escape would be seriously diminished. Decker struggled up onto the roof of the Nissan as his accomplice emptied another magazine at Jupiter. He lent over, propped an arm against the side of the camper and gave a deep grunt as he swung himself across. The cover fire came from the support car now as Decker scrambled onto the roof of the camper and his companion began to clamber onto the Nissan. Jupiter was poised behind the Mercedes, eager to take a shot, unwilling to wait for support to arrive.

Decker let out a growl of pain as he thrust himself over the fence and fell heavily to the ground below. A deep laceration had opened along his thigh and began to stain the sandy ground red. His more agile companion sprang onto the cab of the camper, placed one foot on the roof and released a final barrage as he readied himself for the jump. The gunshots from south of the fence continued to ring out as Jupiter planted both feet, stood calmly amid the hail of bullets and began to fire. The man on the camper staggered in his run-up. His arm, thrust out in front to brace himself on the carpet, slipped, and he pitched forward face first into the concertina of steel barbs.

'John!' Decker yelled through clenched teeth.

John's arm slid between rolls of razor barbs and hung down, his body suspended on the top of the fence. The 'Carpe Diem' tattoo on his forearm was quickly obscured with splashes of blood that fell from his obliterated face.

Mangle was by Decker's side, attempting to drag him to his feet. The cargo of men and guns spilled from the three cars on the north side of the fence. A tripod-based assault rifle was slammed down onto a roof and the gunman immediately opened fire. Mangle thrust an arm around Decker's waist and pulled Decker's arm around his neck, and they staggered towards the waiting Dodge.

The windscreen bucked then shattered as the first two bullets penetrated, showering shards of safety glass across the dashboard. A rear door was thrown open and Mangle shoved Decker onto the back seat, squeezed in as best he could, then slammed the door. The driver spun away as the blunted thuds of three more shots lacerated the side of the car.

They drove for a couple of miles before the driver pulled into the parking lot of a multiplex cinema. The two men in the front jumped out.

'We're more than even now, Decker,' one of them said grimly, looking back through the destroyed side window. 'Here, take the keys to John's Chevy.' He tossed a set of keys at Decker, ran around to the trunk and pulled out a can of fuel. Decker, Mangle and Tatiana had barely cleared the car before he started slopping it generously over the interior.

They climbed into the Chevy as an implosive whoomph of fuel igniting sounded behind them. None of them turned around to watch as the bullet-riddled Dodge was consumed by flames.

17

Mangle struggled to follow Decker's directions whilst concentrating on keeping his speed down, as the slightest contact with the accelerator caused the revs to surge and the car to lurch forward. John had obviously maintained the engine a lot more meticulously than the car's threadbare interior.

He pulled into a housing estate, parked by a cluster of small shops and Decker, with Tazeem supporting him, led the way to a nearby flat. They trooped up the stairs and into a small living-room. Decker took two six-packs of Coors from the fridge in the adjoining kitchen and handed them around. He took a small medicine kit out of a cupboard, cracked open a beer and began to clean his wounds.

'As grateful as I am that you all turned up like that and saved me,' Tazeem said as he popped the tab on his beer, 'I'd still love to know what the hell has been going on.'

'Right,' Mangle agreed. 'It's great to see you again, Decker. We thought you'd died that day at Sadiq's apartment. The news channels reported three bodies.'

'I must have been lucky with some of the shots I fired through the window, which made our friends cautious. At first I panicked at the amount of blood on my shirt, and thought I was on the way out, but after lying there for a few minutes and not hearing anything else from inside, I decided to try and get to my feet. I'd stumbled down a couple of levels before the shooting started up again, but by then I'd put enough distance between us to give me a chance to escape. I fired a shot back every few steps to keep whoever was left pinned down, but if I hadn't been lucky enough to flag down a passing cab I would never have got away.'

'The cab driver picked you up like that? Waving a gun around and covered in blood?' Mangle asked. Tatiana had put down her Coors unopened and curled up against him on the couch.

'Once I got round the corner and saw it coming I stuffed the gun in my pocket and pulled my jacket over the bloodstain. The driver was happy enough to do most of the talking anyway and didn't look like he'd noticed anything.'

'So where did you go?' Tazeem asked.

'The only place I could think of going for help was to the guys I'd been trying to stay away from since I got out of prison,' Decker said softly, and rubbed the palms of his hands across his face. 'Bri knew a crooked doctor who came and looked at the wound. He reckoned the bullet went straight through, possibly just nicked the bowel on the way, accounting for the blood loss. He cleaned it out as best he could, then I chilled out there for a few days while I recovered.'

Decker stood up and unbuttoned his shirt. Medical gauze was taped around the left side of his torso. A fresh bloodstain had begun to emerge in the centre as a result of his fall.

'So how come you ended up down there today?'

'I tried to meet up with you and Tazeem back at the lock-up. We drove up there in Brian's car and almost ran into Tatiana coming out in that camper van. She didn't recognise me, and took some convincing that I was actually a friend of yours, didn't even seem to hear half of what I was saying to her, but eventually she told me what was going on. Said she'd seen Sadiq on the phone making a deal to sell you out, and turned the place upside down looking for keys to the van. Brian and the other two went back to pick up the guns, then we went to find the bakery where Tatiana said the meeting was with that Bryson guy. By the time we found it the only person there was Ermina.'

'Ermina, is she OK?' Tazeem blurted.

'Sorry, man,' Decker said, shaking his head. 'Her car was really smashed up. She's dead.'

Tazeem sat forward and dropped his head into his hands.

'For whatever reason, they must have turned on her, and I knew if I didn't get down there to help, you would both end up the same way. The only thing I could see in our favour was that they'd think the meeting point at the fence was a dead end.'

'You knew that the camper would be high enough so that we could jump over?' Mangle asked.

'No, Tatiana told us about the fence but she didn't know the height. That was the only thing we could think to do, though, so we hoped for the best.'

'But why was Ermina at the bakery?' Tazeem said, straightening up again.

Decker shrugged. 'I don't know what to tell you, man. There was no sign of Mangle, that Bryson guy, Sadiq or anyone else when we got there.'

'Bryson was working for Steiger, so maybe he'd been given instructions to kill Ermina when she came to collect the disks, then deliver them in person,' Mangle said. Tatiana stirred beside him, sat up and reached for her beer.

'Whatever happened, it looks like Steiger is gonna get away with it,' Tazeem said. 'He paid little attention to conversations he had around me, as he never intended for me to be released alive. On the phone he talked of overseeing a final shipment of girls and explosives.'

Tatiana was visibly distressed at the thought of more girls being forced into the life she had barely managed to escape from.

'What's the deal with the explosives?' Decker asked. 'More of those bombs that blew up Latif's shop and restaurant?'

Tazeem nodded. 'Sounds like Steiger's plan is to roll out a wave of terror across the city. Any targets that are likely to get as much media coverage through destruction and loss of life as possible.'

'But why the hell would he do that?' Mangle asked, struggling to make sense of what he was hearing.

'Other than the disks we saw of the mayor, he has other high-profile figures woven into this web of blackmail. He causes utter mayhem, then the people he's controlling step up to the cameras and promise the violence won't be tolerated and they will put an immediate end to it.'

'And then Steiger ceases the attacks, catapulting the levels of popularity and influence of those under his thumb through the roof,' Mangle interjected, with a slow nod of his head.

'That's exactly it,' Tazeem confirmed grimly. 'When the dust settles afterwards, he pulls out a suitable scapegoat to go down for the attacks, blames it on a political or religious insurrection, and the public get their pound of flesh.'

'Which would also help to isolate his people from any suspicion when they began doing his bidding,' Mangle said.

'He's bringing in a shitload more of the Daisycutter bombs he uses, tomorrow,' Tazeem said.

'What was that?' Tatiana asked, looking alert now. 'Daisycutter explosives, did you say?'

'That's what I overheard,' Tazeem confirmed. 'Why?'

'That was the device used in the assassination attempt when my parents were killed. It was commonly used across the old republics in times of political turmoil.'

'Yeah, that's what they said on the news as well,' Mangle added. 'A tightly packed tube of explosives with a copper liner in the device, triggered to fire in a specific direction, then another shell of further explosive and shrapnel that disperses in a circular pattern, cutting through anyone and anything in its path. Kasey Haugh said it was the first report of them being used over here. She speculated that an old cache may have been sold on the black market and shipped over.'

'I think I want to lie down for a while,' Tatiana said and looked over at Decker.

'Sure, take the spare room,' Decker said, and stood to show her the way.

Tatiana got up but held onto Mangle's hand for him to accompany her. Decker pushed open a door on the landing that led to a small box room containing a wardrobe and single bed, with a small patch of dusty blue carpet under their feet.

'I'll leave you two alone, then,' Decker said and closed the door after him.

Tatiana slid down her tracksuit pants, pulled off the sweatshirt and climbed under the quilt. Mangle wasn't sure what his response to that should be and stood uncomfortably for a moment, watching. The fine orange glow from the streetlamps filtering through the thin curtains glistened on her smooth skin, and highlighted some rough areas of healing cuts and abrasions.

'Will you get in and just lie with me?' she asked.

'Yeah,' he said, trying not to think of the experiences she had been forced to endure. He fumbled with the belt on his trousers, kicked them off and pulled his shirt over his head. The bed felt cool against his skin and her sudden warm touch made him shiver. He pushed as far back as he could, but the confines of the single bed pretty much precluded there being a gap in between them.

'Um, sorry,' he said as further attempts not to crowd her probably felt like the opposite.

Tatiana turned to face him. 'What will we do now?' she asked.

Mangle was even more confused, and was glad when his hesitancy prompted Tatiana into speaking again.

'We know everything they have done, and will continue to do, yet we are unable to go to the police. All of the girls there, plus the ones they continue to traffic in, will be brutalised and eventually killed.'

'I don't see what we can do about it. Maybe write down as much as we know and send it off to a bunch of reporters. Hope one of them runs with the story and digs deeper?'

'That will take too long,' Tatiana said hopelessly, 'Steiger is leaving tomorrow night.' Her shoulders began to shake gently as her sobs overcame her.

'Hey now,' Mangle said, tentatively caressing her arm. 'You can't make yourself responsible for the welfare of everyone. Whatever we can give to the press I'm sure will eventually result in some of the girls being freed.'

'And Steiger? Even if he shuts down what he has built here, he will still crop up somewhere else and commit the same crimes again.' Tatiana wiped the tears from her cheeks and brushed her hair away from her face. 'Is it possible that the men behind this are the same ones responsible for the death of my family? If that is true then I will never rest until they pay for what they did.'

'I really don't know, but how could you ever find out?'

'The big man you have described – Jupiter. If he was the one who planted the bomb when my parents were killed, I would know. I just need to get close enough to recognise his face.'

'You think the scars on his face were a result of what happened that day?'

Tatiana shrugged and looked away. Mangle let his hand rest on the warm skin of her upper arm. He could feel scar tissue beneath his fingers, signatures of pain she'd already endured, yet despite this she still strove to help others even if it meant putting herself back in harm's way. There was nothing Mangle could say to make her feel any better.

Tatiana closed her eyes and after a while fell asleep. Mangle lay watching her and wondered if he would be able to sleep if he'd lived through the same experiences that she had.

Sadiq parked a block away and secured the case in the trunk of the Mercedes before cautiously approaching his apartment building. He didn't want to chance an opportunist thief making off with a suitcase full of cash.

No one went in or out of the apartment entranceway as he walked nonchalantly along the other side of the street. The owner of the adjoining clothing store came outside and began to pull down the steel shutters as he closed up for the day. Sadiq turned his back and perused the window display of a baby boutique he'd stopped beside. Once the rattle of shutters had ceased, Sadiq hurried across the road.

He had no key now, but even if he did he wouldn't have risked using it. The police, or anyone else who might be watching the building, would have only a rough description at best of the Asian that apparently lived there, but it would flag their attention for sure if someone unidentified let themselves in with a key. They would certainly have pictures of all key-holders in the building.

Sadiq pressed the buzzer for Mrs Altrecht, the lonely old woman who would let in anyone. Sure enough, the lock clicked open and Sadiq pushed open the heavy door. Mrs Altrecht lived on the second floor, and would be tottering expectantly to her door to see who had come calling. Sadiq strode up the stairs two at a time and hurried to a doorway on the first floor. He stopped outside, took a deep breath to compose himself, and knocked sharply three times.

'I'm finished for the day,' a disgruntled voice barked from within the apartment.

'Mr Petrov, I need to see you for just one moment.' Sadiq knew this was his best chance to get out of Garden Heights. He needed the building's superintendent to cooperate.

A moment later came the sound of latches and bolts being withdrawn and the door opened a few inches, still secured by a chain. The man eyed Sadiq up and down and coughed, making no attempt to cover his mouth.

'Thought you would be long gone by now,' he said gruffly and maintained firm eye contact. Whatever had happened upstairs, Mr Petrov was determined to show he wasn't intimidated in the slightest.

'Is someone there?' a frail voice echoed down the stairwell. Mrs Altrecht had wandered out of her apartment to discover who her guest might be.

'I just need to get something from my place, yeah? And I'll be on my way,' Sadiq said. 'I would much rather have this conversation inside.'

After a moment's contemplation Mr Petrov closed the door on Sadiq. He heard the metallic scrape of a chain being removed and then it reopened, allowing him inside. Sadiq stepped into the gloomy hallway as Mr Petrov shuffled into the kitchen and set about making some tea. Sadiq walked into a cramped living area with too much furniture. He sat down on a scuffed mahogany Louis XVI style chair and waited for the man to return.

A stack of rumpled video game magazines lay on a table beside him. Sadiq picked one at random and began flicking through. Some of the headlines from articles inside had been cut out.

'My nephew, Ralph,' Mr Petrov said returning to the room, by way of explanation.

'I didn't think video games would be your thing,' Sadiq said, dropping it back onto the pile.

'Was it you, then, that shot them?'

'No.'

The old man nodded. A contradictive gesture that seemed neither to confirm nor deny his belief in the truth of what Sadiq had said. 'So you need to get in there, and then you're leaving for good.'

Sadiq re-established eye contact, and nodded in return.

'I want paying in advance.'

'I can't do that, Mr Petrov,' Sadiq lied, having anticipated the old man's stance. If he paid first, there was nothing to stop Petrov from calling the cops before he even left the building. 'I have some money in the apartment. I'll collect it and bring you five hundred on my way out.'

'You will give me two thousand, and I will go up there with you,' the old man said gruffly.

Sadiq agreed and drank a little of the bitter tea Mr Petrov poured from a silver and blue enamelled pot. It had gone exactly the way he had hoped. He'd almost managed to pull the whole thing off.

Crossing the road outside, Sadiq hurried back toward the car. He patted the counterfeit passport and other identification that provided a reassuring bulge in his pocket. He had left Mr Petrov happily leafing through his stack of used notes, but even with his aversion to authority, figured the money wasn't likely to buy his silence for long.

Sadiq jumped into Tazeem's silver Mercedes and started the engine. He indicated and pulled out into the flow of evening traffic. With the briefcase full of money in the trunk and all the ID he needed to disappear, all Sadiq had to do was be sure that no one had spotted him. The police weren't such a concern but Carson Keaton would be more than happy to tie up this particular loose end.

He drove on for a few streets, pulled a U-turn and went back the way he'd come, watching the mirrors intently for any other vehicles making a hasty change of direction. There were no obvious candidates for a tail, and Sadiq had begun to allow himself to feel a little smug before the sight of a grey Hummer three cars behind caught his attention. He was reasonably sure it had been behind him when he had driven away from his building. Sadiq followed a right–left–right–left weaving pattern through the city blocks, always keeping to the speed limit, but never seemed to be more than 200 yards from the following vehicle.

If they were police they would already have pulled him over. It had to be someone working for the Mayor. By now they would have intercepted Mohammed and realised the cases had been switched. If he pulled over and attempted to take the case from the trunk they would undoubtedly pounce. His only hope was that they'd expect him to have already stashed the money elsewhere.

Sadiq drove into the centre of Garden Heights and pulled into a car park in one of the city's most luxurious quadrants.

He got out, purposely didn't pay for a ticket at the machine, and hurried off down the street. Hopefully this would be enough to convince his pursuers he had no intention of returning to the vehicle. They would most likely abandon it and try to follow him on foot.

The obvious disadvantage Sadiq now faced was that he didn't know who to look for. The large, grey, military-style vehicle had been easily identifiable, but now whoever followed would blend into the background. This was a situation Sadiq had been in numerous times over the years, and his inbuilt survival mechanism kicked in as he ducked in and out of doorways and hurried through mostly deserted department stores, winding down to the close of business.

A youth in a brightly coloured red and green hooded jacket looked bewildered as Sadiq thrust a handful of money at him and told him to take it off. He looked around suspiciously, then obediently removed the jacket and handed it over. Sadiq pulled it on as he hurried down a narrow stairwell and out to an adjacent row of shops. He doubled back, and now eagerly retraced his steps toward the car.

Casting furtive glances left and right would only draw attention to him, so Sadiq tried to keep his eyes down and his stride smooth and efficient. He overshot by a block and doubled back to survey the area from a better vantage point. From here he could see all nearby parked vehicles and anyone standing about waiting he would mark as a potential tail.

A slightly hunched figure rushed out from The Walker building, one of the elite apartment complexes. Protectively cradling one of his hands he pushed past Sadiq. Sadiq's heart began to race, but the man obviously had other things on his mind and didn't pay him any interest. Breathing again, Sadiq leant against a huge marble pillar and continued to scan for a threat. Overworked businessmen talked too loudly into cell phones, hurrying along to their favourite bars to indulge in an evening of numbing anxiety respite. Couples linked arms, some weighed down by shopping bags boasting pretentious designer labels, others primped and preened for a night at a restaurant or theatre.

Sadiq had learned to trust his instincts, and right now his were uncapping the lid on the familiar feeling of victory. He began to walk across to the car park. If this were a movie, Sadiq thought, his theme tune would be playing in the background.

The man who had brushed by him a moment earlier climbed into a red 4x4 Toyota and wheel-spun out of a bay in the parking lot. In an effort to control the vehicle he turned the wheel hard, causing the back end to slide out. There was a loud crunch as it careered into the front wing of Tazeem's silver Mercedes. Sadiq stopped dead. The shrill siren wail of a car alarm emitted from the damaged vehicle. All heads turned in that direction as the man accelerated away out of the lot.

Small groups congregated to discuss what they'd witnessed. Cell phones flipped open as emergency service calls were placed to report the incident. Sadiq felt hamstrung. Would he even have a chance to retrieve the money? Forcefully he stepped forward, determined to seize what would undoubtedly be his last chance, but the sight of one couple caused him to pause. They weren't chattering like the others. In fact they were cool and alert, eyes not on each other, nor the squalling Mercedes.

The man, slightly taller than his female companion, looked up and saw him. His arm rose smoothly to his ear, his lips moving soundlessly as he spoke into his sleeve.

18

When Mangle went through to the living-room the next morning he didn't need Decker and the others to tell him what they had already been discussing. It had obviously been on everyone's minds, and Tatiana, Decker and Tazeem looked resolute in a decision that had been made in his absence.

Three cups of half-drunk coffee steamed on the table and Decker went into the kitchen to pour a fourth. There was no jubilation or self-righteous indignation, just a silent acceptance of their fate.

'So what's the plan?' Mangle asked, as Decker put the cup of coffee down in front of him.

What Tazeem had overheard of Steiger's conversation looked to be pretty accurate. A fat Port Authority guard paced back and forwards at the entrance to Eastgate docks, repeatedly checking his watch. At a few minutes before eleven, two vans advertising frozen foods and a dark blue Bentley pulled up outside. A man stepped out of one of the vans and approached the gate. He wore a jacket and cap sporting the same logo as the vans.

'Are the cameras down in the cross section to the shore?' he asked the guard.

'Yes. Now please hurry up. I already said I didn't want to do this any more. At the very least I'll lose my job if anyone finds out.'

'We'll be in and out in ten minutes,' the man confirmed, walked back and climbed into the van.

The three vehicles pulled forward as the guard unlocked and swung open the heavy gates with a shriek of metal. He began to close them again after the vehicles entered, but cast a look over his shoulder and thought better of it. He hurried over the cold, uneven ground to catch up with his visitors.

'Decker, if we're gonna make what they did to John right, we've gotta get in there now,' Brian said grimly.

He broke cover and ran, hunched, out of the scrap yard they'd waited in next to the docks. Tony, not waiting to hear whether anyone else agreed, followed.

'This is what we came here for,' Mangle said. He took Tatiana by the hand and followed the first two. Decker and Tazeem, a few steps behind, made up the rear.

They were equipped with a pistol each at the insistence of Decker's friends, except Tatiana who refused to hold one after shooting the technician at The Club, but none of them had anticipated the number of assailants they would have to face. The idea had been to try and avoid a firefight like the one they had endured in securing Tazeem's release, but Decker now wondered if that would be possible.

They could still hear the overweight guard puffing, his breath expelled in clouds like a steam engine and his stubby arms swinging furiously as he rushed to where the vehicles had halted further down the track. Past a large brick reception building and a shuttered warehouse marked Collection Point D, they'd parked behind another warehouse a short distance from the river.

Once inside the gates, Decker and the others kept out of sight behind rows of huge metal shipping containers and worked their way towards Steiger's men. The guard hovered around nervously as four men wearing the matching caps and jackets got out of the vans and walked the remaining 30 yards down to the shoreline.

Jupiter walked around and opened the rear passenger side door of the Bentley, and Steiger climbed out. He stood straight-backed and confident, inhaled deeply of the cold night air, and then exhaled, his breath a pluming column from each nostril.

'Just ten minutes then. I said after the last time I wouldn't be doing this again,' the guard said again, trying to assert himself over Steiger, who didn't reply and simply held up a hand to silence the man. 'I mean it, I'm not gonna lose my job over this,' he steadfastly repeated, and a cursory glance from Jupiter wasn't enough to deter his protestations.

'Here is your fee,' Jupiter said and tossed him a fat envelope. 'Five thousand.'

'Plus special time with Maria whenever I'm in South of Seven,' the guard added.

Jupiter laughed and nodded.

An old 80-foot fishing boat chugged quietly up the river. Mangle hadn't noticed it at first, as there were no lights on board. The four men in jackets and caps guided the boat in and secured its moorings. A carbon fibre gangway was folded out, wheeled forward and fastened onto the side of the boat. A man in thick, dark grey waterproofs with fluorescent orange stripes strode briskly across the gangway, shook hands and spoke directly to Steiger. Another man followed him and briefly addressed the group of men on the shore before two of them followed him back on board and disappeared below deck at the stern.

'What the hell do we do now?' Brian asked. He was obviously eager to avenge the shooting of his friend, but any direct confrontation would surely result in their deaths.

'I guess we wait for some kind of opportunity,' Decker said unconvincingly, never taking his eyes from the shore.

They positioned themselves behind the final row of containers, peering cautiously around them. Mangle felt Tatiana's hand clasp his own. It might have been the tentative touch of one seeking comfort, but it felt more that she was trying to reassure him that they would be OK.

He turned to look at her and asked, 'Is that the man?'

Tatiana's concentration etched lines in her forehead. 'I can't tell. It's too dark and he is too far away.'

The first two men reappeared a few moments later and walked down the gangway, followed by a procession of slender young women in single file.

'If we are to save the girls we must do something before they are taken away,' Tatiana said as they were led toward one of the vans.

She looked searchingly from face to face but nobody spoke. They knew she was right but none of them could suggest anything that might help.

'There are more girls than you said there'd be,' the guard protested weakly. 'But it's done now, just pack up and go.'

Steiger broke his silence and addressed the guard for the first time: 'We have some crates to offload as well, and then we will leave.'

'This wasn't what we agreed. You said half a dozen women who weren't able to get work permits. You didn't say anything about crates.'

'What is it you want, more money? What is your problem?' Jupiter growled at him.

'No, what's in the crates anyway? Drugs? Guns? I won't do this any more, no, no, no. You need to leave right now before I call the police,' he blustered.

Jupiter withdrew his right hand from his coat pocket, clutching a snub-nosed revolver. In one fluid motion he cocked it, lined up with the guard's head and shot him dead before the man could say another word. Reaching down, Jupiter plucked the envelope of cash from the guard's jacket and slid that and the revolver back into his coat pocket. Then he followed Steiger towards the boat.

The remaining two men continued with their work unaffected; only squeals of fright from the girls acknowledged the shooting had taken place. They were loaded up one at a time into one of the vans. The last in the line continually looked back over her shoulder as they walked from the boat. 'Sasha,' she cried, 'where is my Sasha? I want my sister.'

Tatiana's nails almost drew blood as they sunk reflexively into the back of Mangle's hand. 'It's Polina, oh my God, no. It's Polina.'

Tatiana was on her feet, about to sprint towards them, when Mangle grabbed her arm and Decker helped to wrestle her to the ground.

'Shut the fuck up,' one of the guards yelled at the girl, and slapped her across the side of the head. She staggered but did not fall, turned her tear-streaked face and glared defiantly back at him, bereft of any fear.

'Bring me my sister, you son of a whore!'

Tatiana struggled to get free as Mangle and Decker held tight to her, Decker's hand covering her mouth. 'Any noise we made was probably covered when the guard yelled at that girl,' Decker said quietly.

'She can't be more than 13 or 14,' Tazeem said, shaking his head.

The man laughed as he bundled the girl into the back of the van. His accomplice climbed into the driver's seat while he locked the rear doors and walked around to the other side. Tatiana shook herself free and took off running towards them.

'Fuck, she's gonna get herself killed,' Tazeem said.

Mangle started to run after her, and a step or two behind followed Brian and Tony. They covered the open space between the containers and the van quickly, without being spotted. Tatiana stopped at the back of the van to catch her breath. The engine started up. The cold metal vibrated softly against her shoulders as it idled. Mangle arrived at her side, Brian and Tony too, looking uncertain that following her had been the best course of action. Brian signalled to Tony and both ran around to the opposite side.

Tatiana strode forward until she became visible through the windscreen. She spun around and stood perfectly still. Within seconds, both doors were thrown open as the two men in the van struggled to comprehend how one of the women had got loose, and aimed to rectify the situation before she was noticed by their superiors. Mangle brought the butt of the pistol down onto the back of one man's neck. He slumped into a heap at Mangle's feet. The crunch and succession of muffled thumps he heard from the opposite side of the van indicated that the other man hadn't got off so lightly.

'Take off their jackets and caps,' Mangle said, hoping a surprise attack might give them the edge they needed. The guards' hands and feet were bound with zip ties Tazeem had insisted they bring along. Like Mangle, he did not relish the prospect of more deaths, and given the opportunity they would prove a better alternative to shooting.

'We have to get the girls out of here,' Tatiana insisted, as Decker and Tazeem made it across to where they stood.

'Brian, Tony, drive the van out and blow the whistle on what's been happening,' Decker said, taking charge. 'Take them straight to the press. That lot in the back will be undeniable proof of what's been going on. Once it's all over the TV, no matter how many police Steiger has in his pocket he won't be able to buy his way out of this.'

Polina looked out through the small rear window and pressed her palm against the glass. Tatiana began to cry as she pressed her hand up against Polina's through the glass, and tried to reassure her that she would help Sasha.

Brian and Tony looked uncertain about leaving him in the lurch so Decker spoke up again. 'If none of us make it out of here then all the girls in the van are done for, and besides that, John will have died for nothing.'

'You're still trying to make up for what happened years ago,

Decker,' Brian said softly with a shake of his head. 'You didn't mean to kill that guy despite the threats he was making against your sister. You need to let it go, already, and stop trying to be a hero.'

'You don't know what you're talking about,' Decker snapped, but his hand instinctively moved to the back of his neck and rubbed the tattoo John had inked all those years before. 'This has got nothing to do with what happened back then.'

'It's true, Decker,' Tazeem said. 'You went out on a limb for me and Mangle when we were in jail, and we thought you'd died so we could get out of Sadiq's place that day. You can't keep on like this, man, you should leave with these two now.'

'I'm not leaving till this is done,' he said firmly. 'You and Mangle are still here, we came together, and we're leaving together.'

Brian and Tony could see there was little point in arguing any further. They bundled the two bound and unconscious men into the cab and climbed in after them. Tatiana backed away from the van as Tazeem kept watch to alert them if any of the other men approached.

'It's still clear, but the stack of crates they're unloading is growing by the minute. Once they have them off the boat they'll come and load them into the second van,' Tazeem informed them.

'Watch what you're doing, Decker,' Tony said as he rolled down the window. Decker nodded and the van pulled away.

'Hopefully they weren't supposed to wait for the other van to be loaded up as well, or we're gonna have company up here a lot quicker than we'd hoped,' Mangle said as the van accelerated out of the docks.

Decker, Mangle and Tatiana moved to where Tazeem was keeping watch by the edge of the warehouse. Steiger and Jupiter must have gone aboard with the man who they guessed was the captain. One man struggled over the gangway, carrying a wooden crate, and stacked it along with the others. He walked back onboard, presumably to fetch the next one.

'Now,' Decker instructed.

They ran along the side of the warehouse and through the open doorway. The air smelled damp and crisp from salt and oily deposits. Large coils of rope, floats and mooring buoys were piled haphazardly alongside various-sized gangways, loading trolleys and a fork-lift truck. They retreated to the darkest corner just in time before the man made another laboured trip ashore with a crate.

'Do you have something in mind or are we in here just to get out of the wind?' Mangle whispered as the man went back to collect another.

Decker motioned for them to stay put. He crept outside and ducked down behind the stack of wooden crates. After a few moments the man returned. Decker waited until he heard the heave and scrape of wood as the crate was lifted and placed atop the last. He stepped out, grabbed the man by the neck and thundered a hammer-like punch into his solar plexus.

The startled man crumpled like paper. Decker pulled him forward head first into the crates before he had any chance of recovery. Mangle and Tazeem ventured to the doorway and took this as their cue to drag him inside out of sight. Tatiana fastened zip ties around his ankles and wrists in case the damage Decker had done wasn't sufficient to keep him unconscious.

'I need to go on board,' Tatiana said as Tazeem and Mangle waited for Decker to take charge on what happened next. 'I need to look at the man with the scars to see if he is the one that planted the bomb. If these are the men responsible for my family's death then I have to make them pay. And I must do what I can to free Sasha.'

'Just wait until they leave the boat,' Mangle protested.

'There is still a girl onboard who needs our help. And what if they don't leave the boat? This could be the way Steiger and the other man are to leave,' she snapped.

'Even if it wasn't beforehand, once they see they have a man missing they might cut their losses and run,' Tazeem said with a shrug.

'Alright, but I'm coming with you,' Mangle insisted.

'If anyone comes out looking for the guy we just hid, Tazeem isn't gonna pass for one of them even from a distance, whether he wears the jacket and cap or not.'

'Decker's right, Mangle. Not unless one of them has been spending way too much time in a tanning salon.'

'Tazeem, if Tatiana's determined to get a look at Jupiter, then you go with her. If you're spotted, get off the boat as quick as you can, whether you've found the other girl or not. Me and Mangle will try and find a way to slow them down, hopefully give enough time for Bri and Tony to get word out and for the cops to get down here.'

Tatiana nodded and started toward the gangway before anyone could disagree with Decker. Tazeem scampered after her, muttering what a stupid idea he thought it was. Once onboard, Tatiana walked along the narrow platform inside the gunwale towards what she believed to be the bridge, where a light now shone through foggy rectangular windows. Standing outside, the tremors she felt through the deck as the men moved around inside were enough to convince her that a change of approach was needed in case any of them made a sudden appearance.

She turned back suddenly, startling Tazeem who gripped a support rope tightly to avoid losing his footing.

'Where are you going now?' he hissed at her, but Tatiana pushed past and began to climb up to the observation platform above. Moving as delicately as she could so as not to alert the men below her, Tatiana inched forward and hung over the side, trying to look through the windows below. Catching on, Tazeem followed and held tight to the backs of her thighs, enabling her to edge down a few more inches.

She squinted and peered inside. The captain faced roughly in her direction, but the inside light shining on the smudged glass would show him nothing but a blurred reflection even if he looked directly at her. With their backs to Tatiana were two more men. One she knew immediately as Steiger. The features of the other, the larger man called Jupiter, remained elusive. She could see them talking as their conversation continued, but could make out little of what they said. She felt Tazeem tapping on her leg, evidently keen for her to give up on the suicidal notion and return to the others.

Tatiana didn't hear the loud splash in the harbour behind them, but the men on the bridge did, and so did Tazeem. His hands fisted as they gripped tightly onto Tatiana's jeans and hoisted her back up. Reluctantly, she allowed it, but before the men charged out from the bridge they'd turned their faces in the direction of the sound. Even through the scars, she recognised the face of the man whose actions brought about the end of her previous life.

Decker waited until Tazeem and Tatiana had boarded the boat and he could no longer see them before he stepped onto the gangway. Mangle had been instructed to wait by the pile of crates, and had been told – pointlessly, Decker realised immediately afterwards – to try and look inconspicuous.

His main aim, along with bringing Steiger to justice, was to ensure that all of the explosives were seized. After seeing the devastation they had caused at Latif's restaurant and computer shop, it was unthinkable that any could remain in the hands of men who would use them to bring about huge numbers of casualties. He hoped Tatiana and Tazeem would be able to free the girl, but right now he couldn't let himself get distracted with thoughts of anything else.

He tugged the peak of the cap down level with his eyebrows and flexed his shoulders. They felt tightly restrained within the confines of the jacket that was at least a size too small. He walked to the stern of the ship where two more crates sat beside a set of steel steps and a railing leading down to the decks below. As he was about to descend, Decker heard the sound of heavy boots clumping their way up, and quickly ducked back around the corner. He heard a man grunt with strain, followed by the thud of what he supposed was a crate dropped on top of the pile.

Decker about turned and walked quickly back along the deck. Mangle, who had been watching from the shore, hurried over into the cover of the storage building. Behind him the man cursed and again picked up the crate.

'Where've you been?' he asked Decker as he struggled around the corner.

'Ahh, I had to see Steiger,' Decker said, in what he hoped sounded like a natural response, 'I'm done now though.' Again he tugged at the brim of his cap and kept his eyes low.

'There's another two crates at the top of the stairs. Get this one and I'll fetch the last couple from below.'

'Take it over yourself. You're almost there now anyway,' Decker said.

The man muttered something, but started across the gangway. Decker went to the stern and picked up another box. He hurried back to the gangway but the other man had already begun to cross. There was room for two people to pass so Decker knew if he stood waiting it would look suspicious and draw attention to him. He walked on, hoping the man would push past him without another word.

'Who the fuck are you?' the man asked when he drew level with Decker.

'I've been called down to help, get this finished up quicker.'

'Well, where's the other guy?'

'He's up seeing Steiger?' Decker said, but a rising inflection at the end of the sentence betrayed the lie, turning his statement into a question.

The man lunged forward and seized the crate. Decker struggled with him, unable to reach the gun that was tucked under the line of the jacket down the back of his pants. He looked into the man's face and read the uncertainty as his initial wide-eyed surprise began to lift. The man could see his decision to jump Decker had been the wrong one as Decker was taller and clearly more powerful.

The man gulped in a breath. Decker saw he was about to yell

for help and released his grip of the crate which bought him a few tenths of a second as the man adjusted to the extra weight. Decker swung back his right arm and punched him on the bridge of the nose, drew back and punched him again. The man stuttered and blinked. Bubbles of blood burst from his nostrils as he tried to form words. Decker slammed another fist into his head just below the temple and watched as he tumbled, still clutching the crate, backwards into the water.

Decker shot a look in Mangle's direction and saw him hovering uncertainly by the warehouse before a voice from the boat caused him to duck back inside.

'What the fuck happened?'

Decker spun around and saw Jupiter approaching across the deck. The darkness, jacket and cap had been enough to mask his identity so far, but when he spoke, surely that would blow his cover. The crate bobbed to the surface in the water below him. Decker pointed at it, and angled a cautious look up at Jupiter.

'Fucking idiot! Get it out of there and get them all loaded into the van. We leave in five minutes.'

Decker nodded and waited for Jupiter to withdraw, but something held him in place a moment longer. Decker walked slowly down the gangway to retrieve the crate from the water, but still Jupiter remained. Reaching out he nudged the crate which bobbed and spun clockwise, and after a few seconds he managed to coax it into the side.

Decker heard nothing from the boat and didn't know if Jupiter still watched him, but didn't want to risk another glance upwards. As the crate came within grasping distance, the pale, vacant expression of the man Decker had assaulted floated up from the water beneath.

Heavy footsteps sprinting across the deck confirmed Jupiter's presence, and that they had now been discovered. He looked up just in time to see Jupiter descending below deck at the stern. Mangle was already ahead of him, running across the gangway in pursuit.

*****

After Jupiter charged out from the bridge, Steiger and the captain followed a moment later, moving more cautiously toward the stern.

'Wait for our chance to get back ashore,' Tazeem mouthed once he had Tatiana's attention.

She shook her head and then shook off his grip. Once the two men had vanished at the back of the boat Tatiana climbed down the ladder on the starboard side and followed. Tazeem's heart was racing, but he tried not to panic. Jupiter was no more than 20 feet away, yelling something at one of the men. He had no idea where Mangle and Decker were so Tazeem took a deep breath and slid down the ladder after Tatiana. She had paused and beckoned for him to hurry. Before he caught up, Tatiana had already begun her descent, gracefully taking the cold, wet steps two at a time. Tazeem went after her.

Tatiana paused on the next deck. There was no sign of Sasha, but the gaping door into the prison at the back of the galley brought up an overpowering sensation of grief over Natalia's death. She couldn't allow anyone else to die at the hands of these men.

Tazeem heard raised voices over the engine noise from the bottom deck. He pointed downwards once he caught her eye. She nodded solemnly and they went below. Tazeem gripped Tatiana lightly by the wrist so that he could alert her if he heard an immediate threat, although the droning growl and hiss from the engine pretty much levelled the playing field as far as their senses were concerned.

A host of olive-grey painted heavy machinery filled the centre of the engine room, with white pipes running the length of the ceiling. Down one wall were a line of valves and pressure dials, and the room was lit by a run of murky, flickering fluorescent bulbs. Neither the captain nor Steiger could be seen, but Mangle faintly heard voices from up ahead. Again he pointed to signal his intention to Tatiana and they proceeded around the throbbing machinery and through the underlying cloud of steam.

A girl lay handcuffed to a pipe in a far corner, with blood on her hair and face. He felt Tatiana stiffen and she covered her mouth to stifle a moan. Two of the wooden crates were on the ground a few feet from her, and one stood open with its lid resting against the side. On a table beside them were three shiny, cylindrical metal objects. The captain and Steiger were in conversation.

'You cannot decide to pick and choose from my supply. This arrangement will continue to work with or without your help.'

'I'm sure you can find another captain to bring you the women, but as for these …' Jacob countered, picking up one of the devices from the table, '… there is a much greater element of trust.'

He flicked open a clear plastic cover and pressed the switch underneath. A smug red light began to pulse. The device was in a state of readiness.

'Jacob, we have worked together for many years. As a token of good faith you can keep the girl, but we both understand this will not happen again.'

The captain chuckled and pressed the switch again, deactivating the threat, before putting down the cylinder. The disquieting look that flashed in Steiger's eyes as the captain turned his back indicated that this would be his last trip.

Tatiana was up and on her feet before Tazeem could do anything to stop her. She snatched the explosive cylinder from the table and copied what the captain had done seconds earlier. The light returned, flashing its prophetic promise of destruction.

'Where is Polina?' the handcuffed girl cried, recognising Tatiana.

'Polina got away, she is safe now,' Tatiana reassured her before turning back to face Steiger. 'Release Sasha and cuff yourselves between the pipes.'

'I have neither the key to do that nor the inclination,' Steiger said as a broad smile spread over his face. 'Now put that down before you hurt yourself.'

'You had my parents killed, you bastard. You're the one who ordered it.'

Steiger couldn't have known which incident she spoke of, but shrugged off the accusation. It was obviously not the first time he had been accused of such an atrocity. 'Put it down, I won't tell you a third time,' he said, his tone both curt and demanding.

Tears spilled down Tatiana's cheeks. Her hands trembled. Tazeem willed her to put it down, hoping they might yet find another way out. 'You will rot in hell for all you have done,' Tatiana spat at him and jammed her thumb down onto the red button.

Time appeared to stand still. Tazeem held his breath and cringed, waiting for the inevitable explosion that would undoubtedly kill them all. The next sound he was aware of was Steiger's laughter, rich with mirth, like someone who'd just heard an amusing anecdote at a dinner party amongst friends. He peered around the machinery as a hooded man strode up, snatched away the device from an incredulous Tatiana, and clubbed her over the head with a familiar, deathly white fist.

'The activation button has no connection to the device, it's simply an old design,' Steiger explained, undoubtedly for his own further amusement.

The man who had assaulted Tatiana dangled what looked like a car-key fob on the end of a thin, silver chain. His pale skin almost an extension of the white hooded-shirt he wore. Tazeem was in no doubt that this was the man he'd seen outside Latif's restaurant on the night of the explosion.

'Remote detonation,' Steiger went on. 'Jupiter had a terrible accident a little while ago and we've lost other good men over the years. It was a natural progression.'

Fury surged up in Tazeem and he charged at the hooded man, swinging the butt of his gun in a circular arc which impacted against a pale cheekbone with a crack. The man cried out and fell to the floor, clutched his face and dropped the fob which skittered across the floor.

The captain jumped forward and grabbed at the gun. Tazeem

struggled with him. The captain had a sinewy strength that was in stark contrast to his years. The pale man leered up at Tazeem as he crouched on the deck like an animal. Scarlet blood eagerly explored the indent of damaged flesh. Tazeem and the captain waltzed left and right as they tried to gain control of the weapon. Their arms swung upward and a shot discharged. Immediate pain accompanied a jet of boiling steam as the bullet punctured one of the pipes. Tazeem and the captain instinctively jumped away, protectively clutching areas of exposed skin. The gun clattered harmlessly to the ground.

Urgent footsteps heavily descended the stairs. The cloud of steam was quickly filling the engine room. Tazeem, cradling his scalded hand, regained enough composure to lurch forward towards the gun. A bullet ricocheted off the riveted, steel-panelled floor just inches from his grasp. Tazeem shrank back. He knew he was defeated.

Mangle was oblivious to Decker's shouts from behind as he ran on board in pursuit of Jupiter. He had to find Tatiana and get her off the ship before anything terrible happened. Skidding a little as he rounded the corner, Mangle grabbed the railing and took a second to regain his balance. The hollow sound of a gunshot echoed coldly through the ship. Decker had closed the gap between them and Mangle started down the stairway after the surprisingly agile Jupiter.

Sounds of movement, possibly a struggle, came from the bottom of the boat as Mangle took no more than a brief glance around the middle deck. He turned to the stairs again as another shot was fired. Mangle's heart lurched and he plunged down around the final turn. Jupiter stood just below him, a gun aimed at a figure on the ground roughly 20 feet away, but Mangle couldn't make out who it was through the heavy curtain of steam.

He sprang onto Jupiter's back. The crook of his elbow tightened around a neck as thick as a tree trunk, and he attempted to cut off the air flow as he'd watched Decker do once before.

Jupiter reached back and plucked Mangle off as easily as swatting an annoying insect and threw him down onto the deck. Mangle flailed an arm out just in time to brace his fall. He landed next to Tazeem, no more than a few feet from the source of the steam. The jet billowed insistently beside him, soaking his clothes and scalding his skin.

Jupiter raised the gun again and stepped towards them. He looked determined that the next shot wouldn't miss. A sound from behind, and the instinct for self-preservation caused Jupiter to turn his head just in time to see Decker as he approached. Decker lunged for the bigger man, preventing him from getting a clear shot with the gun. He grabbed Jupiter's solid forearm and forced his thumb into the pulse pressure point, causing him to drop his weapon. Thinking he had the upper hand, Decker relaxed his grip and made to grab Jupiter and put him in a choke hold.

Jupiter reached behind him and grabbed a handful of Decker's shirt with one hand and Decker's left wrist with the other. He dropped to a knee and spun Decker over his shoulder. Jupiter kept hold of his wrist and twisted as Decker was in mid-air. Decker let out a scream as his shoulder was torn out of its socket, and he crashed down onto the steel deck.

A menacing, gleeful expression lit Jupiter's face from within like a Halloween lantern. The scars on his face glistened in the flickering light, milky, like candle wax, as he slowly bent down to retrieve his gun. The pale man had slithered across the floor and sought protection behind the burgeoning presence of Jupiter.

'And order is restored,' Steiger said, stepping around the billowing steam from the broken pipe.

'Not yet, it isn't,' Tatiana said from behind him.

Steiger turned and saw she had again picked up one of the explosives. She held it, weary yet determined, like a player in some barbaric futuristic sport. Tazeem shuffled over next to Mangle and tugged him towards Decker by the stairs. Everyone had forgotten about Jupiter, who stood there uncertainly, the gun clasped in a giant fist that now hung loosely by his side.

Steiger laughed at the simplicity of Tatiana's cognitive process. 'The activation button doesn't work, my dear. Have you forgotten already?' he jibed.

Tatiana pulled the lank strands of hair out of her face and turned directly towards him. 'I've forgotten nothing, you bastard. Perhaps you lose track of something, though.'

Uncertainty swept the room like a forest fire. Steiger, the captain, Jupiter and the hooded man were caught up in flames of doubt. One by one their eyes fell upon the forgotten girl who remained chained and bleeding in the corner. In one grimy hand was clasped the fob that the hooded man had gloatingly flaunted moments before.

Jupiter turned and began running up the stairs two at a time. His pale companion, seeing which way the wheels of fate had turned, was just a second behind him. Tazeem tugged again on Mangle's arm and tried to help Decker to his feet.

Steiger took a step towards the gun that Tazeem had dropped.

'If you move once more I will take out this whole fucking room,' the girl in the corner said. Her strained voice was barely audible above the engine drone.

'Get out now,' Tatiana said to Mangle, who stood with Tazeem supporting Decker as he got painfully to his feet. Tazeem turned and began towards the stairs.

'Put it down and come with us,' Mangle pleaded.

Tatiana shook her head. 'I knew when I stepped on board that I wouldn't be getting off again.'

'Don't be ridiculous,' Mangle pleaded. 'The girls got away, and we'll make sure the men all pay for what they did. You don't have to do this.'

'It is the only way to be sure.'

Tatiana turned her back on Mangle and moved beside her chained friend on the floor who struggled to maintain consciousness; her face was now syrupy red with blood from numerous head wounds.

'Come on, Mangle,' Tazeem said, 'we have to go.'

Reluctantly, Mangle took hold of Decker and they began their ascent. Decker's left arm was useless. Any contact with it sent shockwaves of pain through him, so Tazeem gripped tightly onto the waistband of his pants and helped haul him along. They passed the middle deck and climbed again. Mangle repeatedly cast looks behind them, in case Tatiana had decided to follow.

They struggled out onto the top deck. Jupiter and the hooded man had already disappeared. Tazeem moved onto the gangway and they began to help Decker across.

The whole boat shook violently from the magnitude of the blast. The gangway unhooked and Tazeem was pitched headfirst into the water. Decker fell forwards, grinding his damaged shoulder against the gunwale and let out a ragged scream. Mangle scrambled back to his feet from where he'd fallen, and looked for any sign of hope that Tatiana could have survived. Flames lapped greedily up onto the deck on the starboard side of the ship. The smell of scorched metal and blistering paint permeated the air.

'We have to get off,' Decker said through clenched teeth. 'If the fuel tanks go up we won't stand a chance.'

Mangle knew he was right. He seized Decker by his good arm and managed to get him to his feet. The boat was taking on water from the explosion, and began to tilt drunkenly. The deck lurched suddenly and Decker began to slide. Mangle secured one arm around his friend's waist and hoisted him over the edge. Decker let out a surprised yell as he fell into the water below.

Mangle cast one last hopeful look around the ship before he jumped over the side, just as the air around him reverberated with the intensity of another explosion. He plunged into the freezing water, and quickly surfaced, gasping for breath. He splashed around, looking for Decker. The burning shell of the boat began to sink into the water behind him, creating an undercurrent that tugged insistently at Mangle's legs.

Tazeem reached out an arm from the dock above and shouted to him, 'Give me your hand.'

'I have to find Decker,' he yelled, and spun around again in the water. Pieces of burning debris fell like meteors all around. There was the sound of loud coughing and desperate gulping for air behind him as someone broke the surface. 'Decker,' Mangle said as he reached him.

Decker allowed Mangle to guide him to the quayside, clinging to a charred piece of crate. Between them Tazeem and Mangle managed to hoist Decker out of the water, as the sound of distant sirens diluted the bonfire crackle of the burning ship.

19

Sadiq woke in a small dark room, covered in a cold sweat and surrounded on three sides by looming pieces of heavy furniture. Panic caught in his throat, before memories of the previous day flooded his consciousness and he remembered where he was.

After being outplayed by the Mayor's henchmen, he had instinctively run back towards his old apartment block. No one would look for him here, at least not immediately, but he still couldn't chance returning to the apartment itself. With nowhere else to turn, he pressed the buzzer for Mrs Altrecht, and once admitted, stopped on the first floor landing and again knocked for Mr Petrov.

The old man looked surprised to see him, but not fearful, so Sadiq assumed that after their last meeting Petrov hadn't turned him in to the police. He concocted a quick story and promised the old man more money if he let him stay a few days. Sadiq didn't plan on being there that long. He just needed enough time to think and plan his next move.

After a few hours' rest Sadiq knew what he had to do. All of his bridges had been burned and he had no one left to turn to. There was just one last limb he could crawl out onto, and if it broke, that would be the end of him. He reached for his phone and turned it back on. It was only 5 a.m., but he dialled the number for Raymond Burgess.

'Raymond,' Sadiq said as soon as the call connected.

'Is this who I think it is?' The voice was gruff and thick with fatigue.

'Well played yesterday,' Sadiq said, inadvertently answering the question. Silence echoed down the line. 'I know, despite taking receipt of both parcels you still may feel you have some unfinished business with me, yeah?'

'You could say that,' he confirmed.

Sadiq thought he heard a hint of curiosity in Raymond's voice, which was about the best he could hope for. 'The Mayor isn't out of the woods yet. This whole thing could still come down with him in the middle of it.'

More silence.

'I'm handing myself in to you. I don't want more money. I just don't want to spend the rest of my days running, yeah? If I can help, then I will.'

One of the bound men on the floor of the cab groaned, but didn't try to get up.

'Not long now dick-head,' Brian said with a smile, and prodded him sharply with the toe of his shoe.

Tony didn't take his eyes off the road, fully focused on getting them to the Channel 10 News building. The youngest of the girls in the back continued to weep.

'You think we'll meet Kasey Haugh?' Brian asked.

'I dunno,' Tony said. 'Although yeah, I guess we probably will. She always takes the lead on the biggest stories.'

'You reckon I'll have a chance?'

'With Kasey? No way,' Tony laughed. 'What would she see in a bum like you?'

'Well, there's the hero factor, what with us bringing all these girls to safety, out of the clutches of evil and shit.'

'Yeah, you're right, she will see that. Course then she's gonna look right past you and see me, your better-looking friend who also happens to be a hero.'

Brian laughed, and it felt good. They didn't know what else would happen back at the docks, but their part had now been played. All that remained was to drop off the girls, give their statements to the police, and hope that everything would turn out OK.

A blue light behind caught Tony's attention.

'Are you speeding?' Brian asked, spotting the squad car in the side mirror.

'No, I've kept it just under the limit all the way.'

'There's no reason for them to pull us over, then. What do we do?'

'We have to let the truth come out. It would have been better to get to the news station first, but we can't risk running from a routine stop or we'll look guilty, which puts us right back in the shit again,' Tony said, slowing the van and pulling in under the glowing yellow arches of a fast food restaurant. Despite the unsociable hour, a queue had already formed at the drive-through for breakfast. 'We just tell them what we know and let them take it from here.'

'How do we know they're on the level? Decker said Steiger has cops on his payroll.'

The police cruiser stopped a few car lengths behind and two officers got out.

'There are witnesses,' Tony said, gesturing towards the restaurant beside them. 'It isn't like they could just do away with us.'

'Witnesses to the van, yeah. And to us. But if these guys are on the take, and we get bundled into the back of the squad car, then one of them drives the van away, it's gonna be our word against theirs that the girls even exist,' Brian exclaimed. He pulled off his jacket and used it to cover the two bound men by his feet as best he could.

Tony looked uncomfortable. He checked the mirror again.

The officers were almost at the van. He turned the ignition key, killing the engine, tossed the keys into the back of the van and looked over his shoulder at the women sitting behind. 'Unlock the back door, quickly. When I tell you, get out of the van but don't run. Stay in sight of the people at the restaurant. Do you understand?'

A number of blank faces stared back at him, but one woman nodded her understanding and crouched to pick up the keys.

Three taps on the driver's side window and Tony turned, saw the stern face of the officer and wound down the window at his instruction.

'What are you doing in this part of the city?'

'What?' Tony asked, surprised by the question.

'You've been told to keep the vans away from the city centre. Why are you so far off the normal route?'

'Now!' Tony yelled to the women, who immediately began to scramble out of the van.

There was no doubt that these officers were part of the conspiracy, but once the women were out in plain sight of so many witnesses there would be no way to perpetuate the cover-up. Tony blasted the horn three times to attract as much attention as he could. He smiled back at the startled officer, whose hand hovered uncertainly over his service revolver.

'Hold still, you idiot,' Ted Hamilton snapped impatiently as he tried to manoeuvre himself into position by Decker's shoulder.

'It's easy to say "hold still," but this hurts like a motherfucker.'

'It's gonna hurt you a whole lot more if I don't get this right.'

Decker gritted his teeth and braced himself, then howled as Ted pulled out the dislocated joint, twisted the arm and dropped it into place in a roughly fluid movement.

'Don't do anything stupid and that will probably heal up OK on its own,' Ted said, offering his usual sparse reassurance.

Tazeem handed over what little cash they could afford and Ted shook his head disdainfully before sliding it into his back pocket. 'Next time, don't call me unless you have a lot more than this. In fact I'd rather you didn't call me at all, but I'm guessing that might be too much to hope for.'

Tazeem, rubbing the freshly stitched incision where his chip had been removed, nodded and showed Ted to the door.

In the front room of the bungalow Mangle had turned on the TV. The Channel 10 anchor, Kasey Haugh, looked her usual picture of composure as she spoke about the sex-trafficking operation. Her dark brown hair, swept across her forehead fluttered in the early morning breeze from her vantage point down at Eastgate Docks. Her eyes were grim yet steady, the picture of professionalism.

'The two men taken into custody earlier today, Brian Meadows and Anthony Clarke, have failed to offer anything other than what police are describing as wild fabrications as to their roles in this large-scale operation. On their information, an early morning raid was carried out at a licensed premises known as "The Club". No evidence of involvement was discovered and the move looks to have been a smoke screen to allow the real conspirators to evade capture.'

Decker muttered to himself and winced as he gingerly rotated his left arm.

'Police are also saying that the explosion that first alerted them to the operation at the docks is not linked to the bomb attacks in Garden Heights earlier this month. It is believed to have been an engine malfunction and possible fuel leak that led to the blast, and they say that without this turn of luck the operation would have continued on undiscovered.'

'I can't believe those bastards are going to get away with it,' Mangle said bitterly, 'and that your friends who helped us are the ones who will have to pay.'

Decker walked out of the room and into the kitchen. 'I'm gonna make something to eat. Anyone want anything?'

'There's not gonna be anything else about this on the news,'

Tazeem said. 'It's the same shit she said the last few times it's been on, and the other stations have been no better.'

Mangle got up off the couch, picked the half-empty bottle of vodka from the table and walked back toward the bedroom. Tazeem followed Decker into the kitchen.

The news report cut back to the studio and a white-haired man in a dark blue suit segued into footage of another story. 'Garden Heights Mayor, Carson Keaton, refused to comment on what mayoral aide Raymond Burgess described as "totally unfounded and slanderous lies".'

The picture switched to an elegant, solemn Carson Keaton at an early morning press conference. 'By striving to do the right thing for the people of Garden Heights, it appears I have made some enemies along the way.' His slightly tired looking face conveyed sadness at those who would seek to derail his altruistic leadership. 'All that matters to me is that I retain your ongoing support, and I promise, I guarantee,' he added with a smile, 'that I will deliver a future that the good people of Garden Heights deserve.'